This item should be returned on or before the last date stamped above. If not in demand it may be renewed for a further period by personal application, by telephone, or in writing. The author, title, above number and date due back should be quoted.
LS/3
- 4 APR

A Murder of Crows

Catherine Edison has everything going for her in the town of Kingsport, Ontario, where she has lived all her life. She has a rewarding career, a loving daughter, an ambitious husband—and John, her lover. She also has good friends, who have formed a close-knit group since childhood.

Then John is found dead on a country road. Hit and run? Maybe. Catherine has her doubts, but no one else seems suspicious, and her husband, campaign manager for another member of her circle who is running for political office, is *far* too taken up with raising funds for the campaign to take his wife's fears seriously.

Not even when another member of the group is killed and Catherine herself barely escapes the fatal 'accident' does anyone believe her claim that a murderer is on the loose. Staff Sergeant Warshinsky is sympathetic, but that is all.

Alone in a familiar world grown frightening, Catherine must maintain an outward composure in the face of a mounting death-toll among her friends and her own mounting fears. For the murderer can only be one of her circle—and she loves and trusts them all.

MARGARET HAFFNER

A Murder of Crows

THE CRIME CLUB
An Imprint of HarperCollins *Publishers*

First published in Great Britain in 1992
by The Crime Club, an imprint of
HarperCollins Publishers, 77–85 Fulham Palace Road,
Hammersmith, London W6 8JB

9 8 7 6 5 4 3 2 1

Margaret Haffner asserts the moral right to be identified
as the author of this work.

© Margaret Haffner 1992

A catalogue record for this book is
available from the British Library

ISBN 0 00 232369 3

Photoset in Linotron Baskerville by
Rowland Phototypesetting Ltd
Bury St Edmunds, Suffolk
Printed and bound in Great Britain by
HarperCollins Book Manufacturing, Glasgow

PROLOGUE

The snow fell thickly as John Retson hurried down the country road. The wind's icy fist snatched his curses and thrust them back down his throat. 'I don't damn well believe it!' he swore once again. 'How the hell can the damn spare be flat too?' He kicked at the snow in front of him. 'I just checked the bloody thing yesterday . . .'

He kept his flashlight trained in front of him, illuminating the fast disappearing road. He started to jog but his foot slipped and he crashed to the frozen ground. Howling with pain and rubbing his hip, he struggled to his feet.

Walking more carefully, he continued towards a stand of trees overhanging the road. Just beyond the wood, he knew there was a farmhouse. Warmth. A telephone.

Behind him he heard the throb of an approaching car. 'Now it comes,' he grumbled. 'Why not twenty minutes ago?' He turned around and stuck out his thumb.

The car, travelling slowly, rounded the bend and two blinding white lights trapped him in their glare. The car slowed even more and began pulling to the side of the road. John stepped forward, ready to climb aboard. Suddenly the engine roared and the tyres spat out snow and gravel. Before John could react, the headlights, like terrible, glowing eyes, bore down upon him and the screaming metal beast tossed him skyward.

John came back to consciousness thirty feet from the road. His right leg canted crazily against his left arm. Pain hovered on the fringes and he felt a warm, thick wetness running down his chest. He tried to sit up, but a dozen knives stabbed his body. He lay still, only his chest heaving as he fought harder and harder for each breath.

Panic focused his numbed brain. I'm going to die! Help me! he tried to cry out. Blood gorged his throat, choking him.

Out of the darkness an even blacker shape emerged and

5

a human silhouette formed against the shadowy trees. It whispered a terrible incantation over John's failing body.

'One down. Four to go.'

They were the last words John Retson ever heard.

CHAPTER 1

In her bed, Catherine Edison stirred. The alarm clock buzzed quietly on the night table. Another Monday. With a groan, Catherine swung her feet out of the covers and propped herself on her elbow. Her wide grey eyes looked blind and unfocused as she groped for her thick glasses. Without them she felt defenceless and undressed. Her toes curled as they touched the frigid carpet. Why did Paul insist on keeping the house like an igloo? Just because he had a blast furnace inside his body didn't mean Catherine should have to freeze.

She rolled herself back into her warm cocoon, able now to focus on the dawn just showing at the window. Just two more minutes! In the adjoining bathroom she heard the shower stop and the curtain slide back with the clatter of metal rings on metal. Paul always got up a few minutes earlier than she did and sometimes brought her a cup of coffee to give her a kick start. Catherine could smell the coffee now. That automatic coffee-maker had been a great buy.

Paul Edison emerged from the bathroom amid a fog of humid warmth. Dressed only in briefs, he vigorously towelled his light brown hair. Catherine thought the silver streaks at his temples gave him a needed touch of distinction. She still admired his tall, well-proportioned body. Paul had gained only a pound or two since their marriage thirteen years ago and, though his heavy workload was cutting down on his exercise time, the lack of toning wasn't visible yet. She felt glad of her still trim figure.

'Catherine?'

'Yes?' she murmured from the haven of the warm bed.

'There's an important fund-raising dinner this Saturday night.'

'Mmmm?'

'I'd like you to come.'

7

His wife groaned. 'You know I hate those things. Besides, I haven't a thing to wear.'

'So go see Alicia and let her fit you out. You need some decent clothes—after all, we'll be socializing a lot more once we move to Toronto.'

'If we move to Toronto,' Catherine corrected him. Relocating to Toronto in the vanguard of Calvin Parker's political career didn't appeal to her as much as it did to her husband.

'We will. Calvin'll win the nomination as party chief, just you wait and see.'

Catherine grunted and ran her fingers quickly through her short, chestnut hair before shaking it more or less into place. You have only yourself to blame for this, she told herself sourly. It was you who couldn't wait to introduce your husband to Calvin and the rest of your old circle of friends. And now, with Paul as his chief fund-raiser, Calvin did have a good chance of becoming the provincial leader of the Conservative party. And with Catherine herself an NDP sympathizer, for heaven's sake!

'So what about it, Cath?' Paul had his pants on now and was shrugging into a crisp white shirt.

'Huh?'

'The dinner. Saturday. Will you come?'

Catherine sat up in bed and threw off the blankets. 'Why do you need me? I'm not part of the "Parker Team".'

Paul sat down beside his wife and draped an arm around her shoulder. 'It's Julie,' he admitted conspiratorially. 'Calvin knows public functions make her nervous. If you're there too . . .'

Catherine sighed. For a friend she'd make the sacrifice. 'All right, I'll go, but only if my green wool dress is suitable.' She laced her fingers through her husband's. 'I'm swamped at the university right now. With both my graduate students bugging me about their seminars I haven't time to shop.'

Paul kissed her soft hair and squeezed her shoulders before he got up. 'You'll look fantastic. Thanks, kid.'

'You're welcome. It's time to wake Morgan.'

8

'I'll do it.' He disappeared from the bedroom, leaving Catherine to haul herself out of the sheets. She was not a morning person.

Showered and dressed in record time, she was about to run down stairs when the telephone rang. She picked up the bedside extension.

When Paul came back he found her still sitting on the edge of the bed—staring sightlessly at the telephone. Her hand shook as she hung up.

'What's wrong?'

'It's John Retson. Julie's brother.'

'Oh?' Paul's voice held only polite interest and he turned his attention to his gold cuff-links.

'He's dead, Paul.' She struggled to keep the crushing despair out of her voice and only a slight tremor betrayed her.

'Dead? He can't be!'

They stared at each other and the cuff-links fell with a clunk to the floor.

Paul brushed his hand over his forehead. 'How did it happen? He was only thirty-eight, for God's sake!'

'A hit-and-run accident, I think. Julie wasn't very coherent.'

'No, I suppose she wouldn't be.' He compressed his already thin lips. More work to do, he thought with annoyance. If Julie Parker wasn't able to cope with the funeral arrangements for her twin, and she wouldn't be, her husband would have to take over. With Calvin otherwise occupied, Paul would have to shoulder the extra work.

'Where did Julie call from? Was Calvin with her?'

'What?' Catherine surfaced momentarily from her ocean of misery.

'Is Calvin at home?' Impatience sharpened Paul's voice.

'Yes. He's staying with Julie today. There are lots of things to be done.'

Paul pulled his jacket off the hanger and slipped it on as he rounded the foot of the bed to snatch up the telephone.

'Who are you calling?'

'Calvin, of course.'

9

'About business?'

'Yes.' Paul punched the number pads.

'At a time like this?' Catherine leapt up from the bed and raced for the telephone. John, her own lover, Calvin's lifelong friend and Julie's twin brother lay dead and Paul thought only of business! She thrust out her hand and disconnected the call.

'What the hell did you do that for?' Paul demanded.

'John's dead, Paul. Dead. Ended. Business can wait.' Breathing rapidly, Catherine laid a hand on Paul's sleeve. 'He was my friend. He was our friend.'

Paul clasped her fingers briefly before he slipped away from her. 'I know. That's why I'm calling Calvin. The more work I can take over for him the more time he'll have for his grief. And for Julie.' Paul spoke slowly, picking his words. 'I've known John since I came to Kingsport, but you and the Parkers have known him all your lives. As the least involved, it's up to me to keep things rolling for Calvin until he's back in the saddle.'

'I didn't think of that,' Catherine murmured. 'That's very thoughtful of you.'

'Saint Paul, that's what they call me!' he joked, but already his mind had begun to juggle his day's appointments.

In a daze, Catherine showered and dressed and hurried along her sleepy daughter. Somehow she followed her usual morning routine, preparing breakfast, tidying the kitchen, feeding the canary. She slipped up only once.

'Aren't you going to ask me if I have my lunch?' Morgan called from the front hall.

Her mother jerked around. 'What? Oh yes. Do you have your lunch, dear?'

'Yes.' Morgan grinned. 'Bye!'

'Wait!' Catherine ran to her daughter and enveloped her in a smothering hug.

'What was that for?' Morgan asked when finally released.

'Nothing.' A crooked smile quirked Catherine's lips. 'I love you.'

'Love you too, Mom. 'Bye.'

10

Paul trailed his daughter to the door. 'I may be late tonight . . .'

'OK. Whenever,' Catherine replied. Why didn't he just leave?

Alone at last, she inched open the window to her thoughts. She lay rigid and wide-eyed on the bed in the guest-room thinking of John. Dead John. Her John. Her beloved. How could she possibly bear it? At least Julie could mourn openly. But a secret lover? She'd have to wear a mask to hide her agony, to pretend she mourned merely the loss of an old friend. Life without John loomed grey and featureless before her.

'John,' Catherine whispered. 'John.' She savoured the sound and could almost hear his voice caressing her own name. Never had it seemed so musical, so beautiful, as when John spoke it softly in her ear.

She longed to close her eyes, to imagine him lying beside her, his breath hot on her breast, his strong arms around her. But she couldn't relax and when she did shut her eyes she couldn't picture John's mobile smile and gentle eyes. Instead, she saw a caricature of his face—lips grimaced in rictus and eyes bulging from his skull.

Peggy Brandenburg's day started like any other week day. Even before she'd hustled her own three offspring to school, three small children were delivered to her door, one crying, one drooling and one sniffling from the latest in a series of winter colds. She settled the newcomers at the kitchen table and poured bowls of cereal for them.

'Cheer up, Brandon, she cajoled the sad little tyke. Today's painting day. You like painting, don't you?'

Brandon wailed on, spewing Cheerios across the table.

'Brandon spitting at me, Mrs Peggy. Make him stop!' Pamela, four years old and dressed in a pink corduroy skirt and matching sweater, sounded nasal and whiney. 'He going to ruin my new clothes!'

Peggy picked up the screaming child and held him on her knee where she gently jiggled him up and down, murmuring soothing sounds. Time after time she unwound his tiny fingers from her dark blonde hair. At least he doesn't notice that my roots are showing, she thought ruefully. She had really let herself go, but then toddlers didn't care that she was slightly overweight and carelessly dressed.

Brandon had just heaved a last shuddering sob when the telephone rang. Not daring to put him down, Peggy cradled him in one arm while she lifted the receiver with the other.

'Hello?'

'It's Catherine.'

A smile lit Peggy's face. A friend in need . . . 'Hi! It's great to hear from you. What's up at eight-thirty in the morning?'

The silence at the other end of the line made Peggy nervous. 'Catherine?'

'It's John . . . He's dead.'

Brandon slid to the floor where he whimpered unnoticed.

'What?' A quaver marred Peggy's soprano voice.

Emotionally exhausted, Catherine murmured, 'He's dead. Hit and run.'

Peggy swallowed convulsively. 'Oh no . . .'

'I thought I'd let you know. I told Julie I'd call . . .'

The mention of Julie jerked Peggy back to life. She remembered all too clearly the death, two years before, of her own brother, Brent. 'How is Julie?' she asked.

'Not good. I don't know if Calvin can hold her together.'

Peggy scanned her surroundings. 'I'd like to help but I don't know if I can get away.'

'Don't worry about it, Peggy, there isn't really anything we can do to help. I just wanted to let you know.'

When Peggy hung up, she was oblivious of the chaos around her. Instead of being forty-one years old and besieged by children in her kitchen, she was twelve and labouring up the steep, treacherous side of a sand pit. She followed Calvin Parker and Julie's older brother Danny, determined not to be the last one to the top. John and Julie lagged far in the rear as she, Peggy, screamed insults at them. Slow pokes! Rotten eggs! Dirty rascals! Peggy's cheeks burned as she remembered how cruelly she'd behaved as a child. It amazed her she and Julie had ever become close friends. At that time, so many years ago, Julie and John, four years younger than the rest of them, had seemed like snivelling children. As adults, the four years melted into nonexistence. And now, not only her own brother Brent, but Julie's two brothers, Danny and John, were gone. Death had claimed three out of the charmed circle of eight. Peggy slumped in her chair. Her forty-one years hung heavy.

The painted figure in the coffin didn't look like John at all, but Catherine knew it wouldn't. Corpses reveal nothing of their former inhabitants. That the body had belonged to a male adult human was obvious but John . . . where was he?

And who had given permission to rouge his full, dear lips? She fought the urge to wipe the crimson insult from their familiar contours. Thank God his eyes were closed behind the gold frames! But John hadn't worn his glasses while he slept—he kept them on the bookcase by the bed.

'He looks good, doesn't he Catherine? They did a good job.'

Catherine whirled around, revolted, but it was Julie so she swallowed the caustic retort which sprung to her lips.

'I prefer closed caskets,' Catherine managed through tight lips.

'Do you?' Julie blinked back the tears in her green eyes —eyes so much like those of her dead twin. 'I need to say goodbye to the person, not to a box.'

'This isn't a person any more. This isn't John.'

'No . . .' Julie's voice trailed off as Catherine steered her away from the casket. Catherine intended to keep herself under rigid control and standing by John's empty body severely tested her.

John, in his ornate walnut casket, dominated the chapel of the Gerald Jones Funeral Home. The unadorned walls were white, too white, and the rose carpet too deep, too suffocating. With each step Catherine felt as if she were sinking into a grave. Over the padded rose chairs and their scattered occupants brass lamps threw a mournful glow.

Matching vases cradled a profusion of flowers whose pung-ent odour caught in her nostrils and threatened to choke her. Instead of flowers she had sent a donation to 'Victims of Crime'.

John had not attended any church for years, but since he was nominally Christian, Mr Jones had erected the plain mahogany cross at the side of the lectern. Death, Catherine reflected, drew everyone back to religion no matter how far away they thought they had run in life.

She perched on the edge of a chair near the front of the funeral chapel. Beside her, Julie absently twisted her chunky diamond ring, oblivious of the arm Catherine slid around her slender shoulders. Catherine looked around but didn't recognize the six or eight men huddled at the back of the room. John's colleagues from work, she assumed.

'Where are the others?' Catherine asked in a stage whisper.

Julie knew she spoke of their circle of childhood friends. 'They'll be here. Where's Paul?'

'Talking to the funeral director, I think. He can't pass up a chance to do some politicking for Calvin.'

'Calvin promised he wouldn't be late.'

'He won't be.' Catherine had no worry on that score. Their circle was a tight one and always had been. Calvin would be there to say farewell to one of his own.

'Here's Alicia,' Catherine announced as the door banged and a startling figure glided towards them. A cascade of black feathers billowed around the new arrival as she dropped into the next chair.

'What a shock! I could hardly believe it when you called, Julie!' Her black eyes opened even wider as she leaned forward. 'Is he a mess?'

Before her feathers had settled, Alicia sprang up again to peer at John's remains. 'Not a mark on him! What a relief!'

Alicia brushed John's brow with her finger tips while her effervescence dropped appreciably. She and her feathers floated back to her friends and died to a stillness matching her sleek black hair. 'Do you realize this makes three?'

14

'Three what?' Julie asked in a distracted tone.

Catherine tensed. Alicia too had noticed the same perturbing fact.

'Three of us dead,' Alicia explained. 'First Danny, then Brent, now John. There are only five of us left.'

Julie shuddered and clutched Catherine's arm. Catherine shot a warning look at her friend. Couldn't Alicia Castelvetri see how close to the breaking-point Julie hovered?

'I'm a curse,' Julie whispered through trembling lips.

'Nonsense. You have nothing to do with it!'

'Both my brothers killed. Murdered! And Brent's heart attack at forty. I tell you I'm a jinx!'

'Brent didn't watch his weight, John walked in front of a car and Danny was in the wrong place at the wrong time. You can't take the blame for any of it any more than I can, or Alicia, or Calvin.' Catherine struggled to keep her voice matter-of-fact. Did she really believe John's death an accident?

'Or Peggy. It's not her fault either,' Alicia added.

Peggy Brandenburg. Brent's sister. She completed the circle.

During this whispered conversation more sombrely clad men and women had trickled in. Catherine recognized a few of them as former schoolmates and long-time inhabitants of Kingsport. She nodded at those who caught her eye.

Then someone totally unexpected strode into the funeral chapel.

'Look,' Alicia exclaimed, 'it's Wilson! What the hell is he doing here? He hated John. He hates all of us, for that matter.'

Peggy Brandenburg's estranged husband shouldered his way through the subdued crowd to choose a seat on the far side and back several rows.

'If he makes a scene at John's funeral . . .' again Julie hovered close to tears.

'I'll go speak to him.' Catherine started to rise but Julie clutched her arm.

'Maybe you'd better not. You might make it worse.'

'I've got to try. Don't worry,' Catherine reassured her while denying her own lack of confidence.

As Catherine threaded her way through the maze of chairs and people, she kept Wilson in sight. He was still almost as handsome as the day she'd met him, at Peggy's side, sixteen years before.

When Calvin Parker had broken up with her right after high school, Peggy had been devastated. No one could convince her it was for the best.

The first few times Catherine came home from university to visit, Peggy had pumped her about Calvin's activities.

'I don't know what he's doing, Peggy, honest,' Catherine had sworn time and time again. 'I don't see him that often —the University of Toronto is a big place and we're not in the same programme.'

'You must know if he has a girlfriend,' Peggy pleaded.

'Maybe. I don't know. I've seen him with two or three different girls—no one special.'

But when Catherine came home to Kingsport for winter break, Peggy sounded ecstatic on the telephone.

'Wait till you meet him, Catherine. Wilson's absolutely perfect. He's twenty-six and he's working so he's not a tightwad like the other guys. He has a motorcycle *and* a sports car. He's handsome and sophisticated . . .'

When Peggy arrived, displaying him like a prize bull, Catherine had to agree Wilson lived up to his billing. Tall and lean, he clothed his well-muscled body in expensive black leather. His hair gleamed sleek but not greasy, his mouth pouted full and sensuous and he oozed masculine sexuality and power. While his eyes raked Catherine up and down, his hand possessively stroked Peggy's hip. She practically drooled in his ear. Wilson attracted and repelled Catherine simultaneously, but Peggy was consumed. Catherine instinctively knew the untamed, unbroken Wilson Brandenburg meant trouble for anyone who loved him.

Now as she bore down on him, Catherine reflected on how right she'd been. None the less, his sheer animal magnetism compelled her to pull her five foot five inch figure erect and her stomach muscles in.

16

'I didn't expect to see you here, Wilson.'

He turned around and his dark eyes ran critically over Catherine. She didn't flinch. Appraising him, she noticed the crows' feet around his shifting eyes and the lines of dissipation in his face. Wilson had aged after all. Diet and exercise kept his body hard and fit but his face betrayed his years and his character.

'If it isn't The Professor herself. I'm surprised you've stooped to speak to me.'

'Why are you here?'

Wilson cracked his knuckles, then clasped his fingers behind his head. 'To pay my respects to the dear departed, of course.'

Catherine snorted her disbelief. 'You didn't like John.'

'Untrue. The fact is I hated John. Just like I hate you.' His voice oozed like syrup, cloying, unsuited to the words.

'Not funny, Wilson.'

'Merely the simple truth. Isn't that what you preach? Isn't that what you claim to tell Peggy when you say I'm no good?' He stood up, casting a menacing shadow over her.

She hoped Wilson didn't notice her flinch as she ignored the threat and held her ground. 'Since you didn't like John, why don't you leave?'

'And waste an opportunity to annoy you?' Wilson tried to run his hand down her shoulder but she brushed him off.

'Did the Great Calvin send you to deal with the prodigal son?' Wilson asked with a sneer.

'You're not the prodigal son.'

'True. None of you ever accepted me into your family circle.'

'And you aren't repentant. As I recall, the prodigal son repented his wasted life.'

Wilson emitted a crack of laughter and all heads swivelled in their direction. Catherine bit her lip as Julie turned a worried face towards her.

'Behave yourself!' she hissed.

Wilson sat down in one of the dusty rose chairs and

leaned back, completely at ease. 'Don't worry, Catherine darling. I won't make a scene.'

'You'd better not!'

'I'm here to offer support to my dear wife in her time of grief.'

'All her friends are here. Peggy doesn't need you.'

'Wrong. My darling Peggy depends on me.'

'She depends on you to mess up her life,' Catherine retorted, goaded beyond endurance.

A nasty expression twisted Wilson's face, leaving it cold and threatening. 'You stick your nose in things which don't concern you; you and John and Calvin and the rest of your damn group. Without your interference Peggy and I would still be together.'

Catherine fought to conceal her unease. 'We didn't force you to have affairs, waste your money, walk out countless times, lose your jobs . . .'

'Pressure. You pressured me to be like the rest of you bootlicking conformists. You couldn't stand it when I wouldn't knuckle under and imitate Saint Calvin.'

'All we wanted was for you to treat Peggy properly. But you wouldn't do that would you?' Catherine shook with the effort of containing her rage. 'You don't love her, Wilson, why not let her be?'

'She's my wife!'

'Not for much longer.'

'Is that a challenge? I love a challenge! Peggy still has the hots for me.'

Catherine grimaced in disgust. She should have ignored Wilson's presence after all. Instead, she'd exacerbated the situation.

'Please don't do anything, Wilson,' Catherine pleaded. 'This is a funeral. John's dead and can't annoy you any more. Please let him rest in peace.'

'Your wish is my command.' Wilson bowed with a mocking flourish. 'You can count on me.'

'Thanks.' Catherine felt extemely uneasy but there was nothing to do but hope for the best.

As she made her way back to Julie, a small commotion stirred at the entrance to the chapel.

'The others have arrived,' she whispered, ducking in beside her friends.

Both Alicia and Julie craned backward to see the solemn funeral director deferentially conferring with Calvin Parker, the up and coming politician. Catherine's husband, Paul, and Peggy hovered in the background with a knot of last-minute arrivals.

Breaking from the group, the master of ceremonies made his way to the front of the chapel and took his place behind the simple black podium.

'If you would be seated, please . . .'

Alicia and Catherine moved back a row to leave Calvin and Julie, the deceased's only family, alone in the place of honour.

'What's that reporter doing here?' Catherine asked Paul as he slid in beside her.

'Calvin thinks a few photos would be a good idea.'

'Photos of who? Himself?'

Paul shrugged and put a finger to his lips.

'Dear friends and relatives; Calvin and Julie Parker; we are gathered here today . . .'

Catherine ignored the carefully nondenominational, scrupulously bland words describing John's new life in a better world. John had been an atheist.

Directly in front of her, the taut cords of Julie's neck strained under her red-gold curls. Calvin had threaded his arm through hers, but still she sat rigidly upright, staring straight ahead. Was she listening? Was she remembering? Was she reliving moments she had shared with her twin, her protector?

Then Calvin strode to the podium. Catherine followed his mental checklist as he arranged his body for the proper effect. Feet aligned. Knees straight but not locked. Hands clasped, reverently but not obsequiously, on the podium. Broad shoulders squared but not rigidly at attention. Square chin lowered ten degrees from its usual confident pitch, but not enough to obscure his fine brown eyes. Narrow, but well shaped lips composed into a commiserating curve. A lock of dark hair tumbled artfully out of perfection on to his forehead.

'My dearest Julie, so courageous in your bereavement,' his gaze dwelt on her for a few seconds and then swept the rest of the crowd. 'Faithful friends. It is a sad, sad day for all of us.' Dramatic pause. Moist eyes. 'John Retson has left us. John, who has been a part of our lives for thirty-eight years, has gone home.'

A camera flashed, highlighting Calvin's brave endurance.

'John has been a central part of my life since early childhood and while our lives took different paths, mine to business, John's to the factory floor, we remained close friends through the years.'

Catherine tuned out the eulogy which dwelt on Calvin's own character as much as that of the late John's. Surreptitiously, she turned to check up on Wilson Brandenburg. Noticing her hostile stare, Wilson yawned insolently and slouched further into his seat. Catherine's stomach knotted. Would he control himself or was he planning to transform John's funeral into a circus? Wringing her hands helplessly in her lap she forced her attention back to the speaker. Would he never end?

At the podium, Calvin theatrically dropped his voice a note or two. 'John never married. We, his sister and his friends, were his family, and he gave us all he had. Why was a man like John Retson taken so prematurely from us? Why was he mown down in the prime of his life by a hit-and-run driver? Only Our Almighty Father knows. Here, on earth, all we can do is work together to strengthen the law so that it can deal firmly with criminals like the man, or woman, who took our John from us.'

Every face mirrored sorrow and indignation as the echo of Calvin's words died to stillness. But an unnatural chill invaded Catherine's body. Her eyes flickered among the crowd, seeking the source. Someone, someone in the room, did not mourn John's death. Someone was not surprised at all. Catherine shuddered but the other mourners sat passively, pinned by Calvin's piercing gaze, until he finally bowed his head.

'My friends; join me in a moment's silence to remember our beloved, John Retson.'

Since it was January, with the ground frozen to granite hardness, there would be no interment, but Julie had asked the inner circle to gather again at her home. Paul, his arm wrapped around his wife's waist, urged her towards the door. 'We'll be over in an hour or so, Julie. There are just a few things I need to do,' Paul explained. 'Great eulogy, Calvin!' Paul slapped his man on the shoulder.

'Catch you later.' Calvin turned back to the reporter. Julie smiled wanly at the other mourners as they filtered back into the grey, cold day.

Peggy and Alicia lingered in the background, waiting for Calvin to complete his duties.

'Here comes Wilson,' Peggy hissed nervously.

'Take it easy; I'll stay with you.'

Wilson slunk up to his wife and slid a hand around her hips. 'How's my little woman?' he leered. 'Missing me?'

'Let go, Wilson.' Peggy squirmed.

Aware of her ambivalence, he possessively tightened his grip.

'A nice funeral, don't you think?' Alicia asked, stepping closer to him.

'Beautiful. I like funerals. I look forward to yours—it should be even better.'

'Wilson!' Peggy squeaked.

Alicia chuckled. 'It will be. I'm making fabulous outfits for all the expected guests to wear. Shall I make you one?'

'Yes, please.' Wilson's white teeth flashed. 'Make mine in leather.'

'Good idea. Snakeskin would suit, don't you agree?'

Wilson laughed with genuine amusement. 'I always preferred you to the rest of them, Alicia. At least you have some wit.'

He turned back to his wife who had slipped out of his embrace. 'Shall I escort you home, my darling?'

Peggy refused to meet his eye, worried that she would

21

weaken yet again. 'No, thanks. I'm going with Alicia.'

Alicia grinned in triumph. 'Foiled again, Wilson?'

Peggy hated it when her friends sparred with her husband. He reacted viciously if he lost and she had to bear the brunt of his frustration. She was frantic to get away.

'Come on, Alicia, let's go warm up the car.' As Peggy turned to leave, Wilson caught her hand and brought it to his lips. '*A bientôt, ma chérie . . .*'

Peggy pulled her hand away and ran for the door.

'And if you ever need my services, Alicia, don't hesitate to call!'

Freezing rain turned the road to a skating-rink. In the passenger seat, Catherine bit her tongue as Paul raced down the busy street. Her nerves, already stretched taut from the funeral, threatened to snap completely.

'Be careful, Paul!' she shrieked as he swerved to miss an oncoming truck. Paul took his hand off her upper thigh to attend to the wheel but, imminent danger past, he went back to rhythmically kneading her flesh.

After her adrenalin level returned to somewhere around normal, Catherine allowed her thoughts to return to the funeral, although not to John himself. 'Calvin's talk sounded more like a campaign speech than a funeral address, didn't you think, Paul? John hardly got a mention!'

'Great speech,' Paul grunted. There was a thin sheen of sweat on his forehead.

Catherine relapsed into silence, knowing it useless to talk until Paul obtained the release he needed.

Once home, Paul urged Catherine up the stairs, shedding his clothes as he went. In dismay she heard her dress rip as Paul clawed away her clothing. Ignoring even a nod to foreplay, Paul lunged on top of her, straining and pumping. As a final salute to John, Catherine imagined it was his body joining with hers. She shuddered in a confusing combination of pain and pleasure. At last her body, tense for so long, relaxed.

Later, she curled a strand of Paul's golden chest hair around her fingers. 'Why do funerals turn you on?'

Catherine had noticed this odd behaviour over the last two years as first her parents, then his and then Brent had died.

Paul stroked her hair for a moment before he replied. 'I need to prove to myself I'm still alive, I suppose. I hate death.'

'You fear it too.'

'Don't you?'

Yes. She did. She hated John's death and feared life without him. How could he have become so necessary to her in just three miraculous months?

Catherine pulled away, drawing the bed sheet with her. She didn't want Paul's sated eyes on her nakedness. She searched for a pin to mend her torn clothing and then slipped the black linen dress back on. 'I'll miss John,' Catherine softly murmured. 'He added a little vitality to our otherwise oh so proper lives. He and Alicia.'

'I don't know what you see in those two. Or Peggy. Now Calvin, on the other hand . . .'

Paul hadn't met her Kingsport friends until just before they were married but he'd pinned his fortunes to Calvin's within weeks of their arrival in Catherine's home town. The others, Peggy Brandenburg, Alicia Castelvetri, Julie Parker and her brother, John, he accepted grudgingly as part of the package.

'Calvin! He's the only person you ever think of!' Catherine accused. 'Well now there's one less person to compete for his attention. John won't take up any more of Calvin's valuable time.' Catherine sniffed and reached for a tissue. 'That must make you happy!'

'Of course it doesn't.' Paul gave her a quick hug. 'I liked John well enough but he just wasn't very stimulating company, that's all.'

A matter of perspective.

They drove to Calvin and Julie's much more sedately. There, Marie, the domestic help ushered them into the salon where a subdued buzz of conversation enveloped them. Julie popped out of the confusion and gripped Catherine's arm like a lost child finally locating her mother.

'Who are these people?'

Julie shrugged. 'I don't know very many of them but they're Calvin's business associates.'

'They weren't at the funeral, were they?'

'No. A couple of them were here when we got home.'

'Did Calvin invite them?'

Julie smiled automatically and shrugged again. 'Maybe not. But Calvin never refuses to see a member of his team no matter what. He's very considerate.'

'Obviously.' Through the crowd Catherine glimpsed Paul in earnest conversation with a portly man in an expensive suit. Nearby, Calvin shared a laugh with another well-padded gentleman.

'Why don't you and I go into the sitting-room, Julie?'

'I might be missed . . .'

'Anyone here because of John will find you. Tell Marie where you'll be.'

In the sitting-room, Peggy and Alicia were chatting in a desultory fashion, sipping white wine and forming a study in contrasts. Alicia reminded Catherine of a black crane, dark-haired, white-skinned, tall, very thin and never still, her outrageous black feather dress magnifying her every gesture.

Alicia bounced up, the ash on her cigarette tip wobbling dangerously as she planted a hasty kiss on Julie's cheek. 'Julie! How ghastly! Who are those people? They're certainly not John's friends!'

Peggy, pale and permanently exhausted, echoed the sentiments. 'We thought we'd come in here and reminisce.' She pointed to a thick book on her lap. 'We're going through your photo album, Julie. I hope you don't mind.' She patted the sofa beside her. 'Come sit. You look beat.'

'May I join you?' a calm voice asked from the doorway. Susan, Brent's widow and Peggy's sister-in-law, stepped into the room.

'Of course!' Catherine smiled at her.

'Come on in,' Julie invited, while Peggy and Alicia tried to imitate her warmth.

The four women spent a soothing hour reliving their

childhoods and even Susan, who hadn't been part of the group, joined in.

'I heard so much from Brent,' she explained, 'and he had a photograph album too. Bigger than this, I think.'

'I'd love to see it sometime!' Catherine exclaimed amid other murmurs of assent.

'Brent had a camera before the rest of us,' Alicia added, 'so he must have some even earlier shots.'

'As soon as I get it back,' Susan said with a smile.

'Back?' A chorus.

'Some reporter wanted to borrow it. He said he was doing a piece on Kingsport in the nineteen-fifties and needed some photos from that era. I don't know if he'll use any of them . . .' Susan shifted in her chair. 'Come to think of it, he's had them a long time—over six months. I'd better give him a call.'

'Who was it? Tourney?' Catherine asked. 'He usually covers local history.' Eric Tourney taught English at the university and Catherine liked to know what her fellow professors were up to.

Susan shook her dark brown hair. 'No, it was something like Millin, or Milkin.'

'Millikin?' Julie's voice cracked and an expression of horror settled on her delicate features.

'That's right!' Susan's smile faded. 'What's wrong?'

'Oh no,' Julie moaned and her already wan complexion turned grey.

'What is it?'

'Giles Millikin. That's the guy who's doing what they call an "unauthorized biography" of Calvin. He's calling it *Clawing to the Top* or some such awful thing. Calvin has tried to stop it but he can't. How could you, Susan? How could you!'

'I didn't know!' Susan defended herself. 'All I gave him were some pictures of you people and your houses and stuff. They can't do any harm.'

'Calvin's going to be livid,' Julie wailed.

'About what?' In the doorway, timing perfect as usual, stood Calvin himself. Behind his elbow, like a shadow, Paul hovered. 'What am I going to be livid about?' Calvin asked again, striding into the room.

Susan broke the awkward silence. 'I lent Brent's photograph album to a man named Millikin. Julie says you know him.'

The line of Calvin's jaw tightened. 'So that's where the sneak got the pictures. I never figured you for the traitor, Susan.' Calvin laughed without humour. 'Yes, I've met him, only once, but I know his type. He's a damn muckraker.' The hard edge to his voice shook Susan.

'I'm not a traitor,' Susan protested. 'He seemed very charming when he visited me.'

'Because he wanted something. His kind always do.'

'All he got was a few faded pictures. Really, Calvin, you've nothing to worry about—you were very photogenic even then!'

'That's not the point! I won't have anyone prying into my life without my permission! And those photos will add credibility to any garbage Millikin may write. Brent would be very disappointed in you.'

As he paced around the room in the ensuing silence, the soles of Calvin's lustrous black shoes squeaked rhythmically. Calvin so far forgot himself that he ran his fingers through his perfect hair.

Susan stood up to confront him. 'I lent the pictures for an article about the history of Kingsport, or so I thought. I had no intention of betraying you, as you see it. I didn't mean to offend any of you.' Her gaze swept her small audience.

Only Catherine didn't waver before those steady hazel eyes as she tried to read the emotion behind their shuttered façade. Contempt? Dislike? Anger? Fear? She couldn't tell. Susan had learned self-control from her very upper-class mother.

'I'll ask Mr Millikin to return the photographs,' Susan assured Calvin. 'And I won't give him permission to use them in his book.'

'Fat lot of good that'll do,' Paul scoffed from his position at Calvin's side. 'I'm a lawyer, and he wouldn't even listen to me!' Under his breath Catherine heard him add, 'Stupid woman!'

'Can't you get an injunction or something?' Catherine asked.

'No.'

'But what can this Millikin say without committing libel? You've nothing to hide, have you?'

'Of course not!' Calvin's head came up and he regained his power stance. 'But he'll make perfectly innocent activities look suspect. And that can hurt, believe me! Remember Montforten? His career was trashed by rumours alone. People look for the sensation. They want the dirt.'

'Have you seen the manuscript?' Alicia asked.

'Paul and I have seen excerpts . . . I have a friend in the publishing industry.'

'And?'

'Innuendoes. Nothing I can sue over,' Calvin grudgingly admitted.

'Is it malicious?'

'Not entirely. As Catherine pointed out, there isn't much dirt to dig up.'

'Probably if you don't make any fuss, the book will die a quick death.'

'Maybe, but I'd rather suppress it completely.' Calvin turned on his heel and stalked out of the room, shoving Susan aside with his elbow. 'Come on, Paul. We've work to do.'

Paul followed. Would he have elbowed Susan too? Catherine hoped not, but Susan had already moved out of his way.

'You've certainly put the fat in the fire,' Peggy remarked with sour satisfaction.

'So it would seem. I think, under the circumstances, I'd better leave.' Susan turned to Julie. 'I'm truly sorry about John. He was a lovely man.'

'Thank you.'

'I'll walk you to the door,' Catherine volunteered, following her friend into the hall where Susan's composure cracked a millimetre.

'I struck out again, didn't I? God, how I keep putting my foot into it with that bunch!' Susan exclaimed bitterly. 'They've never forgiven me for marrying Brent. Peggy especially.' She slumped against the brocade-covered wall. 'Why are you so different, Cath? You're one of this crowd too.'

'I don't know. My kid likes your kid.' She smiled. 'I like you, I suppose. And you were good for Brent. Before he married you he was much too wild.'

'And I turned him into a boring accountant?'

'You helped him mature into an interesting, responsible adult.'

Susan laughed drily. 'You're the only one here who reads it that way.'

'Susan, you faced an uphill battle marrying into such a close-knit group. It's not you, it's the fact you married Brent and changed the balance that the others hold against you. As for Peggy . . . , even a canonized saint wouldn't have been good enough for her darling brother!'

Susan sighed. 'I've tried so hard.'

'I know . . .' Catherine paused. 'Peggy finds it difficult to accept that Brent died and you're still here.'

'I find it difficult to accept too!' Susan retorted. She shook off the shadow of sorrow which brushed her mind. 'You have to admit your husband fits into the group better than I do.'

Catherine nodded. 'That's because Calvin took Paul under his wing. Calvin is our unacknowledged leader, you know. Look on the bright side, Sue—you've been accepted more readily than Peggy's Wilson!'

'I should hope so! What a cretin.' Susan started walking slowly towards the door.

Catherine stayed in step. 'Don't let them upset you,' she pleaded. 'And as for that damn book, it would be written with or without Brent's photos. Don't let Calvin get to you. When things don't go exactly the way he wants, he has a tantrum and overreacts. He'll cool off.'

'Thanks, Catherine.' Susan briefly clasped her friend's hands in both of hers before grabbing the handle of the front door. 'Oh yes, I almost forgot.' She turned. 'Tennis tomorrow as usual?'

'Wouldn't miss it.'

'. . . in fact, I barely remember what Danny looked like,' Alicia was saying as Catherine returned to the salon.

'I remember. I picture him showing off that black leather jacket he got for his birthday,' Julie whispered. 'He was so proud! He thought he was the next Elvis Presley.'

Catherine remembered too. After all, she'd been his date for that birthday party. At seventeen, they had just started pairing up; Danny and Catherine, Peggy and Calvin, Alicia and Brent. Danny had been Catherine's 'first'. In the bushes, by the side of the ravine, they had fumbled away their virginity. The next night, hours after his seventeenth birthday party, Danny was dead; shot by person or persons unknown.

'. . . and Danny could sing pretty well too,' Peggy was saying when Catherine flicked back to the present. 'The high school band wanted him to audition didn't they?'

They nodded.

'He would've been someone,' Julie declared. 'Danny had drive . . . ambition . . .'

'And he would have been as handsome as John,' Catherine contributed.

By now they had opened their third bottle of Chablis and were getting maudlin. Memories budded and blossomed in the warmth of their shared history and their past glowed with the rosy hue of imperfect recollection. Even the tragedy of Danny's death had lost its bitter sting.

'Poor Danny. Poor John,' murmured Alicia.

'Poor Brent,' Peggy added, saluting her beloved older brother.

'Poor Julie.' Calvin reappeared. 'How are you holding up, my love?' He sat down beside his wife and put his arm around her.

'All right, I guess.'

'This is all that's left of Our Crowd now, Calvin. Just the five of us. Three gone already.'

29

'Look after yourself, Calvin,' Alicia warned. 'You're the only male left.'

'Yes do, please!' Julie huddled against her husband and squeezed his arm. 'I couldn't bear it if anything happened to you.'

'It won't. I've a great future in front of me and I intend to enjoy it.'

'And I'll see he does, Julie.' Paul slapped Calvin on the shoulder. 'We make quite a team, don't you think, old man?'

'With Paul and the rest of you behind me, I feel unbeatable!'

Despite the bonhomie, Catherine shivered with apprehension. How many of them would still be alive to witness Calvin's success? For that matter, would Calvin himself live to reach his goal?

CHAPTER 2

'Hurry up, Morgan, you'll be late, and at art class you'll be throwing on a smock, so it doesn't matter what you wear!' Catherine called up the stairs.

As Morgan bounded down the stairs, the look she threw her mother was withering. What did she know about clothes?

Morgan pointedly tapped her foot as Catherine hunted for her car keys and handbag.

'Where are your boots, Morgan?'

'I don't need them—I'll only be taking a few steps outside.'

'It's January, dear, the car will be cold.' Catherine's voice was muffled as she shrugged into her quilted coat.

'Oh Mom . . . please . . . I hate them.'

'Hate them? I took you to a dozen shops and spent over a hundred dollars for those boots just three months ago!'

'Really, Mom, I don't need them and we're late, so please let's go.'

30

Clumping in her Kodiaks, Catherine followed her strong-willed daughter's pink suede runners out to the car and wondered yet again where to draw the line between dictatorship and guidance. She was too soft, too demanding, too lax, too regimented; but never, Catherine was sure, right.

'I'm dropping in on Aunt Alicia while you're at your lesson. It's not worth driving all the way home.'

'Great! Can I visit after?'

'We'll see.'

'I need a new skirt and . . .'

'No way, kid! You already have five times as many clothes as I do and you don't need anything.'

'But Aunt Alicia sells such awesome clothes and she always gives us a great discount,' Morgan wheedled.

'Even so, her clothes are still the most expensive in town.'

'They're worth it!' Morgan declared. 'Tracy goes wild when she sees me wearing an A. C. "original creation".'

'How can such a clothes-horse be my daughter?' Catherine wondered aloud, swivelling to glance at the girl beside her. Morgan had her father's curly hair and her mother's fair skin but without the freckles. Her complexion glowed clear and translucent, just like in an ivory soap advertisement. Already as tall as Catherine, her body was stretching out and just starting to swell in interesting places. Catherine felt she had barely coped with a child. How would she manage as the mother of a popular, pretty teenager?

Morgan laughed. 'Maybe you should let Aunt Alicia choose some clothes for you this time. Daddy said you weren't fashion-conscious.'

'He meant it as a compliment.'

'Maybe.' Morgan's cheeks dimpled as she smiled.

Catherine pulled up as close to the studio as she could so Morgan's shoes wouldn't be ruined by the salt-saturated snow. 'See you in two hours.'

''Bye!' Her daughter waved a dismissal.

As the boutique's gold door closed behind her, Catherine was immersed in the sybaritic atmosphere of Alicia's Originals. Out of the depths Marsha, the head saleswoman, glided. When she recognized Catherine, her welcoming smile took on genuine warmth.

'Catherine! We haven't seen you in ages! How are you? Where's Morgan?'

'Hi, Marsha. Just fine. Morgan's at her art lesson, so hopefully I can visit Alicia without it costing me ten dollars a minute.'

Marsha chuckled; she had a deep musical laugh. 'But she wears her clothes well. Morgan has style.'

'Unlike her mother?'

The saleswoman shrugged her elegantly clad shoulders. 'You have style when you want to . . . you just don't want to very often.'

'Tactfully put. Is Alicia upstairs?'

'Yes. She was swearing at some lilac linen when I last saw her.'

Alicia lived and worked above her elegant shop but to get to the stairway Catherine had to weave her way through racks of Alicia's distinctive creations. Their designer used rich, sensuous fabrics, cut along deceptively simple lines. Wearing them, women felt beautiful, desirable and astonishingly comfortable. The garments hung singly or in pairs on wooden hangers suspended from fantastic wire sculptures. No dress was crushed, no silk blouse crammed among twenty clones. Jumpsuits did not jostle brocade jackets in this store.

Along the back wall, in individual mirrored alcoves, Alicia Castelvetri displayed her quirkier fashions. Only very confident women could wear these outfits—women like Alicia herself.

A drape in swirls of rose and burgundy caught Catherine's eye. Woven from fine wools of different hues, rather than printed, the material felt rich and exotic in her hand. She held it to her cheek.

'It suits you.' Marsha slid the cloth from the hanger and wrapped it around Catherine. The colour did bring some life into her sallow complexion.

'What exactly is it?'

32

'An overdress. A kind of long poncho to wear over evening pants.'

Fighting her way out of its folds, Catherine was already shaking her head. 'Not for me.'

'Take your coat off and try it,' Marsha urged.

'No. No, thanks.' She backed away. 'It isn't me.'

'It could be . . .'

When Catherine arrived upstairs in the workroom, Alicia was slumped into an old leather armchair, pulling desperately on a cigarette.

'It's been one shitty day, Catherine.' Two jets of smoke pulsed from her nostrils. A cloud billowed from her scarlet lips.

'Hello to you too.' Catherine dropped her coat on top of a box of buckles and plopped into the matching chair. It shaped itself to fit like an old, comfortable sweater. 'So what's the problem?'

'Everything. Suppliers who don't supply, inventory that doesn't move, designs that won't work.' She kicked at a mauve cloud on the wooden floor and took another drag on her cigarette. 'Forget it!' Alicia's arms flailed the air. 'I'm glad you're here. Want some wine?'

'Sure.'

Alicia vanished through the heavy door which separated the workroom from her living quarters, leaving her guest to contemplate the chaos surrounding her. How could anyone work in this mess? When Catherine had asked this question, the designer claimed disorder was necessary to the creative process.

'You're a scientist, Catherine, you seek order in chaos. I'm an artist so I do the opposite. I hate order, discipline, categorizing. I need to "let it all hang out".'

Which she did with a vengeance. She ignored Catherine's warnings of the dangers of clutter, particularly on the floor.

Alicia returned with two glasses of red wine and they sipped in companionable silence, relishing the unaccustomed peace.

'You were having an affair with John,' Alicia murmured.

Catherine managed to not sputter into her wine at this bald pronouncement. 'Why would you say that?'

'John told me.'

Emotions simmered inside Catherine like gas bubbles in the mud pits at Yellowstone Park. Anger at John's betrayal flashed and died as Catherine remembered his dead face. Grief and loss swelled in their turn while bemusement hissed on the periphery.

'Why?' Catherine whispered.

'Why did he tell me?'

Catherine nodded.

With her long fingers Alicia coaxed another cigarette from her case. Why did the red nails against the white paper remind Catherine of blood droplets on snow? Drawing her feet up beneath her, Alicia lit up with practised, economical moves and sucked in a lungful of smoke.

'John and I were lovers too.'

A protest sprang to Catherine's lips but Alicia waved her down.

'Not now. Years ago. But we remained close. He told me lots of things over the years.'

'About me?'

Alicia shook her head slightly. 'No. He just mentioned that you were seeing each other. He didn't gossip about his women.'

Catherine said nothing. What was there to say?

'Aren't you surprised?' Alicia cocked her head to one side.

'About what?'

'That John and I were lovers.'

Catherine felt the blood seep into her cheeks, but Alicia wasn't pulling any punches so why should she? 'I did think you were lesbian.'

Alicia smiled—red mouth, sharp, white teeth. 'I'm versatile. John thought it added an exotic dimension to our relationship.'

'Oh.' Catherine took another gulp of the now tasteless wine, giving herself time to find a rudder in her sea of emotions. Silently Alicia refilled the glasses.

'Who else did he sleep with?' Catherine's voice cracked.

Alicia hunched her shoulders. 'No one we know. Did you think you were his only affair?'

'No . . .' She had tried not to think about his past when they were together. Or her own.

'You acted pretty callous at the funeral,' Catherine accused.

'I have my image to maintain.' Alicia tossed her head. 'You were pretty composed yourself, all things considered.'

Anger flashing and dissipating in a matter of moments, Catherine smiled instead. 'We played our parts so well— maybe we should've gone into acting.'

Her hostess leaned forward conspiratorially. 'Wasn't the funeral awful? I thought it would never end! And Calvin . . . What a performance!' She threw herself back in her chair. 'John would have died laughing if he weren't already dead. He found Calvin's self-importance very amusing.'

Silence descended again. Catherine heard a faint murmur of voices from the shop below where Marsha reassured a customer. The ornate cuckoo clock in the corner of the workroom was ticking as loudly as her heart.

'You know that I see a psychic from time to time?' Alicia spoke languidly, swirling the red wine this way and that as she stared into its crimson soul.

'Yes?'

'She warned me someone close to me was going to die.'

'So? It's bound to be true sooner or later.'

'She predicted it three days before John was killed. She said a man I knew well would die violently within the week.'

Catherine shifted uneasily but scepticism ran deep in her scientifically trained being. 'Coincidence.'

'Mrs McKeown is rarely wrong.'

'Mrs McKeown? Don't you mean Madame Zora? Or Swami Shankar or The Great Oswald?'

'No. Her name is Mildred McKeown and she lives in a high rise apartment on Rosewood Drive. Except for her psychic ability she's an ordinary, middle-aged lady—dull, in fact.'

Catherine snorted. 'A psychic Edith Bunker.'

'I knew you'd scoff but her prediction was horribly accurate. John died. Violently.'

Catherine's heart and the clock ticked on. Like a distant cowbell on a summer's breeze, she heard the chime at the shop door signalling the arrival or departure of a customer.

'I was with him that night, Alicia.' Catherine felt the words being drawn out of her against her will.

'The night he died?'

Catherine nodded. Images whirled around her mind and she chose only those fragments of memory which would form the bones of a story.

'We met at the Riverside Motel that night. When we rendezvoused at a motel instead of his place, John arrived first and put a silk butterfly in the window so I'd know which room he was in.' Catherine smiled. John's practical streak couldn't hide his romantic soul.

In her memory the room was indistinct—just a typical B class motel room: one window with print curtains pulled shut, two plastic armchairs, a formica desk and a matching chest of drawers. The tiny ensuite bath had an ashtray and two glasses, inevitably greasy despite their hygienic paper covers. And, centred in the room, the double bed where John sat, shirt off, smooth muscles bulging discreetly beneath the sheen of his golden skin. Remembering sent a surge of tingling warmth through Catherine's body. She sipped her wine before she spoke again.

'We had wine. We made love.' Catherine shivered at the memory. 'We talked . . . a little, but never much. We kept our lives separate . . . no threads to entangle us and lead back to our real lives. John was a wonderful lover; warm, giving, demanding, playful . . .'

Her gaze turned inward, Alicia nodded in agreement and somehow Catherine didn't mind. She paused, savouring the intimacy of the moment, but when she resumed speaking her voice echoed with desolation. 'I left him about eleven-thirty and went straight home. I never saw him again.'

They gave John more than three minutes of silence.

'Does Paul know?'

The inevitable question. Catherine shook her head.

'Where did you say you were going?'

Catherine sighed. Having to recite the mechanics of her affair cheapened it. 'I told Paul I'd be at the botany library. I often do my reading there in the evening—fewer distractions. Anyhow, Paul has completely taken over our study.'

'And he didn't notice anything when you got home?'

'I didn't even see him.'

'Maybe he was out having an affair too.'

Panic shot through Catherine for a split second and then dissipated. 'I doubt it. He's working pretty hard these days and we don't see much of each other. When I got home he was still hard at it in the study; at least I assume so since I heard the radio in there. I just slipped upstairs and went to bed.' Catherine flushed remembering what happened later. 'I was almost asleep when he came up and judging by his amorous mood he hadn't just come back from a late-night prowl.'

'And now?' Alicia asked, tilting her sleek head to one side and fastening her bright eyes on Catherine's face.

'What do you mean?'

'Are you looking for a new lover?'

Catherine slammed her glass down on the wide arm of her chair and a few drops of wine spilled out. 'No! John wasn't just a lover—he was . . . John.' Two spots of fury burned on her cheeks. 'How can you ask such a question? He wasn't merely a sexy body to be replaced by anything wearing pants!' She poised on the edge of her chair for another moment and then subsided, drained. 'Besides, I have Paul,' she whispered. 'I love Paul.'

'Ok, OK. Sorry. Calm down.' Alicia attempted to placate her friend. 'I know John was special to you. He was special to both of us.'

Catherine relaxed, slightly mollified, but her mood had changed and she turned the conversation back to Alicia's business woes for the few remaining minutes of her visit.

When Catherine left, Alicia didn't return to the lilac fabric. She hadn't been sleeping well since John's death and felt tired and dispirited. And uneasy.

She had first had her fortune told, just for fun, at a third-rate travelling circus. The grubby tent was lit only by the grey light filtered through the dirty canvas. Peering short-sightedly at Alicia's palm, the old woman mumbled the usual drivel about dark strangers and money. Alicia felt impatient and unimpressed and wished she hadn't come despite her friend Angela's dares. Suddenly, the crone's grip tightened painfully and she poked her sharply carved face into Alicia's.

'Don't fly, girl. You have no feathers. You have no wings! Don't fly! Stay away from Chicago—it is death if you go!'

Alicia struggled to tear her hand from the talons of the ancient one. 'What are you talking about? I'm not going to Chicago!' Alicia backed away but the woman and her skeletal, clutching hands didn't pursue her. Instead, the crone slumped, disoriented, into her chair and Alicia escaped into the fresh air.

Angela, the first of her woman lovers, waited outside. 'What's wrong? You look like you saw a ghost!'

'No. Just a silly old woman trying to trick people out of their money.' Laughing nervously, Alicia pulled her friend away from the tent. 'Let's go!'

Two days later, she was invited to show a few clothes at a convention in Chicago—her first move into the international world of fashion. Only as she boarded at Pearson Airport did Alicia remember the fortune-teller's warning. She scoffed at her twinge of fear. Fortune-tellers . . .

The plane smoothly took off and Alicia began to relax again. But while she poured a glass of Coke, the brown liquid altered course and started flowing sideways down her arm. Lurching wildly, the plane slid down the sky. Alicia's heart pounded erratically. Her mouth went dry.

Don't fly, girl! You have no wings! Don't fly! The fortune-teller's warning shrieked in Alicia's head and she clapped her hands over her ears.

'Put on your oxygen mask, miss, and take the crash position!' Her seat-mate clung on to the back of the seat ahead and yelled instructions at her. The man held the mask to Alicia's nose and mouth while she slipped the elastic around her head with palsied fingers. She took shuddering breaths and braced herself. All around the passengers hunched pale but compliant, grimly following instructions. Only then Alicia realized the seats near the missing wing door were gone. She'd been sitting there just minutes before but moved to allow four friends to sit together . . . Those four teenagers and one stewardess were sucked into oblivion. Alicia stretched her mouth wide open in a soundless wail.

The remaining passengers and crew made an emergency landing at Detroit, physically undamaged.

As soon as she got back from Chicago, Alicia started seeing a psychiatrist but gave it up almost immediately. She didn't need to analyse her pre-natal emotions. A year after that, however, still troubled by the harrowing event, she visited another fortune-teller, Mildred McKeown. Until the last appointment, Mrs McKeown had confined her advice and predictions to Alicia's business and social affairs. But on the night when she foretold John's death she'd worn the same haunted expression as the gypsy fortune-teller. Alicia had been afraid then. She was afraid now. And if, like the psychic, she could see the future, she would have been terrified.

CHAPTER 3

Catherine manœuvred her car into the one tiny spot left in the lot beside her husband's law firm. She didn't bother to lock it since her errand would take only a couple of minutes.

'Pick up the file on Neilson Manufacturing,' Paul had asked her. 'I'll call Gretchen and she'll have it ready.'

Catherine's schedule was already crowded, but she agreed. After all, the office lay just a few blocks from the university. It wouldn't be a long detour.

She raced up the stairs of the graceful limestone building to the second floor where Keigelmann, Edison and Purdy had their offices. The gold lettering on the heavy glass door gleamed richly in the subdued lighting of the hallway. Catherine didn't stop to admire it.

'Dr Edison, what a pleasant surprise.' Jeanine, the receptionist smiled a greeting. The sparkle in her startlingly blue eyes belied the formality of her carefully coiffed grey hair and tailored tweed suit. 'What brings you here today?'

'Hello, Jeanine. Gretchen has some papers ready for Paul. I'm here to collect them.'

'Have a seat and I'll call her.'

The navy brocade cushions of the waiting-room chair enfolded Catherine in their soft embrace while Jeanine spoke quietly into the telephone. Catherine nodded to the one other occupant of the room, an elderly gentleman dressed in the fashion of the nineteen-forties. He, in turn, graciously inclined his head in her direction. If he'd been wearing a hat he would have tipped it.

When Jeanine looked up her grey brows hung low over her eyes. 'Gretchen will be right out. She says Paul hasn't contacted her about any papers.'

'Damn,' Catherine ejaculated under her breath. The elegant gentleman's eyebrows snapped together in disapproval.

Gretchen Busch swept through the door dividing the waiting-room from the private offices as energetically as decorum would permit. Paul's secretary, her long, full skirt swirling around her shapely legs, pushed back her straight honey hair as she waded through the deep pile of the rug. 'I'm sorry, Catherine, but Paul didn't leave me any instructions. Do you know what exactly he wants?'

Catherine hesitated. 'The Nelson . . . no, Neilson Manufacturing file is what he told me.'

Gretchen's grey eyes loomed large behind her wide, red-framed glasses. 'Huh.' She compressed her lips to a thin line. 'You might as well come with me to his office while I look.'

Catherine followed the whirlwind into the hushed atmosphere of the inner sanctum. The second suite on the left was Paul's and Gretchen commanded the outer office. Mountains of papers stood in neat rows, indicative of Gretchen's orderly mind.

'Do you have enough work to keep you busy?' Catherine asked.

'Lots. I take the overflow from the other partners and I do the real estate work for the entire office.' Gretchen smiled. 'It's like being my own boss.'

'Sounds like you're enjoying yourself,' Catherine remarked.

'I am.' Gretchen crouched over a low drawer and rapidly fingered through the ranks of legal-sized manilla folders.

She straightened, empty-handed. 'Sometimes when Paul comes in on the weekends or evenings he doesn't refile things properly,' Gretchen said. 'I keep telling him to just leave the stuff on the desk and I'll look after it.' She slammed shut the last drawer. 'Come on.'

Catherine meekly followed Gretchen into the huge inner office. It made her own room at the university look like a messy closet but Catherine preferred the lived-in atmosphere she maintained. She picked up the framed photograph on the corner of Paul's desk—the picture of Morgan and herself was four or five years old. I'll have to get him a new one, Catherine thought, if and when Paul comes back to work here. She wandered aimlessly while Gretchen flew around the room flipping open every folder she came across.

Since Catherine's last visit to the office another small table had been added to the side of Paul's desk. A sleek computer and a printer waited for someone to switch them on into purring life. 'Does Paul use the computer, Gretchen?'

'Oh yes, we're all into computers now; every law office is. Paul's very good with them, actually. Before he left to go politicking he was more computer literate than the rest of us.' Gretchen paused to frown at the disarray in one of the desk drawers. 'But I'm getting better—I feel quite comfortable with them now and the others come to me for help.'

'Good for you,' Catherine murmured. Paul hadn't mentioned to her that the office was computerized. Another symptom that communication between them was in difficulty.

'Eureka!' Gretchen waved a folder at Catherine. 'I found it. Neilson Manufacturing.' She turned to the last page in

41

the file. 'The most recent date on this is two years ago. I wonder why Paul needs it?'

'Think of a political connection, Gretchen, and you've got the reason. Politics is his *raison d'être* right now.'

'So I gather.' Gretchen handed over the file. 'I hope this is it. Too bad Paul didn't get around to phoning me—you wouldn't have had to wait so long.'

'It's OK. I haven't been here in ages. I enjoyed seeing the place again. *Plus ça change . . .*'

Gretchen turned off the light and shut the door behind them. 'I saw you at John Retson's funeral,' Paul's secretary said. 'I'm sorry about your friend. He was a wonderful man.'

Catherine's head snapped around. 'Oh? Were you there?' Her question came out more sharply than she intended. Was Gretchen one of John's other 'affairs'?

'My husband works at the aluminium plant. He and John usually took the same shift.'

'Oh.' A flush of embarrassment rose in Catherine's cheeks.

'I didn't know John very well myself,' Gretchen continued, 'but Ray—that's my husband—and John were drinking buddies. John came over to our place a few times to watch the football games on TV. I gather he didn't have cable out his way.'

'No, John lives . . . lived in the country,' Catherine replied, forcing back her tears. She turned to stare out of the window so Gretchen couldn't see her moist eyes.

'How's your arm these days, Catherine? All better?' Gretchen sat down at her desk and swivelled her chair around to face Catherine.

'As better as it's going to get.' Under control again, Catherine turned and flexed her left hand in front of her. 'I have all the movement back but absolutely no strength. A cup of tea is about as much as I can lift.'

'You should've gone for a larger insurance settlement,' Gretchen admonished, flicking her hair out of her eyes. 'The accident was the other guy's fault.'

'Oh well.' Catherine smiled. 'I'm not the vindictive type.'

'If it had been your fault I'll bet the other guy would've tried to take you to the cleaners.'

'Maybe, maybe not,' Catherine responded, 'but I did all right. I've learned to live with this little handicap—it makes a great excuse for not taking out the garbage!'

Gretchen laughed and escorted Catherine to the doorway of the suite. 'Say hello to Paul for me. Tell him I'm doing OK holding the fort.'

'He's lucky to have you. 'Bye now.' Catherine lifted a hand in farewell and returned to the lobby where Jeanine winked a bright blue eye at her. 'Get what you wanted, Dr Edison?'

'Yes, thanks.' She couldn't resist smiling at Jeanine.

'Nice to see you again . . .'

Catherine descended the stairs thinking about Gretchen Busch and John. Had they been lovers?

CHAPTER 4

Catherine sweated in the kitchen all Sunday afternoon preparing roast beef, Yorkshire pudding, potato salad, lemon pie—all the stuff Paul liked. He was busy in the study, but when called he attacked his dinner with gusto and even lingered over coffee.

'Great dinner, Cath.' He patted his stomach. 'It should keep me going for another week at least.'

'Thank you, kind sir.' She made a little bow. 'By the way, I picked up a video for the three of us to watch tonight.'

Paul examined his watch with a worried frown. 'I don't think I've time. I've a whole lot more to do tonight.'

'I suppose you're working on something for Calvin,' Catherine remarked bitterly. 'He seems to rate higher in your book than Morgan and I do any more.'

'That's not true!'

'It sure looks that way from where I'm sitting! You haven't spent two consecutive hours with either of us in months.'

Paul slapped his palms down on to the table, rattling the dishes. 'You're exaggerating.'

'I am not. When was the last time you inquired about my research? Or Morgan's school work? Do you remember what grade she's in?'

'Of course I do!'

Catherine leaned closer and stared him in the eye. 'Well? What grade?'

'Uh . . . six. She's in the sixth grade.' Paul, in his turn leaned forward challengingly. 'Right?'

'You had to think about it.'

'But I'm right. I'm not as out of touch as you think.'

Catherine subsided into her chair and drained her coffee cup. 'What are you working on that's so damn important?' she asked at last.

Paul relaxed, acknowledging the truce. 'Calvin's speech for the Oakwood Chamber of Commerce dinner and I'm trying to hit just the right note. I need to glorify private enterprise without alienating the more socialistic-minded reporters and constituents. It's not easy!'

'Why can't Calvin write his own material?' Catherine sulked. 'I hope he appreciates all your effort.'

'He does appreciate it—especially since he is abysmal at speech-writing. But, Catherine, you have to admit he can deliver a speech better than anyone around!'

'I suppose . . . but then he gets all the kudos for your work. You should go into politics yourself, instead of getting behind Calvin and boosting him.'

Paul leaned back in his chair and shook his head decisively. 'No way. I'd freeze out there in front of the crowd. I don't have any of Calvin's charisma. I'll settle for being a backroom boy—the power behind the throne.'

He sprang energetically from his chair and kissed Catherine on the top of her head. 'And you can be the power behind the power behind the throne!' He strode off towards the study.

'There's no throne yet!' she called after him.

Sitting alone with the ruins of dinner, Catherine sighed and poured herself another glass of wine. While Paul

44

worked day and night on Calvin's still 'unofficial' bid to become the new party leader, his own law practice slipped away. More and more of his clients were being absorbed by his partners, Wilf Purdy and Jan Kiegelmann and so, since Calvin didn't pay Paul, the Edison family income was dwindling alarmingly. When Catherine had mentioned billing Calvin, Paul had been adamantly opposed.

'When Calvin gets elected I'll get my reward. He promised to put me in charge of his private office.'

'A glorified secretary!'

'Power broker. I'll be at the centre of activity. We can tighten our belts for another few months, honey. Calvin will soon be the front runner.'

'The race has barely started. Things can change. And have you a written guarantee that Calvin won't just cast you aside when you've got him elected?'

'That's a hell of a thing to say about one of your oldest and dearest friends, Catherine, and not much of a vote of confidence for me! I can still be of use *after* he wins the leadership.'

Catherine flushed. 'I know. It's just that you're working so hard and I never see you . . .'

And here was yet another weekend devoted to Calvin. She was beginning to hate that man!

She sipped the white wine and smiled bitterly. Paul resembled a bloodhound pursuing the scent. He couldn't be distracted from his path and Calvin's election as Premier was his current target. That the Conservative Party had suffered a humiliating defeat in the last election didn't even give him pause.

Calvin, in fact, was the indirect reason for Catherine's affair with John. Driven himself, Calvin had turned Paul into a workaholic. Now that Morgan had matured to the point where she didn't need her mother's constant attention, Catherine had free time—time she would have spent with Paul, given the chance.

Three months before John's death, Catherine and Julie accompanied their husbands to a fund-raising dinner. 'To add an air of informality and family values,' Paul explained.

But when the gala affair concluded Paul and Calvin huddled with their associates and the women were left cooling their heels in the empty, barnlike room.

'We should just take the car and go home,' Catherine declared. 'I have to prepare my lecture for tomorrow.'

'Do you think we should?' Julie wondered timidly. 'Calvin'll be really angry.'

'So what?' Catherine demanded. 'However, I didn't bring my keys since they don't fit in this ridiculous little handbag. You don't have to worry.'

Julie sighed, pleased to avoid annoying Calvin. 'What about a taxi?'

'Way out here?' Catherine said with a snort. 'I don't know why they hold these affairs in the middle of nowhere. Maybe they need a captive audience.'

They sat in gloomy silence. Catherine toyed with her empty wine glass and tapped her nails impatiently on its rim. She watched the tired-looking waitresses sweep the soiled tablecloths from the long wooden tables and scrape the chairs across the floor to stack them along the far wall. The room smelled of stale smoke and human sweat. Catherine wrinkled her nose in distaste. Suddenly she sat forward and stabbed a finger at Julie. 'John! His place isn't far away. He'd give us a ride, don't you think?'

'Sure he would!' Julie smiled in relief. She wanted to get home as much as Catherine and if her twin brother, John, gave them a lift it wouldn't inconvenience Calvin. John always came when she called.

Twenty minutes later the women ran out into the chilly night to climb into John's jeep. The shock of fresh air accentuated the slight high Catherine felt from the wine. She tossed her hair and skipped a couple of steps.

'You'll both have to sit in the front,' John announced. 'All my camping gear's in the back.'

Somehow Catherine found herself in the middle, wedged between brother and sister as they sped through the magic darkness. For a split second the headlights impaled a small animal, frozen in fear, by the side of the road. Then they rushed to illuminate another ephemeral tableau.

46

John's knee touched Catherine's. Their thighs exchanged warmth and, for Catherine, John ceased being Julie's brother. For an instant he took on the persona of his dead brother, Danny, and then his own unique maleness pressed itself on Catherine. She shut her eyes and abandoned herself to the frisson of excitement. Danger. Did John feel it too?

She opened her eyes a slit and peeked through her lashes. John's profile glowed dimly in the blue light from the dashboard. He kept his gaze on the road but his right foot shifted on the gas pedal and his thigh pressed more urgently against hers. Catherine didn't move away. When John down-shifted for a tight curve his hand brushed her knee, bare except for thin nylon hose. Unobtrusively she hiked her skirt a little higher. Julie breathed softly as she slept, her head resting lightly on Catherine's shoulder.

'I'll drop Julie off first,' John said, his voice thick. He cleared his throat. 'She's really tired.'

'That's fine.' To Catherine's ears her voice sounded artificial and it jolted her. What on earth am I thinking of, she asked herself? I'm a happily married woman and John is a childhood friend!

Drawing away, she crowded Julie who murmured in her sleep. Catherine knew John was looking at her but she kept her eyes fixed on the side of the road. She could feel John's presence; he emanated a sexual force which at the moment made her giddy. She hadn't felt so sensual in years.

The jeep coasted to a halt in the Parker driveway.

'Wake up, Julie.' Catherine shook her friend gently. 'You're home.'

Julie sat up, bleary-eyed, and fumbled for the door handle. 'Thanks, John,' she mumbled and staggered out of the jeep. Her good training kicked in as she mechanically asked, 'Would you like to come in for coffee or something?'

'No, thanks, sis,' John quickly replied. 'You look dead on your feet. I'll just run Catherine on home. See you soon.'

Julie sketched a wave, hunched her shoulders against the bitter night wind and soon vanished into her house. Catherine was alone with John and her unchained emotions. She licked her lips.

47

Silence hung over them during the drive to the Edison house. They eyed each other furtively. Catherine sat erect with her knees pressed tightly together but she hadn't moved over to occupy Julie's vacated spot.

'Where's Morgan?' John asked, his voice sparking the charged atmosphere.

'She's having a sleepover at a friend's house,' Catherine whispered.

'Guess Paul's going to be tied up for hours with Calvin and his cronies.'

'Likely.' She swallowed. 'It looked like an all-nighter to me,' she tried unsuccessfully for a nonchalant tone.

He pulled up in front of Catherine's house and switched off the engine. For the first time since leaving the restaurant they sought each other's eyes.

'Would you like to come in for a drink?' Catherine's voice sounded steady but husky.

'Thanks.' John got out of the jeep, locked the doors and then followed her to the front door where she fumbled with the keys.

'Let me.' He slipped the keys from her trembling fingers. Once inside, Catherine held out her hand to take his coat, knowing they would somehow manage to touch each other. The electricity coursed through her body as his hand brushed hers.

'What would you like?' She led the way to the living-room but, when she paused, John placed his hand in the small of her back and propelled her down the hall to the guest-room.

After shutting the door behind them, John turned her to face him. He removed her glasses, folded them carefully and placed them on the dresser. He put his own beside hers, aligning both pairs parallel to the dresser edge. Then he returned his attention to Catherine, his eyes unfocused and soft with desire. They stared at each other. Catherine felt her nipples straining against her camisole and her breath came in shallow gasps through her parted lips. John moved towards her. As a groan escaped her, his hands and lips inflamed every pleasure receptor in her skin. Catherine couldn't even remember undressing but once naked their

48

lovemaking consumed them and Catherine's senses over-loaded until she lay shattered on the bed. When John rose to leave she didn't have the strength to protest.

'You'd better go up to your own room,' John suggested quietly. 'It would be wiser than staying here.'

They kissed languidly and John traced Catherine's nipples with his finger. 'See you soon.'

When Catherine awoke in the morning, to find Paul stretched out beside her, it took her a few moments to figure out why she felt so relaxed, so fulfilled. As soon as she remembered, however, a sick feeling flooded her body. What had she done? She vaulted out of bed and ran for the shower but she couldn't wash away her guilt. 'I'll make it up to you, Paul,' she whispered into the rushing jet of water. 'I'll be a perfect wife. I'll never even speak to John again.'

Her resolution lasted until John appeared in the doorway of her office a few days later. 'Tonight?' he asked.

'Yes.' Catherine was addicted.

The ringing of the telephone roused her from her reverie. She answered in a daze.

'Catherine? It's Julie. The police found the car that killed John.'

'At last! Have they arrested someone?'

'Not yet.' Julie paused briefly. 'I know it's Sunday evening and all, but could you come over for a while? I don't want to be alone.'

'Give me half an hour to clean up the dinner dishes.'

'Thanks. I'll be waiting.'

She might as well visit Julie, Catherine thought peevishly, since her family night had gone down the drain. At least someone wanted her company.

As she drove along the familiar streets of Kingsport, huge fluffy flakes of snow wafted down from the black sky. By twos and threes they landed on the windshield and surrendered their essence to the tiny rivulets of moisture running upward on the glass. The air seemed preternaturally silent, even the roar of the car's engine was dampened by the white muffler enveloping the night. Catherine drove slowly through the beads of lamplight that demarcated the road.

Catherine and Paul Edison lived in the older part of town, near the university, where the houses were tall and narrow in their turn-of-the-century architecture. Lining the avenues, spreading elms offered their naked limbs to the elements and worshipped the wind with their ceaseless murmur, cradling the snow in unsuspected crevices. Catherine loved this part of Kingsport and resisted Paul's sporadic attempts to relocate to the sterile suburbs where rambling houses sprawled on manicured patches of green and no tree was taller than fifteen feet.

Calvin and Julie Parker lived in such a neighbourhood, so Catherine drove westward through the night receiving a lesson in the history of Ontario architecture as the buildings got newer and the trees fewer and shorter. She left behind the last of the tall, narrow houses with the wide front porches and passed through a huddled collection of wartime boxes. Whenever Catherine passed an enclave like this, vignettes of her childhood played through her memories. She had grown up in a house just like these. The home where she lived with her mom and dad, had been pale yellow, always bright and clean since her father painted the ribbed wooden shingles every second year. Except for the colour and the landscaping, all the houses on their street looked identical. The living-room and largest bedroom flanked the front door. The kitchen and a small dining-room formed the back wall while the single bathroom and the stairway to the second half-storey were sandwiched in between.

Even now, fifteen years since her mother's death, her sad, desperate voice echoed in Catherine's ears. Tonight a brief, unremarkable interlude replayed in her mind.

'Catherine, could you get me a cup of tea, please, dear, if it's not too much trouble.'

It had been a beautiful summer evening and Catherine was just on the point of setting out to join the other kids at the gravel pit. Danny and Calvin had found an old, rusted rifle in the woods and were going to try some target practice.

As a supreme favour, the rest of them were going to be allowed to watch.

'Sure, Mom, I'll make tea. It's no trouble.'

While she waited for the tin kettle to boil, Catherine picked half-heartedly at a rip in the oilcloth covering the battered table and felt sorry for herself. Her mother was sick most of the time and had been ill as long as Catherine could remember. Except for the handful of days each month when her Mom felt a little better, it was Catherine who did the household chores while her father drove a taxi twelve hours a day.

Mostly Catherine's mother lay hour after hour, day after day, on a daybed in the front room listening to the radio and watching out of the window. Sometimes she knitted or embroidered but mostly her heavily veined hands travelled restlessly over her thin blanket, picking at the countless tiny pills of wool.

'Here's your tea, Mom. Do you want a cookie?'

'No, thanks, dear.' She patted the bed beside her, wordlessly begging her daughter to keep her company.

Catherine sat, hiding her disappointment as well as she could.

'If you had other plans, Catherine, go ahead.'

'Of course not, Mom.' Catherine pulled up a small table. 'Shall we play cribbage?'

'That would be nice.'

They both knew Catherine didn't want to stay but as long as it went unsaid they could pretend to be having a good time. Catherine knew where she would be, given a choice, but she didn't know where her mother's secret dreams took her; she had never asked. This night, driving through the snow, she wished she had.

By the time Catherine shook off the cloying tendrils of the past she had left the 'fifties bungalows, 'sixties ranches, and 'seventies split levels behind to arrive at the neo-Tudor homes of the 'eighties. Julie's looked more authentic than most.

'I shouldn't have asked you to come,' was Julie's greeting. 'It's snowing harder than I thought.'

51

'It's a beautiful night,' Catherine reassured her. 'Where are Calvin and the kids?'

'Calvin's at a meeting and Richard and Melissa are upstairs with Consuelo.'

Consuelo was the children's nanny.

'I thought you said you were alone?'

Julie hung her head. 'I needed a friend. Consuelo or the children wouldn't understand.'

In the sitting-room a fire crackled and hissed and the pair snuggled into the two chairs bracketing the fireplace. A steaming pot of chocolate radiated comfort from the table between them. Julie poured two mugs and handed one to her friend. 'You must be cold.'

'Thanks.' Silence descended but Catherine didn't push Julie into conversation, instead she soaked in the cosy atmosphere, content to wait.

This sitting-room was the only room in the house imprinted with Julie's personality. Flowers abounded. Daisies flourished on the drapes and on the chairs the women occupied. Buttercups danced around the border just under the ceiling. A photograph of yellow lilies flickered in and out of the gloom above the fireplace. Instead of heavy stone and dark wood, the fireplace itself was small, bordered in white, and the mantel, where crystal flowers blossomed, was delicately carved and painted with white enamel. Yellow Italian marble tiles formed the hearth while a white oval rag rug provided the only other covering on the blond wood floor. A friendly room.

'It has finally sunk in, Catherine; John is really dead.' Julie stared at the flames, the misery in her face burned red in the fire light. She spoke slowly, with long, poignant pauses between her thoughts.

'Even seeing his body at the funeral home didn't make it real for me. I don't know why. As for the funeral itself . . . I can't even remember it. Calvin looked after all that.

'It was when the police called to say they found the car which killed him; that's when it hit me. In this city, right now, there's a black Chevrolet Cavalier with a dented fender and a broken headlight and John's blood embedded in its paint. A real, solid object which tore his life away from him. From me.'

Listening to Julie's pain accentuated Catherine's own. Her stomach lurched and her eyes stung. From me, too, she screamed inside. 'We all miss him, Julie.'

'But he was part of me, Catherine! Maybe it seemed to you that we'd drifted apart since I married and the children were born but it wasn't so. John and I were as close as ever. We didn't have to talk—we knew what the other was thinking and feeling. He gave me strength.' Tears were spilling down Julie's ashen cheeks. 'What am I going to do?' she wailed.

'You still have Calvin . . .'

Julie shook her head. 'It's not the same. Calvin's so strong! He expects me to be strong—he can't abide weakness. John was my strength and without him I'll fade away!' The wail dropped to a sigh. 'Fade away,' she repeated in despair.

They were both crying but Catherine knew it was for themselves, for their loss, not for John. The heat of shame soon dried her cheeks.

'Calvin loves you, Julie,' Catherine reassured her. 'He'll understand.'

Julie still shook her head. Catherine poured more hot chocolate and thrust the cup into Julie's freezing hands. 'Drink.'

She drank. Catherine feared Julie's frightening pliability. 'Do you want something stronger?' Catherine asked.

'No.' But from her pocket Julie took two small yellow pills and slipped them into her mouth. As she washed them down the desperation melted from her expression.

In the silence Catherine speculated about the Parker household. In contrast to Julie's gentleness, Calvin presented a formidable personality. Catherine had thought he dominated his family without even realizing it but perhaps his autocratic behaviour wasn't totally unconscious. Calvin expected everyone to bend to his will and most people did. Susan was an exception and Catherine tried to be too, just

53

on principle, since Paul did enough bending for both of them.

'What else did the police tell you?' Catherine's voice croaked hoarsely in the silence. She and Julie both needed to be roused from their respective reveries, and, besides, she wanted to know the details of John's death. 'Why haven't they arrested the guy who owns the car?'

'Because he wasn't driving it. He was in the hospital having chemotherapy and someone stole his car from the hospital parking lot. Poor guy . . .'

Julie raised her head and looked at her friend. 'Do you know exactly where John was killed?'

'On the Bolingbroke Road across from his place, I suppose.'

John had lived in what had once been a cottage. Working sporadically over a couple of years, he had renovated it, installing insulation, hot water and heating. He added a huge glass-walled room overlooking the entire expanse of the lake. In summer he had plenty of company in the other cottagers, but in winter he enjoyed virtual solitude. The only drawback to this idyllic retreat was the very real possibility of being snowed in. To guard against this, John parked his jeep in a nearby farmer's barn and traversed the long driveway by foot or snowshoe. Catherine assumed he'd been hit crossing the main road to reach the cottage drive.

But Julie was shaking her head. 'No. He was about six miles from home.'

'What?'

'He had a flat tyre. He was walking to get help.'

Catherine's brow wrinkled. 'John could change a tyre by himself . . .'

A sob convulsed Julie. 'The spare was flat too. Can you believe it?'

'But John said he'd just checked all the . . .' Catherine bit her lip as she saw the puzzlement in Julie's eyes. 'I mean . . . he told me last winter he checked everything at least once a week.'

Julie nodded. 'John was very thorough. Especially in the winter.' She got up for more tissue and wiped away the tears streaming down her cheeks. She pressed her knuckles into her temples. 'How could they leave him? Maybe he didn't die right away . . . maybe he lay there for hours . . . bleeding . . . in pain . . .'

Gathering Julie's grief-racked body in her arms, Catherine hugged her close and stroked her hair. 'Don't think that, darling. The cold would have numbed any pain almost immediately. I'm sure he died quickly. Don't cry.'

Such inane words, but then Catherine had never studied the etiquette of death rituals and wasn't comfortable when confronted with raw emotion. And the whole story of John's death struck her as odd. Two flat tyres couldn't be a coincidence. And he always carried a powerful flashlight—he would've been far from invisible.

She was still in a sombre mood when she pulled into the carport at home. Paul's Volvo rated a garage but her beat-up Datsun had to brave the elements. For the present her car was sheltered but when the wind strengthened the snow would drift right over it.

A welcome wave of warmth and light greeted her as she slammed the front door behind her. Through the archway she could see Paul and Morgan together on the rug in front of a blazing fire. Only Paul looked up.

'Morgan's beating me, Catherine! Save me from the little fiend!'

They were playing Mastermind and it was Morgan's turn to crack the code.

'Dad won the first game, but I won the second and I've almost got the third,' Morgan crowed with delight, sweeping a lock of hair behind her ear. 'There! I've done it. I'm right, aren't I, Daddy?'

'You are, my little genius. You sure put me in my place!' Paul swooped forward to kiss Morgan on the cheek and then leaned back on his elbows, stretching.

'Bed now, Sweet Pea.'

'Aw, Dad . . .'

'You don't think I'm going to let you stick around to gloat, do you? Next time think twice before you beat your old man.'

55

'I'll be there to tuck you in in a minute,' Catherine promised, giving her daughter a little shove towards the stairs.

'Did you finish your speech?' Catherine asked when Morgan was out of earshot.

'Almost. Morgan came in and asked me to play with her just at the right moment.'

'I'm glad you said yes.'

'So am I. She's a good kid—takes after her mother.'

Catherine was chuckling as she went to say good night to Morgan and the rest of the evening passed in the low key contentment that used to be part of their lives. She chose not to shatter the fragile domestic bliss with questions about John's death.

CHAPTER 5

'Don't jump on the chair, Peter,' Peggy hollered at her nine-year-old son. Exasperation suffused her shrill tone. 'Get off at once, do ya hear?'

Peter scrambled off the battered furniture but hopped back on the minute his mother turned away.

Of late, visiting Peggy was more of a chore than a pleasure but Catherine hadn't figured out how to break off a long-standing routine without hurting her friend. It seemed every time Peggy spoke to Catherine she did nothing but lick the various wounds life had inflicted on her.

'You're so lucky, Catherine.'

Yes, Catherine knew she was lucky, but luck wasn't the only reason her life had evolved more satisfactorily than Peggy's. But her friend never gave her any credit.

'Wilson's still bugging you?' Catherine asked.

'Bugging me! He spies on me, he lets the air out of my tyres, he wanders around outside the house at night . . .'

'Why don't you call the police?'

'They can't do anything.'

'Have you tried them?' Catherine knew the answer was

no. However much trouble Peggy's estranged husband caused, Peggy wouldn't do anything to control him, to get him completely out of her life. When she married Wilson, Peggy had moved straight from her father's home to Wilson's and Catherine didn't think she could face a life totally devoid of dominating men.

'Peter! Stop it! I told you not to play on the furniture!' Peggy came up behind him trailing a wet dish towel which she flicked at the back of Peter's neck. The child dodged with ease, raced across the sofa, dived into his room, and slammed the door behind him.

His mother sighed and reseated herself at the kitchen table. While Catherine made a pattern of circles with the wet bottom of her coffee cup, they both ignored the shrieks coming from the girls' bedroom.

'Too bad Morgan couldn't come. Ashley loves to see her.'

'Yes, too bad,' Catherine echoed. Morgan was not in fact busy, but she hated visiting the Brandenburg household so Catherine didn't have the heart to make her come. Morgan called it the Bear Pit. Her mother knew what she meant.

'The kids don't behave now that Wilson's gone. I can't control them—especially Peter.'

'They're bound to be upset for a while.'

'It has been a year since Wilson left—more than a year. He was getting a little crazy, though; I'm glad he went.' Peggy was still trying to convince herself.

'It's weird he still hangs around.'

Peggy grunted. 'He wants to come back now, you know. Maybe I should let him . . .'

'We've talked this over a hundred times, Peggy.' Catherine leaned forward earnestly. 'Wilson's unstable. Four times you've taken him back and it's time to break the pattern. You know he'll leave again and you and the kids will just got through the agony one more time. Stick to your guns.'

'Peter wants his father back. He blames me for breaking up the family.'

'That's ridiculous!'

'Tell him that!' Peggy shrilled. She went to the stove for

57

more coffee and poured Catherine a refill she didn't want. 'The kids used to mind their father.' Peggy said wistfully.

'Yes. He scared the wits out of them. Ashley and Jennifer don't want Wilson back, that's for sure.'

'But a boy needs his father, Catherine. You don't know —you don't have a boy.'

'No one needs a nutcase around. Peter will calm down over time.' Privately, however, Catherine doubted this. At nine, Peter was well along the way to becoming a younger version of his father.

'Wilson isn't all bad, you know; he can be very charming.' Peggy ended up, as always, defending the jerk.

'I know. But charm isn't the main characteristic of a good husband and father.'

Catherine longed to get off this endless topic if even for five minutes. Out of the window she caught sight of the big pond behind the house. It was frozen now and had been shovelled off for skating. At the moment a thin blanket of fresh snow coated the ice.

'The children you baby sit must love having a skating-rink just outside.'

Peggy smiled and a hint of her basic prettiness peeked through the unkempt hair and extra ten pounds.

'They do. I have skates for all of them but Katie and Bryson are especially good,' she enthused. Peggy loved small children.

Peggy lived in a rambling home on the edge of a small wood. The property was a souvenir of one of Wilson's more affluent periods but somehow they'd managed to hang on to it. There was space enough for pets—rabbits, dogs and cats at the moment. A few chickens (separated from the dogs and cats by a sagging mesh fence) scratched in the yard. Peggy had provided sandboxes, swing sets and climbing ropes. The *pièce de résistance*, however, was the pond—a spring-fed swimming hole in the summer and a skating-rink in winter.

Catherine leapt from her chair. 'Let's go shovel the rink, Peggy!'

'What?' Peggy's head jerked up.

'Have you a spare pair of skates? Let's you and I clear the rink.'

'Are you sure you can manage a scraper with your weak arm?' Warm and comfortable, Peggy felt less than enthusiastic about going out in the cold.

Catherine grabbed her friend's hand and pulled. 'Sure. My other arm's as strong as a wrestler's.'

Ten minutes later, bundled up like papooses, the two women were outside on the ice, each pushing a snow-scraper before her. Peggy's dog, Rex, bounded from one to the other, wagging his tail.

'I've always wanted to do this! Remember when we were kids? At the rink at the end of Earl Street?'

Peggy nodded, her breath already coming in gasps.

Catherine's mind drifted back thirty years. In Kingsport, in the 1950s, outdoor rinks were constructed in all the parks. Around the middle of November the boards went up and the children waited impatiently for the snow to come and the flooding to commence. The city established the rinks and flooded them periodically, but otherwise it was up to the individual neighbourhoods to maintain them. At the rink near Catherine's home the teenage boys took control. The boys decided when scraping was necessary. They ordered the others off the rink and then self-importantly skated up and down in formation, erasing the dust of a hundred skate blades. As a mere girl, Catherine was automatically excluded from the priesthood of this ritual which had appealed to her so strongly. Now, thirty years later, she experienced the rush of fulfilment as her blades stroked rhythmically backward and to the side. She skated like a boy, for power rather than grace.

'Don't go so close to that end!' Peggy called sharply.

Catherine had penetrated an area of deeper snow and was intent on expanding the skating surface into it.

'See those red sticks? They mark off the location of the spring. The ice over it's never thick enough to walk on.'

Catherine swerved away and made a final pass down the centre, accumulating only a thin ridge like white chenille on the end of her shovel. She felt a pool of satisfaction welling up inside her. She had done the job and entered the ranks of the chosen. Catherine was glad, after all, that she'd come.

CHAPTER 6

For the two weeks after John's funeral, Catherine was inundated with work at the university. Her fourth-year class in fungal systematics were handing in their projects on the classification of phytoparasitic mildews. Her second-year students were submitting their lab notes for marking. The first-year students were panicking about their midterm test and lined up at Catherine's door for hints and reassurance. In the few breathing spaces she found, Catherine was frantically wrapping up an experiment to complete her study of interfungal parasitism by *Sporothrix*. She wanted to submit the paper by the middle of February so it would be out of the way before the end of spring term.

Catherine was deep into her data on resistance of *Sporothrix* to commercial fungicides when Julie Parker telephoned. It took her a moment to adjust her thinking.

'Slow down, Julie. You want me to do what?'

'Help me go through John's things. I'm going to spend the weekend at his house and sort through everything. I can't bear to go alone . . .'

Tension knotted Catherine's stomach. She'd been trying to put John out of her mind. 'What about Calvin? Or Melissa?'

'Calvin's busy as usual and the kids would just be in the way. Please, say you'll come.'

Catherine chewed her lip. Could she face the shards of John's life with more courage than his sister? 'I'm really busy here, Julie—it's midterm.'

'Then you need a break and I need you. You knew John . . . he wouldn't mind you seeing his things. Please?'

'All right,' Catherine agreed reluctantly, 'if Paul or Susan can keep an eye on Morgan.'

Fungus forgotten, Catherine's mind filled again with images of John. His auburn hair, wiry between her fingers. His lips, both soft and demanding at the same time. His endless supply of plaid shirts. Catherine's lips twitched. He never had any sense of fashion.

Going with Julie to John's abandoned home would force her to confront the physical remnants of his truncated life. The prospect frightened her. The idea of standing on the very spot where her lover had died terrified her. What would she find? Did John's ghost walk, searching for justice? Revenge?

Friday evening found Catherine driving to John's with Julie at her side. They were both tense. Off the main highway Catherine drove slowly along the Bolingbroke Road. Gravel and ice crunched under the tyres.

'Stop here.'

Catherine twisted to look at her companion. 'What?'

'Stop here. This is where it happened.'

'How do you know?' Catherine whispered without knowing why.

'I can feel it.'

Catherine pulled to the side of the road and turned off the engine. There was nothing remarkable about this section of the road. Here it ran straight, between a rail fence on one side and a ten-foot drop on the other. There was no curve or dip to hide a pedestrian carrying a flashlight, as John always did, and there was enough room to step off the road if necessary. It didn't look like the scene of an accident; it looked like the scene of a crime. Catherine couldn't bear the loneliness. She grabbed Julie's arm. 'Let's go!'

Both women shivered. Catherine restarted the car and turned up the heater but she knew it wouldn't help. Cold wasn't the problem.

Minutes later she turned into a narrow drive and pulled up to a dilapidated barn. 'Can you open it, Julie? I'd like to have the car out of the weather.'

Inside, there was just enough room to squeeze in behind John's jeep. After killing the engine they still sat, motionless and silent, the headlights pinning the salt-caked jeep to their consciousness. The ache of loss saturated Catherine's bones with lead.

'Who brought his car here?' she asked. Her voice hung dead in the still cold.

'Mr Buchanan, the farmer who owns this place. He told Calvin he'd look after it till we decided what to do with it.'

Catherine stared at the vehicle. The last time it was out of the barn John had driven it to see her. Though just a few weeks ago, it seemed a lifetime. Even closing her eyes, she had difficulty picturing John behind the wheel, laughing and gesticulating as he always did.

'Shall we see if there's anything in his car?' Julie asked softly.

Catherine jerkily nodded, took a breath and stepped out into the cold. Even through her gloves the dead chill of the handle burned her fingers as she tentatively swung open John's door. The courtesy light blinked on and bathed the utilitarian interior in a feeble light. A blue silk butterfly lay abandoned on the seat.

'What's that?'

Julie's fingers were reaching for it from the passenger side but Catherine's hand shot out unbidden and snatched it up.

'I'll bring it to the house with us,' Catherine croaked, and slipped the butterfly into her pocket where it was going to stay. It was hers.

Julie opened the glove compartment and began sorting through the few contents. 'Do you have a bag?'

In a daze Catherine returned to her own vehicle where she recklessly pitched her research notes to the floor. She and Julie refilled the briefcase with John's belongings. A packet of cigarettes . . . John no longer had to worry about dying of lung cancer. Three tapes. Pens. A wrinkled shirt. Ownership documents. Magazines. The fishing box and snowshoes Julie left behind in the back along with hamburger wrappers and six paper coffee cups, brown wedges frozen in their bottoms.

'Ready?' Catherine asked finally.

'Let's go.'

They didn't need their flashlights—the stars lit the path with their cold, impersonal light. The only sounds were the squeak of the snow and the swish of their nylon-clad arms against their jackets. The frigid air burned Catherine's lungs and caught at her throat as it hung like cold nothingness over the land. Catherine's nose and fingers were numb long before they got to their destination.

The snow around John's house was trampled.

'Mr Buchanan's been keeping an eye on the place so most of the tracks are his,' Julie commented. 'The rest belong to the type of ghouls who gawk at accident victims and disaster scenes. He tries to chase them off but he can't be here all the time.'

John's home—former home, Catherine mentally corrected herself—didn't feel deserted. Although he had heated mainly with wood, there were baseboard heaters which kept the chill off when John was out. Consequently, when they arrived it was cool but not uncomfortably cold. A congenial scatter of belongings, even unwashed dishes in the sink, spoke of someone gone out for a few hours. After Julie flicked on the lights in the many-windowed living-room, multiple mirror clones of her and Catherine accompanied them on their journey through sorrow. Catherine kept looking for John's reflection to come up behind hers and embrace her. 'I'll make some coffee,' she volunteered, attempting to bring a semblance of normality to the scene.

'Do you know where everything is?'

'I'll manage.'

In the homestead-style kitchen, away from Julie's emotion-charged presence, Catherine relaxed a little and let the familiar motions of preparing coffee soothe her. Usually she had come in here feeling languid and warm after she and John had made love. But this time there would be no amorous exchanges to enliven the coffee-making process. John's favourite mug, black, pedestalled and rimmed with gold sat on the counter. Beside it was the one he had bought for Catherine—scarlet and fluted, wide-mouthed. Catherine reached behind these for two cups less charged with memories and spooned out the coffee crystals while the water boiled. In the stillness she heard Julie's dry sobs. Pain is a tangible thing.

Catherine kindled a fire in the wide hearth and they pulled their chairs up close to it. 'We shouldn't have come here tonight,' Julie whispered, shivering despite the fire. Her eyes darted fearfully around the room, probing the flickering shadows. 'We should've waited for morning.'

'We're here now, Julie, so we'll have to stay,' Catherine answered prosaically, but privately she agreed with her timid companion. The darkness charged the atmosphere with a mystic presence. Beyond the windows the world outside remained invisible, isolating them in a separate realm, in John's lost domain. And John did not rest in peace.

Not surprisingly, Catherine couldn't sleep that night. Beside her, in John's kingsize bed, Julie snored gently. After only token hesitation Julie had taken one of her sleeping pills and so now, at last, Catherine was essentially alone at John's.

The sheets still carried his smell. She and Julie had tacitly agreed not to change the bed. In the dark, in that bed, with the sound of breathing beside her, Catherine could pretend John was still alive and she felt comforted for a time. But when reality trickled like icy rain back into her consciousness, the pain shot through her more cruelly than ever before. Then the questions started churning again in her head.

What happened, John? Who was on the road? Why? Why didn't they see you? Why didn't you move? Did their lights blind you? Did you recognize them? Did someone damage your tyres? Did they run you down on purpose? Why?

Catherine was restless and couldn't lie still, so she slipped out to the living-room and huddled before the embers of the fire.

The police think it was an ordinary hit and run, Catherine told herself. They came and they studied John's lifeless body as it lay in the snow. They didn't have any questions, so why did she? Alicia's talk of a psychic warning might have something to do with her unease.

A crack like a stick snapping startled Catherine from her ruminations. Could the noise have come from the fireplace? She didn't think so.

She could almost feel her ears extending like antennae as she strained to listen. Another muffled crunch whispered through the night and Catherine's heart hurled itself against her ribs.

It's a porcupine or a raccoon, she told herself. She drew her dressing-gown even more tightly around her body and crept to the front door. Stealthily she parted the curtain and peered out into the dark. Nothing. She stood for what felt like hours, willing her eyes to pierce the blackness. Nothing. She had just started to relax when she heard a definite scraping from the other side of the house. Someone was in the porch!

Her heart thudded again and her palms sweated damply while she held her breath and pressed herself back against the wall, frozen in panic. Another sound—a booted foot on the linoleum of the back porch. Catherine's stomach lurched and she felt faint.

'Julie!' she whispered. 'Julie!' But Catherine knew she couldn't waken her drugged friend.

By superhuman effort Catherine moved one foot a few inches forward. Then the other. Six inches. She crept inch by inch towards the door to the porch, each step demanding her lifetime's fund of courage. All the while, through the door, she discerned a faint rustling sound. What was the intruder doing?

Now Catherine was only two feet from the door.

'Who's there?' she croaked. 'Who's there?' she repeated, more loudly this time.

Instantly the rustling stopped. Then a crash rent the night and hurried footsteps raced down the stairs. The outer porch door banged shut and the footsteps faded to silence.

Catherine jerked the door open and switched on the light. Her knees buckled with relief. Whoever it was had gone. She rested her head against the cold wall and trembled uncontrollably. Then she remembered the unlocked outer door which was all that stood between her and the interloper. Galvanized, she raced over, slammed the bolt home and retreated back into the main part of the house. She locked that door too. In the east the sky was tinged with pink when Catherine finally went to sleep.

'What are you looking for?'

Catherine jerked up, startled. 'Oh, it's you.'

'Of course it's me,' Julie replied, perplexed. 'Why are you so jumpy?'

'I'm tired . . . I didn't sleep well, that's all.'

After thinking it over for most of the night, Catherine had decided against telling Julie about their midnight caller. Julie was in no shape to deal with any more unpleasantness. But Catherine was out in the porch having a careful look around.

'What does John keep out here?' she asked.

'He used the porch for storage mostly. He has extra furniture, books, Christmas decorations, that kind of thing. I think we can leave this room for last, Catherine. John didn't keep anything valuable here.' Julie shivered. 'Come on back in the house. It's cold out here!'

'OK,' Catherine agreed. She forgot that she'd been about to track down the source of a faint gasoline smell. She hadn't noticed it yesterday when they arrived.

The two women spent a painful day, each item carrying memories of a loved one now gone. Clothes, they packed up for the St Vincent de Paul Society, along with linens and canned food. The furniture and appliances they inventoried for the auction house Julie had hired to sell the estate. They put aside the few items requested as mementoes. Catherine chose a painting of John's home; Alicia his antique desk. Peggy wanted the ship's clock and Calvin had mentioned a favourite fishing lure.

Julie held up the brilliant yellow and red lure. 'Remember this one?'

'Do I! That's the one that dragged me out of the boat!'

'You could've let go of the rod,' Julie giggled.

66

'Are you crazy? Danny and John would have killed me if I'd lost that damn thing!'

'It took you hours of swimming in the muck to find it.'

'Don't remind me. Ugh!' Catherine shuddered dramatically. 'I was covered in leeches—I thought I'd go nuts before I got the line off that log. And you were no help, as I recall.'

'I couldn't swim at the time.' Julie was still grinning at the memory.

'Convenient excuse! And none of the boys would help. They said it proved girls shouldn't be allowed to fish. Chauvinism even when they were twelve!' And particularly Calvin, Catherine added to herself.

She leaned on John's drier while Julie sorted the laundry-room cupboard and the action triggered a memory. 'Peggy's drier's broken, Julie. Could you let her have this one instead of selling it?'

'Of course! I'm glad you thought of it.' Julie twisted around to look at Catherine. 'Is there anything else Peggy needs?'

Catherine surveyed the scene. 'With all those kids around, the VCR might be useful for rainy days . . .'

'Right. And the cassettes. She can tape over them. I'll label the drier and the video stuff to be kept out of the auction.'

Later that afternoon, Catherine borrowed John's extra set of snowshoes and started out briskly along the edge of the lake. Clouds were piling up in the north but it was still sunny and the rays of light glinted blindingly off the pristine snow. Several black crows laboured overhead and the red glory of a cardinal blazed from the tip of a naked beech tree. Across the snow raced the secret tracks of rabbits and raccoons and mice. The world was still alive, just hidden and mysterious.

Catherine passed in turn a blue, a yellow and then a mauve cottage and at each one she paused. She saw very few human tracks. All the curtains were drawn or the windows shuttered and the cottages appeared undisturbed.

67

It appeared as if only she and Julie had been visited in the night.

When her ankles began to ache from the unaccustomed drag of the snowshoes, Catherine arced northward, around through the woods, to approach the house from the rear. Since the clouds had rolled in by this time, and the wind knifed sharply through her hat and gloves, Catherine tried to pick up the pace. But fallen branches, treacherously hidden just beneath the snow, caught at her snowshoes and repeatedly tripped her up. She shivered with cold and exhaustion before finally reaching the driveway. None the less, she stopped to examine the snow. The rising wind had filled in all the tracks and Catherine couldn't distinguish old from new. Were those fresh imprints leading from the back stairs to the woods? She couldn't be sure and berated herself for not checking them out earlier. But for what, Catherine asked herself? After all, she'd decided to keep quiet, at least for the time being . . .

After an early dinner of canned stew and Pillsbury rolls the two women sat inattentively before the television, each sinking back into the gloom which had lifted briefly earlier in the day. Even the energetic spitting of the fire didn't dispel their lethargy.

'Do you want one of my sleeping tablets?' Julie proffered the brown bottle.

'No, thanks.'

'You said you didn't sleep well last night . . .'

'I'm tired enough now to sleep no matter what.'

'I suppose you think I take too many pills,' Julie remarked defensively from where she'd propped herself in the kitchen doorway. 'But I need them, Catherine, just for a while. I've been so unhappy since John died!'

'I know, dear; it's OK. Take your pill. You'll stop the drugs when you're ready.'

'I will; I promise. Just a few more weeks to get myself together.'

While Julie got herself a drink—wine of all things—to wash down her pill, Catherine worried. She knew Julie had been taking valium for more than a year but she hadn't

68

realized how many other pills slid down that lovely throat. On their arrival, Julie lined up a formidable array of pill bottles on the vanity in John's bathroom. They'd been prescribed by three different doctors. Julie was heading for trouble.

'I think I'll have a dinner-party next weekend,' Catherine announced when Julie returned. 'We need something to snap us out of this depression.'

'I don't think a party would help. And if you invite Susan don't bother asking Calvin and me.'

'Why?'

'Calvin's still furious about those photographs she gave away.'

'You're kidding!'

'I've rarely seen him so upset about something—especially something he can't change. I don't really understand it.'

'I could understand his being angry with the journalist —what was his name—Millikin? But Susan too?'

Julie curled up in her chair and leaned her chin on her knees. It was obvious the pills were taking effect.

'I have the impression,' she murmured, 'that it's the photographs which are bugging him more than whatever Millikin might have written.'

'Why?'

Julie yawned and shrugged languidly. 'I've no idea, but whenever he mentions that "damn book" as he calls it, he always curses Susan and the photographs too.'

Catherine wanted to ask more but Julie was rapidly drifting away from her. 'You'd better get to bed before you fall asleep in the chair,' Catherine suggested. 'I certainly can't carry you!' She regarded her weak left arm with disfavour. 'Come on. I'll help you.'

Catherine didn't feel as if she slept at all but each time she glanced at the luminous dial of her watch an unexpectedly long time had elapsed. Julie was deeply under, so Catherine's ceaseless twisting didn't bother her.

The sleep Catherine did get, if she did doze, was confused and exhausting, her dreams as unsettling as her waking

69

thoughts. Paul's face and body merged with John's as Catherine strove to embrace her husband. The united being pulsed with two disparate personalities, each struggling for supremacy. First John's green eyes, then Paul's brown ones, then one of each stared at Catherine, pleading for help. A moan of utter despair surged from the lips of the mosaic lover as a muted roar and an acrid smell incorporated themselves into her turbulent dreams.

She shifted again under the covers, trying to banish the nightmare. Her eyes popped open in disgust and she fought to untangle her arm and watch from the bedclothes. It was whole seconds before she realized she could see. A flickering orange-yellow light shone luridly through the open door and a hissing dragon's breath blew hot on her cheeks. Fire!

'Julie! Julie!' Catherine ran to the bedroom door where she was stopped dead in her tracks by the wall of heat and smoke and flames. She ducked back into the room slamming the door behind her.

'Julie!' Catherine choked, her lungs and mouth seared by smoke and heat. 'Julie! Wake up! Fire!' Catherine shook her friend, clawing at her neck and shoulder with her right hand. Using her damaged left hand, she twisted Julie's hair tight against her scalp. 'How many damn pills did you take?' she shrieked.

Sobbing and choking, she ran back to the door, dragging the bedspread with her. Desperately she bundled it against the crack under the door where the smoke curled hungrily. Now the door was hot to the touch.

'Julie!' Catherine slapped Julie's face again and again, savagely knocking her head from side to side on the pillow but still Julie would not wake up.

Catherine clambered over the bed to the window and shoved it open as far as it would go. Not far enough. She heaved the bedside lamp through it, mindless of the rain of glass. She flailed the pillow at the jagged edges until the opening was large enough.

'Julie!' Catherine's voice was harsh and raw. The door was on fire, the flames devouring the wood as they climbed it.

Desperately Catherine hauled Julie's inert form, rolling and shoving her across the bed closer to the window. The bedclothes smouldered and then flamed, ignited by a shower of sparks from an exploding light fixture.

The smoke and gases choked Catherine until she could no longer even whisper Julie's name. Still she tried to heave her friend's dead weight up and through the small window. She couldn't do it. With only one strong arm Catherine simply couldn't do it!

Julie's nightdress caught fire and the flames licked up towards Catherine. Now she couldn't even see the window inches from her face but she could feel both her consciousness and Julie slipping away. A scream of defeat and despair filled her mind as Catherine hoisted her own body up and out.

CHAPTER 7

Eventually there came a time when she couldn't slip back into oblivion and Catherine was fully awake. She opened her eyes slowly. She felt as if she were watching the stage curtain rising on a mystery play, but when the curtain was up she still couldn't see anything. She realized this was partly because she wasn't wearing her glasses but it was also because of the darkness of the room. It wasn't pitch dark like a moonless night in the middle of a forest, but only a dim wash of light shone through the half-open doorway. She stared incuriously at the tiled ceiling.

It occurred to Catherine to turn her head. She didn't recognize the fuzzy outlines around her. Odd. Her hands seemed to be swathed in cloth of some kind so she held one of them closer to her eyes. Bandages, Catherine guessed, around three of her fingers and her wrist. A twinge of pain pulsed from them and she knew what she felt was just a hint of what was really there. She knew she was drugged. Her hand fell back unnoticed as tendrils of disagreeable memories brushed the window of Catherine's mind.

Julie.

'Julie!' Catherine yelled, struggling to get up. 'Julie!' Catherine stumbled towards the light on strange, muted feet and was almost knocked down by a white-clad figure.

'Where's Julie?' Catherine shrieked her name over and over until she felt a sharp jab in her left arm and drifted out of knowingness.

From the blank and slightly embarrassed expression on the faces around her Catherine knew they didn't believe her.

'It wasn't an accident,' she repeated stubbornly, sounding like a petulant child even to her own ears. 'Someone broke in and started the fire. I know it!'

'You've been through a terrible ordeal, Catherine . . .' Peggy murmured uncomfortably.

'Yes I have! But I haven't lost my mind because of it—just a little skin!' Catherine was suffering from an unusual combination of first- and second-degree burns and frostbite —she'd been very lucky.

'The fire marshal says the blaze was caused by gasoline —soaked rags stored too close to an electric heater,' Susan murmured.

'In the porch. Right? Under the window?' Catherine demanded.

Susan nodded. 'As near as can be determined.'

'And that's where the intruder was the night before the fire. I told you that! He put the rags there.'

Paul sat on the edge of Catherine's bed and patted her arm. 'There was no evidence of an intruder, honey.'

'How could there be?' Catherine challenged. 'There's barely any evidence left of the house! Or Julie!' She burst into tears. 'Go away!' Catherine sobbed. 'Just go away!'

Paul, Susan, Peggy and Calvin retreated into the corridor. Catherine could hear them whispering.

'She's upset, Calvin . . .,' Paul said apologetically. 'The doctor explained it isn't unusual for the survivor of a fatal accident to try to blame someone or something. It makes it easier for Catherine to accept the fact that she's alive and Julie is dead. The guilt you know . . .'

Catherine saw Calvin's arm go around Paul's shoulders.

'It's OK, Paul. I don't blame her. Julie was the one who insisted on staying at the house for the weekend. If there's anything I can do for either of you . . .'

'Calvin, you're so generous,' Peggy gushed while Catherine clenched her teeth in nausea. 'With dear Julie gone you can still think of others.'

'It is the living who need our help.'

Catherine clamped her pillow over her head. She couldn't take any more of their drivel. Someone had murdered John; she was sure of that now. Then someone had murdered Julie and made a vicious attempt on Catherine herself. And she was the only one who suspected anything was amiss.

After that ghastly visit Catherine kept her thoughts to herself, so it wasn't long before she was considered well enough in mind and body to go home. She'd been out of circulation three weeks but it felt like an eternity. With her perspective skewed so radically, Catherine viewed everyone and everything with a new scepticism. Only Paul and Morgan were exempt from scrutiny but even so, communication between Catherine and Paul had broken down. Both of them were on the defensive.

Just one week after Julie's tragic death, Calvin had officially announced his candidacy for the leadership race. Catherine was appalled and said as much to her husband.

'How could he do this? I thought Calvin would withdraw!'

'Why? Life goes on.'

'That may be, but Julie's barely in the ground!'

'It'll get him some sympathy votes. "Widower, two young children . . . selflessly devoting himself to the good of the party and the people even during his time of grief." It's the stuff image-makers would kill for.'

'What?' Catherine shrieked, temporarily blowing her newly fabricated control.

'Hold on!' Paul backed away, holding his hands out towards Catherine as if fending off the evil eye. 'It was just a figure of speech. Julie's death was an accident. Don't go getting all worked up again.'

'You obviously don't consider her much of loss,' she stormed. 'What about Calvin? Does he consider his wife's death a good career move?'

'Catherine! Think what you're saying! I liked Julie very much. Calvin loved her!' Paul's pacing brought him right up to Catherine and he pointed an accusing finger at her. 'I shouldn't have to tell you that! You've known them all your life.'

'So why doesn't he act like a grief-stricken man? And why are you so full of energy and enthusiasm at a time like this?'

Paul seated himself on the edge of a dining-room chair and spoke distinctly, as if to a slow learner. 'Calvin is throwing himself into his work to try to numb his grief. The least I can do is help him. And you're a fine one to be talking about acting grief-stricken! You're acting crazy, that's what you're doing. Pull yourself together and stop behaving like a child.'

Paul stomped out of the room leaving Catherine white with rage. How dare he walk out on her? How dare he!

She dropped into a chair, trembling with emotion, her anger quenched as quickly as it had combusted. Was she crazy? Was Paul unfeeling? Could Calvin honestly be unmoved by Julie's death? She wanted to cry but refused to give in. Control, she reminded herself. Control. Be objective. Listen. Watch. Catherine took deep, slow breaths and willed herself to calm down. She was resolute. She was not crazy. A murderer walked the streets of Kingsport.

When Paul finally emerged again from his study, Catherine was able to greet him with a smile and a conciliatory suggestion.

'Morgan and I are going over to the Parkers' for the afternoon. Melissa would like a friend around and I thought I'd ask Consuelo if there was anything I could do to help.' Her cheeks ached from holding her false grin. 'Is there any message for Calvin? I'd be glad to deliver it.'

The corners of his eyes wrinkled charmingly as Paul smiled back at his wife and gave her a quick squeeze around her waist. 'If you wouldn't mind taking him some notes,

I'd appreciate it. I'd like Calvin to go over them before the meeting tonight.'

'No problem.'

'That's my girl.' Paul brushed Catherine's cheek with his lips before heading upstairs.

In the car Morgan was unnaturally quiet.

'What's up, Sweet Pea?' Catherine asked.

'Nothing much.' A predictable answer, but Catherine was patient and waited for her daughter to find the words she sought.

'It's Melissa. I don't know what to say to her, Mom.' Morgan turned anxious blue eyes to her mother's.

'But you do want to come with me?'

'Yes . . . But how should I act? Her mother just burned to death!'

'And yours didn't?'

'That's not what I meant, Mom!'

'I know, Morgan, but the fact that I escaped makes it more awkward. Never mind. Just say what you feel; that you're sorry, that you'd like to help, that you care about her. Then just be ready to listen if she wants to talk.'

Catherine held out her bandaged hand to her daughter who clasped it lightly, lovingly. The glance they exchanged shone with love and with gratitude that they still had each other.

'My friends were very important to me when my mother died,' Catherine remarked quietly.

'You were sixteen, weren't you, Mom?'

'Seventeen. My mother had been ill for years so we never did the things most mothers and daughters do.' Catherine smiled at her well-dressed daughter. 'We never shopped, for example, or went to movies or socialized together. Your grandfather and I did most of the housework, grocery-shopping, laundry—all those things I do for you and your dad.'

For a moment Catherine returned to her teenage years and experienced again the resentment she'd felt towards her invalid mother. 'Sometimes, Morgan, I wished Mom would just get it over with and die, so I wouldn't be tied

75

down caring for her.' Catherine bit her lip and avoided meeting her daughter's shocked eyes. 'We couldn't leave Mom alone for long, you know. Dad and I were afraid she'd fall. Or choke. She had a lot of trouble swallowing.'

Morgan's face wore a guarded expression. How could her mom have wanted her own mother to die?

'Then Mom did die,' Catherine said sorrowfully. 'Oh Morgan! How wrong I'd been! Mom's death didn't set me free!' She paused to regain control of her quivering voice. 'I felt so empty. So hurt. I realized too late how much she'd given me without moving from her bed. She always supported me and my goals. And my dreams—however unrealistic. While she lived I always had someone who thought I was the most important person in the world.'

'Oh Mom . . .' Morgan murmured, putting a comforting hand on her mother's shoulder.

'Your grandfather felt as lost as I did,' Catherine continued. 'We tried to comfort each other but we sort of multiplied our misery when we were together.'

Catherine remembered those painful dinners when she and her father faced each other, oblivious of the food, while the third chair sat so poignantly empty.

'What did you learn today, Catherine?' he would ask. Her mother's daily quiz.

Catherine would dredge up an answer. 'The *passé composé* in French.' Or 'Cartesian planes in maths.' Then it was her turn to fill the missing role. 'How was your day, Dad? Busy?'

'Not too bad.'

The stilted conversation limped along as Catherine and her dad gobbled their dinner, anxious to flee the suffocating memories. Why couldn't they share what they felt, Catherine wondered? She couldn't answer the question at the time and she still could not. No doubt a psychiatrist could provide a glib explanation.

'Aunt Peggy and Aunt Alicia, and Aunt Julie too, pulled me through, Morgan. They cried with me, they put up with my moods and my self-pity. They listened to my woes and then cheered me up when I had drained myself. And most of all, Morgan, they made me keep going and wouldn't let me sink into despair.' Catherine turned to her daughter. 'Now it's your turn, honey. Don't let Melissa withdraw from the world. Show her life is still worth living.'

Morgan felt awed by the responsibility. 'I'll try, Mom . . .'

As Catherine turned her car on to the street where the Parkers lived, Morgan pointed out the window. 'Look. Aunt Peggy's here.'

An old blue station wagon straddled the centre of the double driveway, so Catherine had to park on the road. They walked around to the back door and rang the bell. Catherine flashed Morgan a smile of encouragement just before Melissa opened the door.

'Hi, Morgan, Aunt Catherine. Come on in.'

'Hello, Melissa,' Morgan and her mother chorused, entering and removing their coats and footwear. Catherine's boots were monstrous, quilted things, large enough to go over her scarred and swollen feet. She shuffled slowly behind the girls.

'Consuelo's upstairs and Dad's talking to Aunt Peggy in the living-room.'

'Thanks.'

'Do you need help, Mom?'

'No. You two go on. I'll manage.'

Melissa's ten-year-old freckled face was hard to read as she watched Catherine struggle but she turned and led Morgan upstairs without comment. Catherine gave her daughter the thumbs up signal before heading for the living-room. She paused outside the doorway, unnoticed by its occupants.

Peggy and Calvin were seated at right angles to each other across a small corner table. Peggy was leaning forward while Calvin had drawn back into his chair. He was dressed in the casual elegance typical of him but Catherine barely recognized Peggy. Her hair had been stylishly cut and highlighted and seemed to glow with golden health. Instead of jeans and a sweatshirt, she wore a two-piece wool dress in moss green, cut to disguise the extra pounds she carried. Even the small enamel pin, the shoes and handbag were chosen with care. Catherine detected the hand of Alicia in the transformation. Why the sudden change?

'. . . so, Calvin, if you need a hostess for any of your business get-togethers you can count on me. I know I'm not Julie but I could help.'

'Thanks, Peggy, you're very kind, but I won't be giving any parties for a while.'

'You never know. It may be necessary and I'll be there for you.' Peggy giggled nervously. It was not an attractive sound.

'I hardly think it would be suitable for me to entertain at this point, but perhaps sometime in the future . . .' Calvin was rising to his feet and checking his watch. 'I don't want to rush you, Peggy, but I have a meeting in a few minutes.'

Peggy started to reach for Calvin's sleeve but snatched back her hand as she spied Catherine.

'Catherine!' Peggy frowned but Calvin strode over eagerly to greet her. 'Come in, Catherine! Sit down, sit down!' He propelled the new arrival to a chair and hauled up a stool for her feet. 'How are you?' Calvin gave Catherine his whole attention, effectively isolating Peggy on the far side of the room.

'Improving, thanks, but I won't be wearing sheer stockings for a while.'

'Hello, Peggy.' Catherine leaned around Calvin and nodded in her direction.

'Glad you're feeling well enough to be up and about,' Peggy replied. It was obvious Peggy was embarrassed to be found fawning over the new widower.

'I guess we're both checking up on our friend.' Catherine smiled warmly and turned back to Calvin. 'I brought Morgan along to play with Melissa. Did she tell you we were coming?'

Calvin shook his head. 'She stays in her room most of the time lately. Thanks for bringing Morgan—it may pick her up a bit.'

'Our pleasure. Oh, and Paul sent you this wad of notes

to go over before your meeting tonight.' Catherine set the pile on the coffee table. 'I hope you're a speed-reader!'

Calvin mimed horror at the size of the stack. 'That husband of yours is a slave-driver. He never gives me a moment's rest.'

Catherine thought he had the master/slave relationship backwards but held her peace. 'I told Consuelo I'd stop in for a chat if you don't mind, Calvin.'

'By all means.' He headed over towards Peggy. 'I'll walk you to the door before I attack these notes.'

Out-manœuvred, Peggy acquiesced gracefully. 'Goodbye, Catherine. Take care of yourself.'

Moments later the front door closed behind her and Catherine headed for the stairs.

'Catherine?'

Calvin caught up with her. 'May I ask you a favour?'

'Of course. What is it?'

Just for a moment Calvin's eyes dropped and there was a crack in his urbanity.

'Would you . . . would you and Consuelo sort out Julie's clothes and toiletries for me? Throw out the stuff that's no good and send the rest to the Salvation Army?' His eyes held Catherine's for a moment and dropped again. 'I just can't. Her things sit there in our room and I see them and I smell them all the time. I have to get the stuff out of here!'

Catherine brushed his arm gently. 'We'll do it right now.'

'Thanks.' Calvin cleared his throat. 'I'd better get at those papers . . .'

Catherine nodded and started painfully up the stairs.

Consuelo was a tiny, Mexican woman of boundless energy. It wasn't long before Catherine gave up helping her pack Julie's clothes and maintained only a consulting role in the process.

'What you think?' Consuelo held up a soft peach jumpsuit.

'Salvation Army,' Catherine decided. 'Are you sure none of these would fit you?'

'I'm very tiny.'

'You could take them in.'

79

Consuelo shook her dark curls. 'No, I won't keep any. I don't think Mr Parker like seeing his servant in his wife's clothes.'

She had a point, Catherine admitted to herself. Calvin liked to keep the social classes well delineated.

'You're more than a servant, Consuelo, especially now. The family really need you.'

'No kidding!' Consuelo grunted as she hefted the fourth obese bag to the corner of the room. The job was only half done.

Julie and Calvin each had a huge walk-in closet and both were bulging. Catherine was impressed by the amount of clothing Julie possessed but wrinkled her nose at Calvin's wardrobe. Where clothes were concerned, Catherine was fifteen years out of date. She still felt a man could be well dressed with a couple of good suits, three sports jackets and the same number of slacks. Vanity was the only reason she could come up with to explain the muted rainbow of suits, jackets, shoes and accessories filling Calvin's closet.

'The Parkers must spend every free moment shopping,' Catherine commented. 'Have you ever seen so many clothes outside a store?'

'Amazing, isn't it?' Consuelo held a red plaid skirt up for Catherine's verdict. Its hem hung unevenly.

'Toss it out.'

'It be simple to fix it . . .'

'I know, but we have to throw a few things out. The garbage pile is microscopic so far and Calvin thought we'd have some rejects.'

At that moment a red-haired dynamo raced into the master bedroom and bounced on the kingsize bed.

'Get down, Richard,' Consuelo scolded the six-year-old without heat.

'I'm hungry.'

'There are apples and bananas in the basket on the kitchen counter.'

'I want a cookie.' Richard began pawing through the pile of clothes on the bed. 'These are my mommy's. What are you doing with them?' His tiny hands balled into fists as he prepared to defend his mother's property.

'Sorting them out, that's all.'

'Why?' Bright suspicious eyes focused on Consuelo's black ones.

'Because your father asked us to.'

'Oh.' He lost interest.

'Say hello to Aunt Catherine.'

'Hello, Aunt Catherine,' he parroted obediently. 'Can I have a cookie?'

'You'll have to ask Consuelo.'

'Can I?' He turned to his nanny, opening his green eyes wide and cocking his head to one side.

'Have a banana, honey. They better for you.'

'Mommy would let me have a cookie.'

Consuelo compressed her lips. He was right. His mother would have given in to his cajolery despite her better judgement.

'A banana or an apple, Richard, those are your choices.'

'I want a cookie!' he shrieked, stamping his small foot. 'A cookie!'

'No. I don't fall for your tricks, little man. Its too close to supper-time to spoil your appetite with junk food.'

Richard burst into tears and stomped from the room. A moment later Catherine heard his bedroom door slam shut. She threw a questioning look at Consuelo. 'The poor boy . . .'

'I know. I want to hold him and protect him too, and give him everything he want just to see him smile. It would sure be easier!' Consuelo sank wearily on to the bed.

'Does Calvin help with the children?'

'For the first week or so he very good but Mr Parker a busy man . . .'

'And when their mother was alive? Did she spend much time with them?'

A soft smile played over Consuelo's full lips. 'Mrs Julie loved them very much. She played with them, listened to their stories and even laughed when Richard say same joke for the tenth time! She spoiled them, it's true, but she was interested in them. Anyway, they had Mr Parker and me to keep them in line. We no pushovers!' Consuelo paused for a second before continuing. 'Lately, though, Mr Parker didn't want his wife spending so much time with kids.'

'Why?'

'He want her more involved in his political campaign. He chose these clothes for her.' Consuelo's gesture took in the more formal dresses at the far end of the closet.

Catherine tried to picture timid Julie as an aggressive campaigner. It was difficult. Then she remembered the pills. 'So that's what was bugging her! No wonder! She hated being in the spotlight.'

Consuelo nodded in agreement. 'Before each time she go out to one of those . . . dinners . . . she changed her clothes four, maybe five times. And I heard her practising in her room. "Good evening, Mr Smith. So kind of you to come out and support my husband. He'll make a wonderful leader." It was so sad. Mrs Julie wasn't the type.'

'What did Calvin think?'

Consuelo hesitated. Catherine Edison had been very close to Mrs Parker but she was also Mr Parker's friend. How much should she say?

In her mind, Consuelo heard Julie Parker pleading with her husband not to make her go to a fund-raising dinner. She was nervous; she wept; she didn't know anyone; she didn't know what to say, what to do. 'Please don't make me go, Calvin!'

'I married you because you look good beside me. You are—or could be—an attractive accessory. Now, dammit, you'll earn your keep! Charm some money out of the bastards for me!'

Consuelo had heard the harsh crack of an open palm on bare flesh.

'I can't! I don't know what I should say, Calvin. I might make a mistake!'

'You read the stuff Paul wrote, didn't you? Didn't you?'

'Yes!' Julie sobbed.

'Then that's what to say. A two-year-old could do it! Get dressed!'

As usual, Julie had headed for the medicine cabinet before she crawled into one of her dresses her husband had picked out.

'Mr Parker a bit impatient at times,' Consuelo finally told Catherine, 'but he comfortable in a crowd. It hard for him to understand her fright.'

'Calvin can be quite insistent when he wants to be, but there's no harm in him,' Catherine remarked.

And now Peggy was making a bid to replace Julie. She would do a better job, Catherine thought, but Calvin would never give her a chance, not with the taint of Wilson Brandenburg soiling her. But, perhaps Peggy's new goal would help her push Wilson out of her life.

As she and Morgan drove homeward, Catherine's thoughts returned to Peggy. Peggy and Calvin had been a hot number for a while in their late teens but the cooling off had been rapid and one-sided. Had Peggy been carrying the torch for him all these years? Had she chosen Wilson, Calvin's opposite in every way, out of spite or hurt? The idea hadn't occurred to Catherine before, but witnessing Peggy's metamorphosis had been a shock. There was no doubt Peggy was making a play, but for Calvin or Wilson she wasn't sure. Trying to make Wilson jealous was the sort of game Peggy might try, and it was the tactic most likely to succeed with Wilson. Had Peggy finally realized that it was the thrill of the chase that her husband enjoyed?

Or had he discovered a new kind of thrill? Catherine shivered. Wilson enjoyed torturing his family. Had he progressed to the ultimate, evil deed?

CHAPTER 8

Paul and Calvin grabbed one of the rare evenings when they were both in Kingsport to confer on the progress of Calvin's leadership bid. They'd been closeted in Calvin's study for a couple of hours but the mood was upbeat. Calvin felt buoyed by the results of the latest poll—he had narrowed the gap between himself and the front runner, Ivan Dressler.

'My policy speeches are attracting some of Dressler's supporters,' Calvin enthused. 'I'm on the right track.'

Paul shrugged out of his grey lambswool sweater and settled more comfortably. 'Don't get too right-wing,' he cautioned. 'As your Official Agent I'll be thrilled if you can pull over some of Dressler's big money men, but we don't want to lose grass roots support.'

'It's a fine line,' Calvin agreed. 'Dressler's implied he'll slash social programmes so I'm staying away from that topic. Let the delegates assume I favour the status quo.'

'We have to say something about women and minorities —it's political suicide to ignore the opposite sex these days,' Paul reminded him.

Calvin stretched and left his desk to walk around the room. 'Speaking of women, did you know Peggy Brandenburg keeps popping up in my path? She wants to replace Julie, at least in my public life. Says she'll be my hostess.' Calvin grinned, inviting Paul to share the joke. Dropping back into his chair, he swung his feet on to the desk and leaned back.

'Peggy's more outgoing than Julie was,' Paul remarked, 'and not bad-looking when she fixes herself up.'

'I don't need a hostess, nor a wife just yet,' Calvin asserted, locking his fingers behind his head as he relaxed. 'Julie's still in everyone's thoughts. Mine too,' he added hastily.

'Of course . . .' Paul murmured.

'Not to mention Peggy's still married to that loser, Wilson,' Calvin continued. 'She really ought to shake him— she should have done it years ago.' Calvin shook his head. He couldn't understand why Peggy had married Wilson in the first place. 'I thought you had more brains than that,' had been his comment when the nuptial plans were announced. 'He's going to be trouble . . .'

'You and Peggy used to date, didn't you?' Paul knew the answer. He knew the history of the inner circle almost as well as they did themselves.

84

'Yeah. She was really something back then.'

'What happened?'

Calvin shrugged impatiently. 'We grew up; I moved on. Who cares?' Calvin shifted his feet back to the floor and snapped his chair upright, dismissing the topic.

'Now about our anti-pollution policy, Paul. That's the sweetheart cause at the moment, so we need a stronger wording. When the rest of the guys come over tomorrow I want some input on how to give it more punch.'

'Without actually promising any more money?'

'Not much, anyhow. Fiscal responsibility is big in financial circles.' Calvin stood up and rubbed a hand across his forehead. 'Hell, I'm tired!' His eyes felt gritty and he wanted to remove his contact lenses. 'Politics is a tough game. Want a drink?'

'Sure. Scotch, please.' Paul made himself comfortable and watched Calvin pour the liquid gold from its elegant green bottle. Calvin always stocked Glenlivet, something Paul could rarely afford to buy. Thank heavens my beer-drinking days are behind me, Paul thought. As long as I can move in the right circles I'll never have to drink cheap booze again.

'I've noticed you always drink Perrier when *you're* buying,' Calvin remarked as he handed over the glass.

'Not always,' Paul mumbled into his drink.

Calvin settled back in his big leather chair and loosened his tie. Paul relaxed marginally as he sipped the Glenlivet, appreciating as always the golden fire it kindled in his throat.

After he had drunk half the glass Paul felt brave enough to broach an unpleasant topic. 'Uh, Calvin . . .'

'What?' Calvin's red-rimmed eyes glanced at his financial officer.

'The uh . . . coffers are getting emptied faster than I anticipated. We're running out of funds.'

Calvin's eyes narrowed but Paul plunged ahead. 'Do you think you could toss in just a little more?'

'I can't afford to,' Calvin replied instantly.

'What about Julie's money?'

'She didn't have any to speak of.'

'Her parents must have left her something,' Paul persisted.

'They did, but she put it in a trust fund for the kids—against my wishes.' Calvin pulled at his bottom lip. 'I think it was the only time she crossed me.' He stared into his glass and slowly swirled around the three ice cubes.

'Life insurance?' Paul asked. 'Julie was heavily insured —you told me that.'

'The money hasn't come through yet, though with the inquest over the adjuster can't delay much longer.'

'You could borrow against it, maybe . . .'

Calvin sat up straighter in his chair and turned his steady gaze on Paul. His voice had a hard edge that made Paul flinch. 'I said I couldn't put any more money into the campaign. Finance is your department, man, so it's your problem not mine. Why don't you cough up a little more yourself?'

Paul flushed. 'I can't. I don't have any more and Catherine's already upset about how much this is costing us. I've been working for nothing, you may remember.'

'You'll be well rewarded when we win.' Calvin's eyes pierced Paul a moment longer and then released him.

'It's Dressler's fault, you know,' Paul complained. 'Him and his manager, McCarthy. There seems to be no bottom to their wells.' He stood and began to pace. 'They're both from old money.'

'Well, I'm from young money,' Calvin declared, standing in his turn to get on to his soap box. 'My father scrambled to make a buck and so did I. I have the energy and the drive and I know how to fight. With the right financial backing and my street smarts we can cut Dressler's support out from under him. Right?'

'You bet,' Paul hastened to agree. He fetched his glass, took a sip and recommenced his pacing. 'You've already got this part of the province in the bag and the north will support you precisely because you aren't Establishment. Toronto has to be our main target now.'

'And that takes money.' Calvin eyed his agent. 'You've

talked a lot about your Bay Street connections from law school days, Paul. You could hit them up for some financial support.'

Paul wiped his palms on his grey slacks. 'I'm not sure. They don't know much about you . . .'

'But they will after you talk to them, right? If they're as rich and powerful as you claim, you could swing a lot of bucks my way.'

Calvin was standing toe to toe with Paul, jabbing him in the chest to punctuate each point.

'Sure, Calvin,' Paul mumbled, backing out of range.

'So find the money we need and don't bother me with the details.' Calvin sat down and pulled his chair up to the massive desk while Paul returned to the long trestle-table sagging under its load of paper. He reached wearily for the next letter in the stack of unopened mail. It was from the lawyer for Gresthoff Publishing. He scanned it rapidly. What else could go wrong? 'Shit!'

'What is it?'

'That damn book! There is simply no legal way to stop it.'

'You told me you had it in hand,' Calvin accused.

Paul licked his lips with tiny, snakelike thrusts of his tongue. 'Gresthoff's lawyer's sharp. He's countered every one of my arguments and I know they'd win if we took it to court.'

Calvin's knuckles whitened as he gripped the arms of his chair. 'That book *can't* come out!' he croaked.

'But there's nothing libellous in it,' Paul pointed out. 'The facts are correct; it's only the interpretation that's unsympathetic. As their lawyer sarcastically said, we have freedom of speech in this country.'

'That's something I'll change when I get to the top.'

Paul laughed nervously, unsure whether or not Calvin jested. 'We'll work something out.'

'You're sure a court challenge isn't the answer?' Calvin demanded.

'Trust me. All we'd get out of it is bad publicity.'

87

Calvin paced, kicking errant papers out of his way as he strode back and forth, bashing his fist rhythmically into his cupped palm. Paul edged out of his way behind the table.

'I can't let a stupid book stop me, Paul. I'm good. I know I'm good. I'll be a great leader and a great Premier if I only get the chance.' He stopped in front of his aide and continued with steely determination in his voice, all the more convincing because he spoke so calmly. 'I will get the chance. Nothing, absolutely nothing, is going to stop me.'

Paul gripped his friend's shoulder in encouragement. 'You'll get the chance, Calvin. That silly book won't stop you. Lack of money won't stop you. You're on your way to the top!' But to himself Paul added a desperate appendix. 'You'd better be, pal, or we're both in deep trouble.'

CHAPTER 9

It was three a.m. and Peggy was sitting bolt upright in bed, her ears straining to locate the noise which had awakened her. Instinctively she drew the covers to her neck. Her palms were sticky with cold sweat and her knuckles glowed like mother of pearl in the night.

It must be Wilson, she told herself sternly for the tenth time. He'll be shouting in a moment.

On the other three occasions when Wilson had prowled in her night he'd been stumbling around drunk, banging into trees and snow banks and shouting her name. His purpose, if he were capable of sustaining one, was to wake her up and ruin her peace.

The silence beat against Peggy's eardrums. Where was the noise she'd heard? Could it have been a dream? Still Peggy held her pose. She concentrated only on her sense of hearing.

There it was again! The high-pitched squeak of footsteps on the icy, packed snow of the driveway. Someone was outside. Peggy's eyes jerked to the curtained window and she stared, immobile, waiting for . . . waiting for who or what to appear? You're on the second storey, you fool, she admonished herself.

It must be Wilson. He's trying to scare me this time. Cloaking herself in her few wisps of courage, Peggy eased herself out of the warm sanctuary of her bed and willed herself to the window. There, she hesitated for a moment unable to take the final step and open the curtains. Peggy took two deep breaths. She flicked back the drape.

'Ahh . . . !' A white, wild-eyed face stared at her from the darkness. Peggy fell back against the bed. The frantic rushing of her blood blocked out all other sounds. But already her mind was sorting out the visual message. That horrifying apparition had been her own reflection in the glass. Peggy sobbed against her bed. Thank God her cry had been so weak.

As she approached the window for the second time, a muffled crunch froze her to stillness. A foot had broken through the icy coating on the snow. The intruder had deserted the driveway for the lawn.

Again Peggy parted the curtains but this time she dodged through them quickly and then held them closed behind her. Her reflection vanished but still she could see little outside—only a faint glimmer of white from the few smooth patches of snow. Now she strained both ears and eyes.

Was that a human figure there, under the tree? Peggy's heart stumbled in its gallop. No. It was a snowman wearing an old blanket for a coat. She breathed again. Over by the pond—what was that? A man? It moved. A shadow maybe? No sound accompanied the shifting shape as it disappeared into a black stain on the night tapestry.

Crack! A branch snapped over in the copse of trees. Peggy's hand flew to her mouth to smother a choked scream. What would she do? Why didn't she have a telephone in the bedroom? Were the doors and windows locked? Incoherent prayers threaded through her agonized mind. 'I must do something,' she whispered. 'Please let it be Wilson.'

Abruptly Peggy threw the curtains back and rammed open the window. She punched at the screen and never even heard it thunk on to the packed snow below. Sticking her head and shoulders out the window she called, the tension raising her voice to a strident pitch. 'Who's there?'

Nothing.

'Wilson? Wilson? Where are you?'

Still Peggy saw nothing but there was a flurry of skittering sounds as someone ran through the trees at the side of the house.

'Wilson! Get out of here!' Peggy's voice quavered as she fought back terror and tears.

A car door slammed. An engine roared. Tyres squealed. Peggy sagged to the floor, weak with relief. It was ten minutes before the wash of frigid air from the open window revived her and she crept back to bed. The children slept on but their mother lay rigid, her eyes wide and staring.

As the stolen car sped along the dark country roads the lone occupant was smiling with satisfaction. It would work. The set-up was perfect and since only Peggy's room was at the back of the house, the children would hear nothing at all.

CHAPTER 10

Catherine was relaxing at home. She'd propped a cushion under her swollen feet and a large pot of tea steamed by her side. Abandoning a stack of research papers, she luxuriated in a work by her favourite author, Jane Austen. The doorbell brought her back to the twentieth century.

'Drat!' She began struggling up but before she got her feet to the floor, the door opened and Alicia's head popped around the corner.

'Hi, Catherine. May I come in?'

'Alicia! Yes! Come on in!'

'Don't get up.' As Alicia struggled out of her boots and coat Catherine settled back in her chair, a happy smile turning up the corners of her mouth.

'Wow! Let me look at you!' Catherine whistled. 'Quite the duds!'

'You like?' Alicia twirled around.

'Do I!'

Catherine's friend was wearing an eye-catching creation of purple silk and olive velvet. As Alicia turned, the short, full skirt swirled, catching the light and reflecting it in a rainbow of soft greens.

Together with the clothes, Alicia's long, thin body and white skin made a dramatic picture.

'You should model your creations yourself,' Catherine said with admiration. 'You look stunning.'

Alicia smiled but shook her raven head. 'No way. Modelling's hard work.'

'And designing isn't?' Catherine raised her eyebrows.

'Designing's fun. It's a game to me.'

'A very lucrative game,' Catherine remarked.

'Yes. Now it is. Not at the beginning, though.' Alicia swirled the skirt once more in front of Catherine. 'Shall I make one for you?'

'Uh—uh, no, thanks. I haven't the presence to carry it off—or the legs,' Catherine added. 'Particularly at the moment.'

'I knew that's what you'd say, so I brought you this.' Alicia laid a large dress box on the other woman's knee. 'Let me help,' she said as she deftly untied the ribbon so Catherine could open her present.

The gift was buried under layers of filmy paper but before Catherine had peeled it all back, she knew what it was— the burgundy overdress she'd admired in the shop.

'Thank you! It's gorgeous!' Catherine half lifted the wool from its nest and rubbed the soft material against her cheek.

'Take it out of the box.' Alicia grasped the overdress by the shoulders and shook it free of the paper to reveal a second garment.

'What's this?' Catherine gently extricated a pair of ivory silk slacks.

'To wear with the burgundy top. Now you can't plead nothing to wear when people ask you out.'

Catherine laughed. As she stroked the rich fabrics the reflection from the wine red overdress gave colour to her wan cheeks. 'I haven't been doing that, have I?'

'Ha!' Alicia settled herself into a chair, carefully arranging her skirt beneath her. 'The trouble with this outfit is I can't sit down without wrinkling it.' She shifted again. 'One can be truly elegant only when standing up.'

'Another good argument for being a slob like I am! Thanks, old friend. It's beautiful. Paul and Morgan will be impressed for sure. They won't recognize me.' Catherine refolded her new clothes and slipped them back into their box. 'Would you like some tea? I made it just a few minutes ago.'

'OK.' Alicia sprang out of her chair. 'Don't get up. I can find a cup.'

When Alicia returned to the living-room Catherine poured the tea. Handing the cup back to Alicia, she remarked, 'I noticed I'm not the only one to benefit from your fashion expertise.'

'Oh?'

'Peggy. I recognized your touch. She's looking great.'

'She is, isn't she? I've been begging her for years to pull herself together and she's listening at last.' Alicia smiled with proprietary satisfaction.

'Why do you suppose that is?' Catherine queried. 'Could Calvin have anything to do with it? Is she picturing herself as a political wife?'

'Perhaps.' Alicia smoothly crossed her silk-clad legs. 'At least she's thinking of someone other than Wilson for a change, and that can't be bad!'

'True,' Catherine agreed. Even if Calvin were only a temporary distraction—and she couldn't imagine Calvin ever making it permanent—this situation might break the strange bond which tied Peggy to her ne'er-do-well husband.

'Speaking of Wilson, I met the jerk outside the credit union,' Alicia remarked. 'I know he's looking for another loan, though he claims to have a deal of some sort all lined up. He says he's going to be rich and Peggy will be begging him to take her back.'

'Wilson's had a "great deal" lined up all his life but it never comes off,' Catherine said with a snort. 'Does he expect us to believe him?'

'Who knows? But the freer of him Peggy gets, the more he wants her back. Seeing her with Calvin and looking great must be driving him crazy!' Alice laughed. The prospect of soap opera drama delighted her.

'It won't be so funny if Wilson gets out of hand. He's already hassling Peggy, you know. And if Wilson's anywhere in the picture Calvin'll avoid Peggy like the plague.'

'Not necessarily.'

Catherine eyed her friend speculatively. 'What does that mean?'

From her small leather handbag Alicia extracted an elegant gold cigarette case along with a matching lighter. Although neither Catherine nor Paul smoked, there were always a few discreetly placed ashtrays available to accommodate the vices of their friends. Alicia pulled a crystal one towards her and methodically tapped out a cigarette before answering. 'Just that Calvin will never be rude to Peggy, whatever Wilson does.'

'Are you kidding? Calvin would be rude to Mother Teresa if he thought it would further his career, and Wilson is political poison. In fact, I heard Calvin telling Peggy flat out he wasn't in the market for a female companion.'

'Because Julie had just died and he missed her and it was too soon to think about it? Right?' Alicia drawled.

'I suppose so. More or less,' Catherine agreed.

'But Calvin didn't say he wasn't interested in Peggy, did he?'

'Of course not. Not in so many words.'

'And he won't. Believe me.' Alicia spoke with a finality that Catherine refused to accept.

'We're talking about Calvin, Alicia. If Peggy gets in his way he'll mow her down.'

'Not Peggy.' Alicia was firm. 'They were very close once.'

Catherine brandished a finger in Alicia's direction.

'Twenty years ago! And he dropped her, you might remember, as soon as he got out into the wide world.'

'None the less, Calvin will tread carefully where Peggy's concerned.' A stream of smoke curled from Alicia's mouth as she spoke. 'So far that threatened biography is only embarrassing to Calvin. If Peggy were to get mad and tell what she knows it could be devastating. Calvin can't afford to cross her—not right now, anyway.'

All sorts of outlandish scenarios flashed through Catherine's mind. 'What are you talking about? What does Peggy know? What do *you* know?' Catherine leaned forward. 'Is there a skeleton in Calvin's closet?'

But Alicia, now that her friend was wild with curiosity, refused to say anything more. 'It's Peggy's story to tell, not mine.'

'Come on! You can't leave me hanging! What's the secret?'

But Alicia wouldn't be drawn. 'Sorry. I shouldn't have said anything. I've kept my promise this long. I won't weaken now.'

Catherine itched with curiosity. How had a gossip like Alicia managed to hold her tongue? Now that she'd opened up a little, however, Catherine was sure Alicia couldn't hold back the juicy details for long.

'So you think Peggy is the next Mrs Parker?' Catherine asked.

Alicia shrugged and the green shimmering of her dress continued long after she was still. 'Who can say? Maybe she doesn't want to be. Maybe if it comes to the crunch, Wilson's allure is still stronger than Calvin's.'

'Then she's nuts!' was Catherine's last comment on the subject.

CHAPTER 11

Since Catherine's accident, her weekly tennis games with Susan had been replaced by dessert and coffee excursions to various retaurants in the county. Tonight they were meeting at the Grindstone, a newly converted mill on the Cataraqui river. Under the iridescent coverlet of snow, the surrounding fields and trees, and especially the inn and its rustic bridge, shone with postcard perfection. The driveway was designed so that one approached the restaurant from the front, allowing time for full appreciation of its beauty. A hundred feet from the building, however, the drive swung off to circle in behind, which meant the utilitarian parking lot with its mud-spattered metallic anachronisms was well out of sight.

'Great decor!' Susan commented in a subdued voice as she settled in opposite Catherine at their table. 'I appreciate not having to fight my way through a jungle of potted trees.'

'Hardly a green leaf in sight other than at the salad bar,' Catherine agreed, 'but they've accentuated the stone and wood beautifully. I like it.'

Dessert proved to be as delicious as the ambience led them to expect.

'Tennis was healthier,' Catherine murmured through a bite of chocolate and Cointreau torte.

'But not as much fun.' Susan grinned, popping the last of her apricot cheesecake into her mouth. 'Who wants to be fit when getting fat can be so enjoyable?'

'We're going to pay, you realize, Susan. When I'm able, we'll have to work out twice as hard—maybe even take aerobics.'

'No way! Never that! Tennis, badminton, skating, swimming, jogging even, but no aerobics. I wouldn't squeeze my middle-aged body into one of those leotards for any price!'

'You look great,' Catherine protested, and with reason. Susan had that rare type of beauty which got better with

95

age. She'd been bony and thin as a child, with a 'too big' face, but now, with the right amount of padding, the perfect bone structure endowed her with a truly classic look.

Embarrassed by her companion's enthusiasm, Susan sought to change the topic. 'Did you hear about the break-in at Gresthoff Publishing?'

Catherine looked blank for a moment but then remembered Gresthoff was the publisher for Millikin's biography of Calvin. 'What break-in?'

'Along with a bunch of other stuff, the galleys for several books were stolen and the computer system was trashed.'

'Trashed?'

'Its memory was wiped. Totally!'

'What books were stolen? Was Millikin's among them?' Catherine demanded, leaning forward.

Susan sipped her coffee, pleased at Catherine's reaction. 'As a matter of fact, yes.'

'Does Calvin know about this?'

'I doubt it. The whole thing's being kept quiet for the moment. I heard about it from a friend who's an agent and one of her clients was affected.'

Catherine considered the situation. Was it possible Millikin's book was the target of the robbery? 'Is it too much to hope Calvin's damn book is gone forever?'

Susan laughed in genuine amusement. ''Fraid so. There are bound to be at least a dozen copies of the manuscript elsewhere. Publication may be delayed a few weeks but that's all. Calvin will have to learn to live with a little notoriety.'

Catherine shook her head doubtfully. 'He's not looking forward to it. He and Paul start foaming at the mouth whenever that book is mentioned.'

'I know. Calvin's still giving me the cold shoulder—I really blew it this time.' Susan let her head sag on to her hands for a moment. Calvin's ire had an isolating effect on her. Except for Catherine, the other members of the group followed Calvin's lead. With Brent dead and her friends fading away, Susan felt very alone.

96

Catherine played with the crumbs left on her plate as she tried to understand why Calvin was punishing Susan for an unavoidable mistake. Granted he was under a lot of strain since Julie's death and the announcement of his leadership campaign, but that didn't go far enough in explaining his atypically vengeful behaviour. And Paul, naturally, followed his lead. Catherine spared a moment to regret her husband's plasticity. While she had provided the dominant force in his life, this characteristic was to her advantage, but now Calvin had usurped her role. Paul would mould himself to fit any pattern his leader dictated.

Catherine returned to the discussion at hand. 'Did you get your photographs back from Millikin?'

'The originals, yes. He made copies.'

'Did you tell him he couldn't use them?'

Susan pushed a strand of dark hair out of her eyes while an expression of distaste settled on her well-moulded features. 'Oh yes, for all the good it did.' She stirred the dregs of her coffee absently. 'Mr Millikin reminded me I signed a release.'

'To use them in an article about Kingsport's history,' Catherine interjected hotly, 'not for a scurrilous attack on Calvin!'

'Always read the fine print, Catherine. I gave permission for him to use them in any way he wished.'

'Damn.'

'Precisely.'

Into the pause in their conversation the subdued hum of the restaurant inserted itself. Threads of Pachelbel's Canon wove in and out of the tapestry of murmured voices and the muffled clatter of dishes. Against this relaxing backdrop, Catherine found it hard to worry about a few faded photographs. Calvin would no doubt forget about them as suddenly and unpredictably as he had angered. But the situation was bothering Susan and Catherine wanted to see Brent's entire album. Could the answer to Calvin's reaction be hidden somewhere in the photographs? 'Do you know how many of Brent's pictures are going to be in Millikin's book?'

Susan shook her head. 'Millikin originally selected a dozen photos but he may have chosen more than he really needed. Calvin appeared in most of them—the others were general shots of Kingsport.'

'And just what was Calvin doing in those photos? Anything compromising?'

'Let's see . . .' Susan frowned in concentration. 'In one he's alone, riding a bicycle past Brent's house and grinning like he'd just hit a grand slam. Two are of him and his parents, one taken in front of their store and one on their front porch. Another shows Calvin and Danny in the woods. Calvin's holding a rifle of some sort.'

'Likely that rusty old thing Calvin found in the ditch,' Catherine surmised. 'It never did work. But I can't understand how any of those photographs do any harm.'

'Neither can I, but Calvin doesn't see it that way. I almost wish the damn book was out now so we'd know the public's reaction.'

'It will be a one-day local wonder and then it'll sink into oblivion,' Catherine assured her friend. 'All this fuss will be for nothing.' Unless, she mused, Peggy really did have some dangerous information and had talked . . .

CHAPTER 12

The doctor's optimistic prognosis pleased Catherine but the effort of making her way downtown to the medical clinic and back had tired her. She plopped down into her favourite chair as soon as she got home.

'Damn!' she exclaimed. 'I forgot my book.' She glanced at the mantel clock. Morgan wouldn't be home from school for at least twenty minutes. If she wanted to read she'd have to fetch the book herself.

Groaning, she hauled her weary body out of the chair. Before heading for the study where she'd left her novel, Catherine detoured by the kitchen to put on the kettle.

Welcome sunlight poured through the window, flooding the white and yellow kitchen with a cheerful glow. Outside, ice glittered on the tall elms. Her spirits lifted. Good news, sunshine, nature's beauty—it was a good day. She felt better than she had since John's death.

In the doorway of the study Catherine hesitated. An unfamiliar scent lingered in the air, tantalizing her nose, defying identification. 'Strange,' she murmured, but then put it out of her mind and went over to the table beneath the window. Her book wasn't there.

I could've sworn I left it here, she thought. Maybe it slid down the side of the chair cushion. She ran her sensitive fingers carefully around the cushion. No book. Puzzled, she flipped through the stack of magazines on the table. The oldest ones were on top. Now she felt truly perplexed. Her cleaning lady knew not to touch books and papers in the study and besides, it wasn't her day. Could Paul have come home and left again while she was at the doctor's office?

Catherine scanned the room. Everything was in its place and yet not. The lamp sat on the left side of the desk, as always, but closer to the edge. Her scientific reprints filled the other corner but were stacked more neatly than Catherine customarily managed. The usual muddle of unanswered mail lay in the centre of the desk but it seemed too neatly piled as well. She looked around uneasily. What was going on?

Sitting down at the desk, Catherine opened one drawer after another, studying the contents. A quick check suggested nothing had been removed. She next turned her attention to the filing cabinet she and Paul shared. After a cursory examination Catherine was certain the two upper drawers, which were hers, had been searched. She opened Paul's drawers but, less familiar with their usual state, she couldn't be sure about them.

Catherine shivered. She no longer felt safe even in her own home.

*

'Mom? The kettle's boiling.' Morgan poked her head into the study. 'Shall I make you tea or something?'

Catherine raised her head to stare blankly at her daughter.

'What's wrong, Mom?' Morgan examined her mother more closely. Catherine sat huddled in a chair, her arms wrapped protectively around herself. 'I think someone's been in the house,' she whispered.

'What do you mean?' The young girl knelt by her mother's chair and anxiously stroked her arm.

'I think this room's been searched.'

Morgan looked around. 'Anything missing?'

Catherine shook her head. 'Not that I can tell, except for the book I was reading.'

Morgan's gaze returned to her mother. 'Everything looks the same as always to me.'

'I couldn't find my book,' Catherine said in a threadlike voice. 'I left it right on this table.'

Morgan's eyes flickered to the table beside her and then down to the floor. The blue cover of a book peeked out from under the edge of the floorlength tablecloth. Morgan's agile young fingers fished out the volume and she waved it in the air. 'Is this it?'

Her mother focused on the book. 'Yes.' She reached for it and clutched it to her breast.

'It was under the table. It must've fallen and got kicked out of the way.' Morgan put her arms around her mother and hugged her tightly. 'Don't worry. Everything's all right.'

Catherine stroked Morgan's silken hair. How lucky I am, she thought, to have a daughter like this. She felt comforted and shook off her paralysing fear. 'Thanks for finding my book, honey. I guess I did overreact.'

Morgan gave her mother's shoulders a final squeeze. 'Shall I make us some tea? Then I can tell you about Gwen's new video game. It's awesome!'

Catherine sat curled up in front of a cheery fire later that evening. Although she had almost burned to death, a controlled blaze in a stone fireplace still appealed to her. Its welcoming warmth seemed totally unrelated to the scorching, ravenous beast which had claimed Julie's life. Catherine had sped Morgan off to bed with a kiss and a hug and now tried to find the energy to get herself ready to retire. She felt too exhausted to move.

On the sofa, Paul rubbed his eyes with his thumbs and then ran his fingers through his tousled hair. 'Too much to read, too little time to do it,' he commented, flinging one more densely written report down on to the coffee table. 'I need a nightcap. How about you, Cath?'

She looked up. 'A nightcap? Good idea. It sounds lovely.'

Paul returned a few minutes later balancing two brimming glasses in his hands. Catherine rescued the nearest one and took a quick gulp. 'Ahhh . . . Thanks.'

Paul settled into the chair beside hers and extended his feet to the blaze. 'We're almost out of firewood. Could you order some more? Two cords should do it.'

'No problem. I'll call Richardson's in the morning.' Catherine leaned back and let the alcohol relax her. 'Paul?' she said presently.

'Uh—uh?'

'Have you been into the study today? At any time?'

'Nope. Too busy. I've barely had time to go to the bathroom. Why?'

Catherine chose her words carefully, unwilling to reawaken Paul's concerns about her emotional state. 'It looks to me as if the room was searched. Very carefully searched.'

Paul choked on his drink. 'What?'

'I'm not sure, but everything seems just a little bit out of place—as if it were moved and then put back. I didn't touch your files so perhaps you could check them and see what you think; see if anything's missing.'

Paul hurried to the study wearing a worried frown. Catherine forced herself to stay put and await his verdict. Above all she didn't want her husband to think her paranoid.

Ten endless minutes later Paul returned.

'Well?' Catherine demanded, uncurling her legs and studying his face intently.

'Nothing's missing,' Paul replied slowly, 'but I know what you mean. All the files are there, more or less in the same order, but they're not the way I put them. Are you sure you didn't touch them?'

'I'm sure.'

Paul sat down again beside her and only the crackle of the fire punctuated the silence.

'Should we report it?' Catherine asked eventually.

'No! Of course not.' Paul spoke sharply but then he moderated his tone. 'Nothing's missing and it would be very hard to prove anyone rifled the files.'

Catherine's fear, allayed somewhat by the cosy domesticity of the evening, knotted her stomach again. 'The doors were locked while I was out.'

Paul gripped his wife's hands lightly in his own. 'Let's not overreact,' he urged her. 'No harm's been done. We'll just make sure we use the security chain at night and double-check the doors when we go out. And the windows too. I'll remind Morgan to be sure her window's locked except when she's airing her room.' Paul gave his wife's hands a final pat and sat back, rubbing the stubble on his chin.

After draining his glass, Paul regarded his wife anxiously. 'All right, honey? Is that good enough?'

'I suppose so . . .' she agreed reluctantly. 'As you say, there isn't much else we can do.'

'Then let's turn in. It's been a long day.'

Paul fell swiftly to sleep but Catherine lay awake, flinching at every tiny noise which scratched at the night's black shroud. Paul was mistaken. Something had been taken—the last shreds of Catherine's peace of mind.

CHAPTER 13

Since John's death, Catherine had been fighting the memory of another fateful day in her life—the day his brother Danny had died. But as fear closed in, the memories did too.

It had started out like so many other beautiful summer days. It was a Friday and the kind of day where the air is so clear it almost sparkles. The grass glowed with living light and the insects hummed in harmonic chords. After Catherine had cleared up the breakfast dishes and tidied the house she burst from the gloomy indoors to add her clear note to the crescendo of life.

Her Danny was seventeen and she, Catherine, was his chosen one! They had proven it the night before and only a very faint niggle of worry clouded her emotions. She pushed it aside. They had only done 'it' once—nothing would happen.

For the moment Catherine was wearing slacks and a T-shirt but her painstakingly chosen party dress was hanging crisp and new in her closet. Tonight she and Danny, Peggy and Calvin, and Alicia and Brent were going to the YMCA dance to celebrate. The young Catherine Dumont knew the world belonged to her and her chosen companions. The frustrations she often suffered due to her mother's illness disappeared like tenuous vapour into the brilliant morning. Catherine literally danced down the street.

Running up the back stairs to Alicia's house, Catherine yelled to her friend. 'Alicia? Are you ready?'

An upstairs window flew open and a curler-festooned head popped out. 'My hair's not dry yet!'

'Put a kerchief over it and come on!' Catherine paced impatiently below the window. 'We told Peggy we'd be at her place by eleven.'

'It doesn't take four of us to bake one cake,' Alicia retorted. 'Peggy and Julie can start without us.'

'This is Danny's cake. I've simply got to be there. Come on, Alicia.'

Catherine and Alicia, her head wrapped in a Paisley scarf of her mother's, ran to Peggy's house where the other two girls were waiting.

'It is going to be chocolate, isn't it?' Catherine asked anxiously. Danny loved chocolate.

'Yes.' Peggy was the chief baker, having the most experience, plus a mother on call who was an excellent cook. 'Here, Catherine, you get the flour ready.' Peggy handed over a sifter and a canister of flour and Catherine eagerly began.

It was a culinary triumph, that cake. All four girls were bursting with pride as they put the finishing touches to the icing. Peggy's mother wrote 'Happy Seventeenth, Danny' on top in ornate blue letters. In the years to follow, whenever Catherine smelled freshly baked chocolate cake, this was the scene which rose to her mind's eye.

They lowered the cake into a cardboard box which they took turns carrying over to the Retson house.

'Mrs Retson said to hide it in the front closet,' Alicia reminded them.

Julie led the way. 'Danny'll never find it here,' she giggled. 'My brother's never hung up a coat in his life!'

'Be back here by five o'clock in time to hide,' Catherine warned her friends. 'I sure hope the guys keep their mouths shut.'

'Brent will,' Alicia said smugly. 'I told him I wouldn't let him kiss me or anything tonight if Danny found out about the surprise party.'

'Me too,' Peggy smirked. 'That's what I told Calvin.'

'Will John tell?' Catherine glared at Julie.

'Nope.' John's twin shook her red curls vigorously. 'It's a surprise.'

'It better be!' Peggy threatened with some menace.

When the group gathered later that day at Danny's house, his mother directed operations. 'Danny's dad took him over to the farm for a few minutes. He told him his grandfather needed some help loading the wagon. They'll be back at five-twenty.'

By five o'clock all the guests had assembled at the Retson house. Catherine had donned a skirt and blouse as had the other girls, but her new party dress still waited in the closet. Catherine didn't want to chance getting chocolate cake on its pristine folds before the all-important dance. Brent and Calvin pretended to be too old for childish things like surprise parties, but their occasional whoops of high spirit revealed their excitement.

As the hour approached, the five guests hid in the living-room while Julie and John tried to look natural in the kitchen.

'Hush!' Catherine whispered fiercely as a fit of giggling broke out in Calvin and Peggy's corner. 'They're coming!'

An indistinguishable murmur of voices emanated from the kitchen until Mr Retson's voice rose above the others. 'Go in the living-room and get the newspaper for me, will you, Danny?' his father requested loudly. 'I think it's on the table.'

Danny was grumbling under his breath as he crossed the threshold.

'Surprise!'

Catherine smiled to herself as she remembered the stunned expression on Danny's face. He really was surprised! But by the time his blush faded to brick red he began enjoying himself.

The high point of the party for Danny came when he opened the box from his mom and dad. At first he said nothing; he merely stared, unblinking, at the contents. Then, with a reverence alien to him, he removed the black leather jacket from its bed of tissue.

'Wow!' A hushed whisper of admiration coursed through the room.

'Put it on, Danny.' His mother smiled at him.

He slipped into it as if donning a ritual robe, stroking the glowing leather time and time again with his fingers.

'Like it?' Mr Retson asked.

'Yes. Yes! Thank you!' Danny self-consciously kissed

each of his parents. 'I thought you didn't like leather jackets,' he mumbled.

'We don't, but you do and it is your birthday after all.'

At six-thirty Catherine, Peggy and Alicia prepared to leave the Retsons' to change for the dance. They were to meet up again with their boyfriends at Peggy and Brent's —the most central location.

Danny walked Catherine to the door. 'See you soon . . .' he whispered. 'I can think of only one more present I'd like for my birthday . . .'

Catherine blushed and touched her lips fleetingly to his. They tasted of chocolate cake. 'See you later . . .'

But she did not see him later. Catherine did not see Danny ever again.

Stood up at Peggy's, she felt furious and humiliated but was determined to hide it from the others. 'No, Peggy, Alicia, you go ahead. I think I'll go on home. Danny can find me there. If he wants to.'

After waiting for a few minutes with growing impatience, the other four continued on to the dance and Catherine, her self-esteem in tatters, trudged home alone to fling herself on her bed and unloose a deluge of tears. She sobbed long and violently. Danny's name mingled with both curses and endearments as she pummelled her damp pillow. Finally, drained to a numbness, she fell into a fitful sleep.

She awakened much later to a blinding headache and unfamiliar voices speaking in urgent tones in the living-room. She lay on her bed, trying without success to discern the words. Defeated, she thrust her pounding head under her pillow and tried to get comfortable—an impossible task. In exasperation she leapt up and dragged her starched net crinoline from under her skirt and threw it on the floor. She jerked off the constricting garter belt and stockings and added them to the heap. I'll never wear this stupid dress again, Catherine decided as she strained to pull it off without undoing the zipper. As for Danny, the creep!

'Catherine?' Her father knocked furtively at the door.

'Yes?' she responded crossly as the dress parted at the seams with a satisfying rip and she stepped free.

'May I come in?'

Despite herself, Catherine's curiosity was aroused. Her father hadn't entered her room in years. Not since she was six or seven. 'All right. Just a minute.'

She opened the door to see her father's expression frozen into solemn lines. Unnatural hesitation marred his step as he crossed the threshold.

'What is it? Who's here?'

Mr Dumont answered the second question first. 'The police. There's been an accident . . .'

Catherine knew right then it was Danny. Her stomach lurched sideways and bile rose, burning, in her throat. In her ears the buzzing whined so loudly it drowned out all else. 'Danny.'

Her father nodded. A sheen of sweat coated his grey features as he grabbed Catherine's wrists and held them tightly, so tightly she was bruised.

'Is he badly hurt, Daddy?' Instinctively she called him Daddy. She was a little girl again, begging for reassurance.

Mr Dumont dropped his eyes from the intensity of Catherine's pleading stare.

'Daddy?'

'Danny is dead, honey. Shot in the neck.'

Catherine's head exploded in one last burst of pain and she could remember nothing more until the next morning.

Her recollections of the days that followed were piecemeal, like still photographs from someone else's past. The police returned after the shooting to question her. She couldn't remember the beginning of the interview but the core of questions had indelibly imprinted themselves on her mind. Even twenty years later she still dreamed of that cross-examination.

Catherine and her parents sat stiffly in a row on the faded red horsehair couch—pigeons on a fence waiting to be picked off. Even now she could feel the prickling of that worn upholstery on the backs of her legs.

'When did you last see Danny Retson?'

'Yesterday, at his house. About six-thirty.'

'You left the Retson place at that time?'

107

'Yes. Peggy Wellwood, Alicia Castelvetri and I went to change for the dance. Danny was to meet me at Peggy's at eight-thirty.' Because her throat was so dry Catherine's voice was breaking but she didn't want the policemen to think she was crying. She couldn't bear the thought of those two unyielding men witnessing her grief. Her pain was all she had left of Danny. 'Could I have a drink, please?'

While Catherine's father scurried to the kitchen the two policemen, Catherine and her mother created a living tableau. No one even shifted his feet until Mr Dumont returned with a glass of lemonade. Catherine sipped eagerly and then cradled the cool glass in her burning hands.

'All right now, miss?'

'Yes.'

'You didn't expect to see Danny Retson before eight-thirty? Here, perhaps?'

'No.' Catherine sensed a tension in the atmosphere. 'Why?'

'According to Mr Brent Wellwood, Retson mentioned coming over here.'

'No.' The silence battered Catherine's mind. 'Who saw him last?' she whispered.

'Mr Calvin Parker and Mr Brent Wellwood, most likely, miss. They walked to the end of the street together with the victim.'

Catherine flinched. Victim.

'Parker and Wellwood went home via the ravine but Danny Retson didn't go with them. They said he planned to come by your place.'

'Well, he didn't!' Catherine's mother's voice was shrill with worry. 'I was here. I'm always here and Danny did not come!'

Catherine felt the policemen's eyes on her and knew what was going through their minds. They thought Danny might have sneaked in past her mother. Their dirty minds pictured Danny and her pawing each other, grasping and panting on her bed. They suspected she knew more than she was saying. She straightened her back and held up her head. 'Danny was not here last night,' she stated clearly.

108

'The last time I saw him was at his house at six-thirty. That's all I have to say.' With this statement Catherine left the room, walking slowly with dignity. The policeman had not called her back.

The impact of Danny's death on the future of his friends was incalculable but their life-stories were altered irrevocably. What would our lives have been like if Danny hadn't been murdered, Catherine mused from time to time. Oddly enough, the harrowing event had drawn them together, not driven them apart and from that point on Julie and John were full members of the group. Would it have made a difference if the murderer had been found? Could the whole episode have been laid to rest if guilt had been assigned? If Danny hadn't been killed would his brother and sister still be alive today?

CHAPTER 14

Settling back in the soft leather chair, Catherine waited as Alicia paced around her cluttered workroom and lit up yet another cigarette.

'I know what you'll think . . .' Alicia spoke jerkily. 'You'll think I'm crazy.'

'Until you tell me what's bothering you, I can't think anything,' Catherine responded calmly.

Abruptly Alicia ceased her pacing and perched on the end of her massive worktable. 'I went back to see Mildred McKeown.'

Noting her friend's air of incomprehension, she explained impatiently, 'You know the psychic. The one who predicted John's death.'

'Oh.'

Alicia seemed incapable of continuing.

'And?' Catherine prompted.

'I know I said I wasn't going to go back but I had to! Julie's dead, you almost died too . . . Who's next? I had to know.' Alicia's blood-red nails traced endless circles on the varnished wood and she sucked on her cigarette like a drowning woman presented with an air hose.

'So what did Mrs McKeown say?'

Alicia recommenced her restless pacing, circling the room like a trapped cat. 'She warned me . . . said I was next. There's a "cusp" in my lifeline which I may not get past.'

Catherine maintained her *sang-froid*. 'Did she say you were going to die?'

'Not for sure,' Alicia replied, hoarse with worry, 'but danger is approaching, stalking me, she said.'

'And you believe her.' It was not a question.

'She was right about John. She was right about my design award last year. She was right about the best location for my third boutique.' Alicia stopped directly in front of Catherine and challenged her disbelief. 'I have reason to be worried!'

Catherine was silent. She was worried too, though for different reasons. She didn't feel comfortable about dismissing Alicia's fears which so closely mirrored her own.

'Did your psychic say anything about the fire?' Despite her scepticism, Catherine wanted to know.

'Mildred said it wasn't an accident,' Alicia mumbled. She blushed. 'She claims evil is on the loose.'

Catherine wasn't sure she was comforted to have some crackpot as the only person who believed her own theory. 'Nice to have someone who agrees with me,' she finally remarked before proceeding. 'But Mrs McKeown didn't predict Julie's death, she just spoke of it after the fact.'

Gesturing excitedly, Alicia rushed to Mildred's defence. 'But I didn't visit her until after the fire. I stayed away a long time after she foretold John's death.'

The two friends sat in silence. Catherine's fears had reawakened. Was someone stalking her friends? Would there be a third victim? Or were there already three? Was Danny's death connected? Or Brent's? No, she decided, it wasn't possible. 'So what will you do?'

'I don't know. I've been considering going away for a while.' Alicia hurled a crumpled match into the brimming ashtray and ripped another from the book to light her next cigarette with desperate haste. 'Am I nuts?'

'You haven't had a holiday in a long time—it might be a good idea.'

A crow of nervous laughter escaped Alicia's red lips. 'You, Catherine Edison, are advocating running away? I can't believe it!'

'Why not? Whether Mrs McKeown's right or wrong, a change would do you good. Go some place warm and soak up the sun.' Catherine smiled warmly at her friend. 'Have fun. Shake the shadows from your mind.'

'Maybe I should.' Alicia sat down in the second chair and relaxed for the first time since Catherine arrived. 'How long should I go for?'

'Did the psychic mention a time-frame? How long is the glitch in you lifeline supposed to affect you?'

'Mildred didn't say, but I couldn't be away for more than three or four weeks. I need to complete my fall line and I can't spare more time than that.'

'So go, then. A holiday is a perfect solution.'

Alicia smiled at last as relief flooded her soul and she basked in the warm glow of companionship. 'Thanks.'

'Any time. Got anything to drink?' Catherine was still worried. If a murderer was really after Alicia, a month's wait wouldn't stop him. Or her.

The shriek of the electric sander stopped abruptly. From behind the empty shell of a 1954 Cadillac, an overweight hippy in stained overalls emerged. The grease monkey patted the rusted hulk fondly. 'She's really gonna be somethin', Wilson, when we got her fixed up.'

Wilson Brandenburg hoisted himself off the dilapidated chair from which he'd been watching Orville work. He joined his buddy at the metal corpse and ran a dirty finger along its clean lines. 'Yeah,' he agreed. 'She'll be a beaut.'

Wilson took three rapid swallows from his beer can, crushed it and tossed it towards a box in the corner. The can rattled against others of its kind sprouting from the garbage bin, but then it clattered to the cement floor.

Wilson wiped his mouth on his sleeve. 'What you doing tonight, Orv? Got a hot date?'

Orville glared sourly at Wilson. He hadn't had a date, hot or otherwise, in years. 'I'm gonna watch the game down at Mick's. Have a few beers . . .'

Wilson slapped Orville's overhanging belly with the back of his hand. 'Too much beer; too little exercise.'

Orville flailed at Wilson who had already retreated out of range. 'Shit, you drink more'an I do. What yer talkin' about?'

'But I keep fit.' Wilson exhibited his firm stomach, pirouetting like a fashion model before a gaggle of buyers. 'The girls just love my body.' He dragged out the word 'body' suggestively. 'Know what I mean?'

'Fuck off,' Orville said, but without heat. He was immune to Wilson's displays of vanity. 'That's why Peggy threw you out? 'Cause she loves your boooody?' Orville did a credible imitation of Wilson's drawl.

'Go to hell, Orv.' Wilson yanked open the door of an ancient refrigerator, grabbed two cans and then kicked the door shut with a cowboy-booted foot. He tossed one can to Orville and snapped the tab on the other. The contents disappeared down Wilson's throat in seconds and the can joined its predecessors.

Zipping up his black leather bomber jacket, Wilson headed for the door. 'Catch you later, Orv.' He thrust out his pelvis lewdly. 'There's some babe out there just dying to get laid.'

Using his smouldering good looks and well-worn lines, Wilson found his babe within a couple of hours. Cassie had noticed Wilson before at the Cinnamon Heart lounge but she'd not been quick enough to advertise her charms. Tonight, she'd homed in as soon as Wilson appeared under the red lights of the bar. Wilson needed no particular encouragement and he took over the initiative. Small talk wasted time so Wilson pulled Cassie straight to the crowded dance floor, manœuvring her expertly through the sea of perspiring humanity. Wilson touched Cassie's body lightly at first, fluttering his fingers down her spine and along the swelling of her breasts. She responded exactly as Wilson expected, allowing her hands to cup his tight bum and pressing her pelvis into his groin. She assented eagerly when Wilson suggested, 'Let's go some place quieter . . .' while kissing her neck.

Driving around in the truck, Wilson plied Cassie with rum, so when he strutted into Mick's house, with her in tow, she'd lost whatever inhibitions she might have had. Wilson dragged the giggling Cassie into the living-room where Orville and his clone, Mick, slouched in front of the television, beer cans balanced on their swollen bellies.

'Me and the lady are just gunna use the bedroom, boys. Don't let us disturb you.' Wilson draped one arm over Cassie's shoulder to fondle her breast and with the other he stroked a shapely thigh. Cassie leaned back against Wilson and rubbed her shining hair against his neck. 'Ummm,' she murmured.

'Give Mick a kiss, honey. He's letting us use his bed,' Wilson said, guiding the girl up to her bemused host.

Obediently she bent to kiss him, allowing Mick a perfect opportunity to ogle her cleavage. Wilson jerked her back up as soon as Mick and Orville had seen enough to be impressed.

'Come on, honey. I won't make you wait any longer.' Wilson winked broadly at Orville. He dragged his rubber girl towards the hallway and up the stairs to complete his mission.

Two hours later Orville and Mick were still sitting on the couch. The television, sound off, flickered before their drunken stupor. Mick belched as Wilson sauntered into the room, doing up his belt with elaborate care.

Mick burped again. 'She wear ya out, Wilson?'

'Hardly.' Wilson jerked his head towards the upper floor. 'She's sound asleep. Done in. As for me, boys, I've worked up quite a thirst. Gimme a beer.' Wilson strolled over and dropped into a sagging armchair.

Orville grabbed a can from the ice chest at his feet. 'I don't know why ya can't take yer women to yer own place,' he complained, tossing Wilson the beer. 'Why bring 'em here?'

'Mick's bed's bigger. And girls like the pink sheets.' Wilson grinned, exhibiting his sharp, white teeth.

Mick flushed. 'You know them's the sheets Sherry left behind . . .'

'They suit you, Mick.' Wilson crossed one ankle over the other and jiggled his boot.

Mick, fists balled, half hoisted himself out of his chair.

'Just kidding, Mick.' Wilson laughed. 'Sherry was a bitch to leave you but at least you got some good bedding out of the deal.' Wilson's good humour died abruptly. 'That's more than I got out of Peggy. So far.' He scowled at the flickering television screen. 'Why don't you shut that damn thing off?'

'Remote's busted,' Mick grunted.

'You're a lazy son of a bitch, Mick.' Wilson got up and savagely snapped off the set. 'I don't know why I hang around with you guys . . .'

'Free beer,' Orville commented. 'You haven't bought a case in weeks.'

Wilson moved restlessly around the room, kicking the furniture and smacking the wall with an open palm. He dismissed Orville's complaint without a thought. He knew Orville and his brother needed him. Wilson's charm managed to keep a lot of their creditors at bay.

Wilson's mind returned to Peggy. 'Bitch,' he hissed. He kicked the chair one more time before he threw himself into it.

'Who? The broad upstairs? Wasn't quite as sweet as she looked?' Mick asked.

'No. Peggy. She's got everything except my goddamn truck.' A nasty grin transformed Wilson's handsome face into a devilish caricature. 'But she's going to pay. In fact, she's already made the first couple of instalments.' Wilson snickered. 'Stupid bitch. Peggy and those goddamn friends of hers think they're better than me. We'll see who's laughing in the end.'

CHAPTER 15

Wilson Brandenburg stuck his foot in the door jamb. 'Aren't you going to invite me in for coffee?'

'I'm busy.' Peggy blocked the doorway, not giving an inch to her estranged husband. 'I've packed a bag for each of the children and I wrote the times of Peter's hockey games and the girl's swimming lessons on this paper.' Peggy thrust a clearly written sheet into Wilson's hand. 'School's out at three-twenty and I told them you'd be there to pick them up.'

'Don't we need to discuss their progress?'

'You were never interested when you lived here, so why would you care now?' Peggy sniffed with resentment.

Wilson used his most ingratiating tone. 'Now I realize just how much I care. Absence makes the heart grow fonder, my angel. I've missed you.' He let his eyes go soft and his lips part ever so slightly.

'I'm busy.' But Peggy's voice lost a little of its stridency.

'Let me come in, angel, just for a few minutes. It's cold out here.'

Peggy hesitated. She still felt the physical attraction as strongly as the day she met him. But pragmatism cooled her enthusiasm now. Sex wasn't everything and money and stability were more alluring with every passing day. Should she let him in?

Suddenly an unexpected shiver of fear crackled through her and a flashback of the horrible night of the intruder snapped into her mind.

'No! Go away! Stay away from me and stay away from this house or I'll call the police.' She cringed away and tried to slam the door.

An ugly, predatory expression replaced the melting look on Wilson's face. 'Don't shut the door on me, you bitch!' He threw his weight against the door and shoved.

Peggy fell back into the foyer, panic flooding her. He's

going to kill me! She cast wildly around for some form of weapon. The umbrella! Still retreating, she snatched it up and stabbed viciously at her husband's stomach. 'Get away!' she shrieked.

In pain, Wilson bent over to protect his soft belly while he grabbed for the dancing umbrella. He missed. Peggy thrust again and Wilson dodged back, his teeth bared like fangs.

'Miss Peggy! Miss Peggy!'

At first neither combatant noticed the shrill voice calling from the living-room doorway.

'Miss Peggy!' This time both Peggy and Wilson heard the terrified screeching and they eased apart, taking up wary stances on opposite sides of the room.

'I have four small children here with me, Wilson. Are you man enough to fight them too?'

Wilson clenched and unclenched his fists, breathing heavily through his open mouth. 'Bitch . . . hiding behind babies.'

Two more voices joined the original wail from the living-room.

'I'm coming, kids,' Peggy called out without taking her eyes off her husband. 'I think you'd better leave,' she hissed at him.

'So you can throw yourself at Calvin Parker? Is that why you're letting me have Peter and the girls for the weekend —so you can replace me with Mr High and Mighty?'

'I thought maybe you really wanted to see them, Wilson, believe it or not. Now I wish I hadn't agreed.'

'Too late! I intend to tell them just what kind of a bitch you really are!' Wilson's face was flushed as he spat the words at his wife.

'And just what's that supposed to mean?'

'You figure it out.' Wilson spun on his heel, threw open the door and then slammed it as hard as he wanted to hit his wife.

Ignoring the increasing cacophony from her charges, Peggy followed him outside.

'Peter and the girls are to be back Sunday night by seven

o'clock!' she called out anxiously, but Wilson didn't answer. A rooster tail of snow spat out from under his tyres as he roared out of the driveway in his dilapidated pick-up truck.

Peggy collapsed into a chair, unaware of the toddlers clamouring around her. What would he do now? Harm the children? Kidnap them? That possibility bothered her even more than the prospect of his hurting her. In his present mood, Wilson was capable of anything. Even murder.

CHAPTER 16

In her studio, Alicia viewed her three pregnant suitcases with satisfaction. Done! She'd managed to cram in all the clothes essential for a southern cruise. And tomorrow morning . . . off into the wide blue yonder!

Alicia executed a few intricate dance steps. Already the pall of dread which had been weighing her down and tainting every moment of her days was beginning to lighten. Soon, away from the fear and the sorrow, she'd be able to sleep without the aid of pills. She wouldn't startle at every unexpected sound.

Alicia peered into the mirror of her make-up case. The smudges under her eyes were as black as her sleek hair. 'Ugh!' Fortunately, her sunglasses would hide this defect until the warm breezes and holiday atmosphere had erased them.

Smiling, Alicia snapped shut the lid of the case. The tracing of worry lines faded from her clear complexion. She would be safe on the SS *Jubilee*, cruising through the languid, azure waters of the Caribbean.

She'd planned on making it an early night, but she'd also promised herself she'd leave a tidy studio behind her. With a heavy sigh she surveyed the clutter. Not even Superwoman could clean it up and be in bed before one o'clock. The heck with it, she decided. Why pretend she could ever be neat? Let her vacation start now.

Alicia plugged in her white kettle and rummaged in the

cupboard for a teabag. Just as she emerged triumphant with one crumpled gauze pillow she heard a sharp knock at the little-used back entrance to her flat. The block of ice reformed in her stomach. Who the hell could it be?

Skirting the rows of shoes lining the steep stairway, Alicia made her way to the bottom and peered anxiously through the frosted window into the alleyway. Thank heavens!

'What are you doing here so late?' Alicia opened the door and let in the caller who stamped hard on the mat to dislodge the clinging snow.

'I know you're leaving tomorrow for some well-deserved rest so I came to ask if there's anything that needs looking after while you're gone. Plants to water? Furnace to check?'

'That's very thoughtful of you, but Marsha can take care of all that. She's in the boutique five days a week.'

'Great.' The visitor paused. 'But maybe you should leave me a key in case something happens on the weekend or at night. In the winter you can never be too careful . . .'

Alicia considered for a moment. 'OK. I'll give you my spare key just in case. Come on up for a sec'.'

Behind Alicia's receding back her unexpected guest allowed a flicker of a smile to escape. Waiting until Alicia returned would have been very inconvenient.

CHAPTER 17

Catherine pounded in frustration on the door of the boutique. 'Where are you, Alicia?' she grumbled aloud. 'I got up at seven o'clock on a Sunday morning to take you to the airport and you're not even awake!'

She punched the doorbell one last time and gave up banging on the door. She stepped back, hands on hips and stared at the dark second-floor windows. If Alicia didn't get cracking she'd miss both her flight and her cruise.

Catherine nibbled her lip as she pondered her options. 'Telephone!' she exclaimed. That was it. Phone the apartment. Maybe that would wake up sleeping beauty. She crossed the street to a grubby diner. Its weathered façade may have lowered the tone of the neighbourhood but at least Leo's Café was open.

'May I use your phone?' she asked, exasperation evident in her voice.

'What's wrong?' A spark of interest fought to remain alive in the worn face of the pear-shaped man behind the counter. 'I seen you bangin' on Ms Castelvetri's door. She's not open on Sunday.'

'I know that! I'm supposed to be taking her to the airport for an early flight and she's not answering the door.'

Leo nodded and his heavy jowls shook like grey gelatin. 'Yeah, I remember her tellin' me she was takin' a cruise. Down south somewheres.'

'Well, she won't be going anywhere if she doesn't get her act together. Can I use the phone? I want to call her.'

'Go ahead.' Leo jerked his head towards the kitchen.

Catherine swiftly located the telephone on the corner of a cluttered but none the less clean counter on the far side of the room. She dialled. Alicia's telephone rang. She let it ring fifteen times before finally hanging up and returning to the front of the café.

'No luck?' Leo grunted.

Catherine shook her head, a tiny furrow of worry creasing her high forehead.

The sole customer glanced up from his newspaper but decided the sports scores were more interesting than this minor local crisis and went back to his paper.

'So what do I do now?' Catherine asked. 'Go home? Call the police?'

Leo scratched at his oily scalp where it gleamed through his sparse grey hair. 'Maybe I got a key.' The man disappeared back into the kitchen and Catherine could hear him rummaging around in drawers and cupboards. A minute later he returned with a Yale key gripped triumphantly in his sausage-like fingers.

'I used to look after the store sometimes for the guy who rented the place before Ms Castelvetri did,' he explained.

'Is it the same lock?'

119

Leo shrugged. 'I dunno. Likely. It's a good one so why replace it?' He threw the key on the counter where it clattered up against the napkin dispenser. 'Try it if you like.'

'Thanks.'

The key turned with a satisfying click and Catherine entered the boutique. She raced through the dark store, then mounted the stairs as quickly as she could with her damaged feet. But the door at the top of the stairs was locked.

'Damn!' She began hammering again. 'Alicia! Wake up! You're late!'

Nothing.

Without much hope of success, Catherine inserted the key into the second lock. It turned and Catherine invaded Alicia's workroom. Without pausing to find the light switch, she sped through the gloom towards Alicia's living quarters. Rounding the end of the long cutting table, she tripped over a bolt of rippled black cloth. She caught the edge of the work table to prevent herself from falling. As she paused to regain her balance, she noticed a shoe sticking out from the end of the bolt. Catherine froze. Two shoes. And a black-stockinged leg. Her mind refused to assimilate what she saw but her eyes followed the roll of cloth to its other end.

It was no wonder Catherine tripped over Alicia before she saw her. The long black skirt, the black jacket and the tumbled black hair shrouded the white body, masking it in the dim light, disguising it as one more discarded item on the cluttered floor.

'No . . .' Catherine mewed piteously. 'No . . .'

Oddly, she was not, at first, afraid. She crouched by her friend—hand outstretched to brush back Alicia's shining ebony hair.

'Alicia,' she whispered. The white cheek was cold. Dead cold. Catherine shuddered. She became aware that her other hand, resting on the grey rug beside Alicia's head, felt wet. In slow motion she drew it up before her hollow eyes. In the dimness her fingers looked like they'd been dipped in black syrup, molasses perhaps. But the black stickiness had the metallic smell of blood.

'Oh my God!' Catherine screamed. She scrambled away from the body, holding her bloodstained hand outstretched, trying to escape its horrifying stigmata.

Still thrusting her arm rigidly out in front of her, Catherine plunged back down the stairs, unwilling to stay another moment alone with death. In the darkness of the shop she lost her bearings and careened into displays and racks of clothes, leaving devastation in her wake. Outside the door, the slap of the cold dawn air made her draw in her breath sharply. Awareness seeped back into her and she slowed her headlong flight.

Leo, watching for lights from Alicia's apartment, saw Catherine explode from the shop. He was at the café door by the time she had crossed the street.

'What's wrong, lady?'

She tried to speak but no sound came out as her dry lips struggled to form words. She swallowed and tried again. Leo's eyes locked on Catherine's bloody hand and he backed away from her.

'She's dead,' Catherine blurted out as she broke through her speech blockage. 'Dead!' She gasped for breath as her chest constricted. Panic rose again in her throat and threatened to gag her. Cold sweat beaded on her forehead. 'Police. Ambulance.' Catherine lurched towards the café kitchen.

'I'll phone.' Leo pushed quickly in front of her. He couldn't bear the thought of that bloody hand touching anything in his kitchen. 'You sit,' he ordered, thrusting a chair at the distraught woman.

Catherine's knees wobbled and she fell into it. A low moan rose unbidden from her very soul.

The single customer put down his paper and stared at Catherine as she sat shivering convulsively. He got up, walked around to the other side of the counter and poured a cup of steaming coffee.

'Here. Drink this.' He plunked the cup in front of Catherine. 'You're in shock. You need to stay warm.'

The stranger's words didn't penetrate but Catherine

121

responded to the arrival of the coffee. Using her unsullied hand to grasp the cup, Catherine took huge gulps. She scalded her mouth but the pain revived her. The terror receded marginally from her eyes and her face lost its rigid, set expression.

'Maybe you should wash,' the stranger suggested, nodding towards her bloodstained hand.

Catherine's gaze darted around, unfocused.

'The washrooms are over there.' The customer pointed to the back corner.

Catherine jerked to her feet and stumbled to the ladies' room where she watched, mesmerized, as the water ran red, then pink, then clear. 'Alicia's going down the drain!' She howled with anguish in the moment before the tears came.

CHAPTER 18

'So what is it you wanted to see me about?' Staff Sergeant John Warshinsky eyed Catherine Edison with impatience barely concealed behind his ruddy, freckled complexion and his unlikely dark eyes. He'd already interviewed her at length about the death of Alicia Castelvetri and knew she was going to fight the official position of death by misadventure. His protruding upper teeth gnawed at his lower lip as he waited for his guest to speak. Catherine had marched decisively into the room and now sat calmly erect in the straight-backed chair facing his desk.

Catherine knew this was her last shot and took her time, assimilating the ambience and allowing this impersonal office to become less foreign and intimidating. To her left, through the venetian blinds, she could see the market square, deserted now under its soiled, wrinkled sheet of snow. Faintly she could hear the swish of tyres on wet pavement—the salt trucks had been out in force. Inside, Warshinsky's office had not enjoyed the services of an interior designer. No one concerned with the aesthetics of life could have chosen the sallow paint or the stark, fluorescent tubing which threw shadowless, cold light on the Staff Sergeant's rabbit face. The policeman kept his grey metal desk surprisingly neat. A green felt pad lay squarely in front of him and two stacks of papers and folders aligned themselves with military precision on either back corner. Warshinsky tapped the eraser end of a stubby pencil rhythmically on the felt pad.

As Catherine watched him, the policeman's face blurred. For an instant he became the blue-uniformed officer who had interrogated her about Danny's death so many years before. The same leaden feeling threatened to drag her down but she shook it off.

She cleared her throat. 'It's about Ms Castelvetri's death. There are two points I would like to bring up,' she stated in her best, no-nonsense, lecture voice. 'First the wine glass. You contend, am I not right, that Alicia, while alone for the evening, poured herself one or more glasses of wine, drank them while she worked, and then slipped on the rug, hit her head on the table and died.'

'Correct.' Warshinsky's voice was a high tenor with a slight sibilance in it. Why did he have to deal with the difficult ones, he wondered.

'Wrong.' Catherine enunciated clearly. 'She was definitely not alone in drinking the wine.'

'We found only one dirty glass.'

'But Alicia would never have used that glass if she were alone. It was one of a pair—a pair my husband and I gave her three years ago for her birthday. She used them only when she had company, when there was someone around to use the other glass.'

Warshinsky shifted in his chair. 'A glass is a glass, Dr Edison.'

Catherine leaned forward a fraction. 'Are you married, Officer?'

'Yes. So?'

'Ask your wife if a glass is a glass. Ask her if she would us one of a pair of crystal glasses if she were alone, working.'

'I'll note your concern, Dr Edison. Now if that's all you

123

want to tell me . . .' He half rose before Catherine cut him off.

'It's important!' She would not be brushed off so summarily. 'Alicia was definitely not alone when she had the wine. And someone washed and put away just one glass. Why?'

Warshinsky sighed and settled back in his chair. 'All right. You tell me why.'

'Because that someone killed Alicia and wanted it to look like an accident; wanted to hide the fact that he'd ever been there!'

'And do you have a candidate to play the part of this mystery visitor? And a motive? Why did this alleged guest kill Ms Castelvetri?'

Catherine bit her lip and fought the urge to drop her gaze and huddle defensively. 'I don't know.'

'I thought not.' Warshinsky allowed a complacent smile to settle on his lips.

'But Alicia wasn't his first victim!' Catherine insisted.

Warshinsky didn't even raise an eyebrow. 'Oh?'

'John Retson and Julie Parker were murdered too.'

Warshinsky leaned his elbows on his desk and looked steadily at Catherine. 'I read the reports on those deaths —in fact the Retson incident is my case. And I can understand why you find it hard to believe the two deaths aren't related. But you and your friends are not being stalked by some crazed killer.'

'Three close friends have died in less than three months, and they've all died violently! You can't tell me that's coincidence!'

'Oh yes I can. Accidents happen. Coincidences happen. As a scientist, you know that better than most people.' Warshinsky ran fingers through his thin hair and tried for a father confessor tone. 'I'm sorry your friends died but there's no evil plot here—just tragic coincidence. There is simply no need to be afraid.'

'And what about that hit-and-run driver?' Catherine challenged. 'Why hasn't he been caught? Aren't you trying any more? Is John just one more statistic?'

124

'We found the car.'

'So? Who was driving it? Find the driver and you've found a triple murderer. It would be worth your while to put a little effort into the search.'

Both Catherine and Staff Sergeant Warshinsky clung to their tempers like climbers to a rope.

The policeman mentally rehearsed the rules on how to deal with hysterical witnesses, then responded with what he considered commendable calm. 'The investigation into Mr Retson's death is ongoing but we haven't any leads at the moment.' Unable to stop himself, he gestured sarcastically. 'Maybe you could give us some pointers, Dr Edison?'

Catherine held her anger under tight rein but her knuckles whitened with the effort. 'I know that you needn't look for a random killer. Obviously it's someone somehow connected to our group.'

'But you don't know who, or what the connection is. Or when your paths crossed or why this person's so upset he's picking you off one by one. Or even that it's a man. Right?' He slapped the desk with his open palm. 'You're not giving me any facts. There's nothing to support your contentions. In my job evidence is as important as it is in your scientific research. No proof, no conclusion.'

Catherine's cheeks burned with humiliation. He didn't believe her. No one did. Why couldn't they see the obvious? 'How many more bodies will it take to convince you that I'm right?'

Warshinsky ignored the question. 'I believe you said you had two points . . . Maybe you'll convince me yet.'

Catherine hesitated, but decided she might as well say her piece. She perched on the edge of the chair. 'The rug —the one you say skidded under Alicia's feet causing her to fall?'

'Yeah?' He stretched out his legs and crossed his ankles.

'The table legs are always on it. Alicia knew it was dangerous and always kept it anchored. It couldn't possibly have skidded.'

'Maybe she'd just cleaned and forgot to put the table back.'

Catherine snorted. 'Did it look like she'd just cleaned? Alicia's workroom was a mess as usual.'

'So you're suggesting someone freed the rug and waited for Ms Castelvetri to slip on it? A pretty unreliable method for a cold-blooded killer, I'd say.'

'He likely pushed her against the table and then moved the rug so it looks like she slipped.'

'We found no marks on the body to indicate any such thing.'

Catherine shuddered at the impersonal language. Alicia —the body. 'It wouldn't take much of a shove, especially from a strong man. Alicia was tall but very thin and light.'

Warshinsky was shaking his head as he pushed away from his desk and stood up. 'Sorry, Doctor, you've really given me nothing to go on—nothing to make me change my mind.' He walked around to stand by her. 'Don't think we weren't suspicious of the second, and particularly the third death. We were. At first. But we've examined the evidence with a fine-tooth comb and there's simply no indication of foul play.' Warshinsky looked at Catherine, sympathy in his eyes. 'I've an open mind. If you come up with something concrete . . .'

Catherine stood up, her knees shaking with the fatigue of defeat. 'I won't keep you any longer. Thank you for your help.' Her sarcasm was wasted on the Staff Sergeant.

He ushered her to the door. 'Any time, Dr Edison, that's what we're here for.'

Closing the door thankfully behind her, the policeman couldn't know that within days he'd be wishing he'd listened more carefully.

It was almost midnight but Paul still hunched over the computer in his private office at the law firm. On the screen, like digital snakes, ranged lists of numbers—financial figures and account numbers for the trust funds he administered. Paul shifted the cursor up and down, altering single digits here and there. He was performing the last step in a long series of intricate numerical alterations which had taken him the better part of Sunday.

126

'Done.' Paul switched off the computer, leaned back in his chair and mopped his brow with a white linen handkerchief. He massaged the tense muscles in his neck, sighing with relief. Now he had half a million dollars to add to Calvin's campaign fund; donations from his mythical Bay Street connections. The 'borrowing' had been harder this time because he had to raid some of the more active accounts. Covering his tracks was more involved. None the less, he felt satisfied with his day's work. And when Calvin became Premier in a few months, Paul would suddenly have those elusive connections and be able to replace the missing money before anyone found out. He avoided thinking about the consequences if Calvin failed in his leadership bid.

Paul looked at his watch. Damn! He'd told Catherine he'd be home by nine for a late supper. Her patience with his irregular hours was wearing out and this certainly wouldn't help. Maybe the fact that he was working at the law office instead of campaign headquarters would prevent an explosion. Crossing his fingers, Paul shrugged into his overcoat, switched off the light and started for home.

CHAPTER 19

'Zip me up?' Catherine stood with her back to Paul and waited for him to fasten her black dress. It was getting a lot of wear lately.

Paul jerked up the zipper. 'Now you're not going to mention the word murder, OK? Try not to embarrass us, for God's sake, Catherine!' He had tried, unsuccessfully, to talk his wife out of attending Alicia's funeral. 'It was an accident —the police are certain. Alicia fell and hit her head. The coroner pronounced Julie's death an accident. The fire was an accident. John was killed by a drunk driver.' Paul had twisted Catherine around to face him and now gripped her shoulders painfully hard. 'There is no murderer. There is no plot to wipe out your damn group—you're all doing a good enough job without any help.'

'You're hurting me, Paul.' Without her glasses, Catherine's eyes loomed huge and unfocused. Tears pooled in their inner corners.

He eased the pressure of his hands but didn't let go. 'I've been patient with you, honey. I've listened to your endless, circular arguments. I haven't stopped you from hounding the police and making a fool of yourself, but frankly, I've had enough. There isn't a shred of evidence to support your crazy theory!'

'But I'm right, Paul. It's me you're talking to, remember? Practical, unimaginative Catherine? As much sensitivity as a bag of cement—that's what you said about me. Have I ever acted irrationally?'

'Yes! Right now.'

'Before now? Have I? Have I?'

'No, but . . .'

'But nothing. I'm as sane as I ever was. It's just that I can see the truth!'

'And everyone else in the whole world is too stupid to understand?' Paul demanded. 'That seems just a little unlikely, don't you think?' His voice grew softer and he slid his hands upward to gently cup Catherine's face. 'Let it be, darling. We'll attend Alicia's funeral, mourn our loss, and then get on with our lives. All right?'

'I need your support.' Catherine felt forlorn and alone as her hopeless quest drained ever more of her energy. 'Everyone else is gone!'

'You have my support in everything but this, and everyone else isn't gone. You have Morgan, Peggy, Susan, Calvin, your colleagues at work . . . We're all here. But you have to put this tragedy behind you and go forward with us.'

Paul cradled Catherine in his arms as he stroked her soft hair. 'As time passes it'll get easier for you.'

'Until someone else dies,' Catherine murmured against Paul's chest.

'What did you say?'

'Nothing . . .'

*

128

On the drive to the funeral home Catherine sat quietly, renewing her faith in her husband. Paul did support her in most things, she realized. But he'd always been a realist, dependent on facts and figures, not intuition and hunches —exactly what he had accused her of being not so long ago. Why should she expect him to change now? Paul's impatience with her flight of illogic merely reflected his character.

Catherine smiled crookedly and stole a glance at Paul's profile. It was hard to believe fifteen years had passed since she'd first admired it!

While researching for her PhD at the University of Windsor, Catherine had rarely looked up from her books and her petri dishes. Regularly she refused invitations to parties but her room-mate, Heidi, finally beat down her resistance.

'Come on, Cath. Keeping your nose to the grindstone only results in a sore nose. Live a little! Lighten up! You're becoming very grim company, you know.' Heidi tossed her long blonde hair and unconsciously posed to best show off her new leather miniskirt. 'The Law Faculty's throwing a party at the Student Union. There'll be lots of MEN there!'

'I've too much work to do,' Catherine prevaricated.

Heidi marched over, slammed her room-mate's book shut and then dumped it into her own desk. She locked the drawer with a flourish and pocketed the key. 'Now you don't. You have fifteen minutes to get ready!'

Willy-nilly, Catherine let herself be hauled off to the party. Mid-term examinations had wound up that afternoon and even the most dedicated law students had decided to let loose. The room was packed.

Heidi knew everyone. Her casual style eased her shy friend painlessly into the group of ten people crammed around a table on the fringe of the minuscule dance floor. The insistent beat of the music vibrated through Catherine as she relaxed, content to listen to the energetic banter of the crowd. Judging by the shop talk, they were all law students. Males heavily outnumbered females, as Heidi had predicted, so even Catherine, who considered herself unattractive and dull, soon had the attention of the two men to her left. That quiet one is kind of cute, she thought. Her heart beat a little more quickly.

'Wanna dance?' asked the taller, louder man, leering drunkenly down Catherine's blouse. The sour smell of beer assailed her nostrils and instinctively she drew back. 'No, thanks. Not right now.'

'Sure you do!' Eddie staggered to his feet and grabbed her arm. 'Let's go, babe!'

'I don't want to dance!' She tried to pull her arm free but Eddie had a good grip.

'Baaa, ba, ba, baaam; baaa, ba, ba, baam.' Eddie pulled her to her feet, keeping inaccurate time to the music.

Catherine threw a look of entreaty at Eddie's cute companion but he had turned away.

She danced. Eddie jived awkwardly, throwing her around like a rag doll. Two minutes later Eddie stumbled, almost dragging her down on top of him, but a hand reached out to steady her and detach Eddie's clutch.

'Want to dance?' It was the cute, quiet young man.

It was a slow dance. Self-conscious at first, Catherine gradually relaxed into his arms, absorbing his warmth, his nearness. It had been a long time . . .

Paul Edison, as her rescuer turned out to be, was in his last year of law school and he waxed enthusiastic about his chosen profession.

'I'm going to be articling at Shaffer and Higgens,' he told her later as they walked arm in arm along the Detroit River. 'They do a lot of legal aid work and juvenile cases as well as corporate law. Then, when I'm qualified, I'll set up my own office and help the underdogs.' They paused to admire the twinkling lights of the Detroit skyline and enjoy the crisp night breeze blowing against their faces. 'You can save the world's food from disease, Catherine, and I can do my part to balance the administration of justice in this country.'

But even then, in the throes of youthful idealism, Paul showed his pragmatism. Even then he'd pictured himself working with corporate clients. 'To subsidize my legal aid work,' he explained. 'We'll have to eat—I've been poor long enough.'

Two months after Catherine met Paul, they moved in together. Their sex life was great. Surprisingly, Paul was a practised lover, and he coached Catherine gently and lovingly. He peeled off her layers of shyness and inhibition and taught her freedom.

Over dinner, over candles in bottles and canned beans on mismatched plates, they endlessly discussed philosophy, politics, sociology and ethics.

Paul introduced Catherine to his lawyer friends, calling her 'my darling doctor' even before she'd earned her degree. And when she did get her PhD and landed a job at the university in her old home town, Paul followed. Without complaint, Paul left his Toronto firm behind, to set up practice in a new city.

Catherine studied her husband. Physically at least he hadn't changed much—just a few interesting creases in his handsome face and a little distinguished grey at his temples. When they had more time, when the damn leadership race was decided, his warmth would resurface.

She took Paul's hand. He looked over, frowning, but seeing the gentle smile on her face he grinned in return.

'We're doing OK. Right?' she asked.

Paul squeezed her hand in reply. 'You bet.'

She gazed out of the window at the grey landscape. 'Things haven't turned out exactly as we planned, have they?'

'In what way?' He glanced quizzically at his wife before turning back to the road.

'You were going to open a store front office and I intended to work for CUSO in the Third World . . .'

Paul smiled ruefully. 'The rat race sucked us in, I guess, but basically our values haven't changed.'

Catherine wondered. She enjoyed her secure, comfortable job at the university. And Paul was in charge of fund-raising for a right-wing politician.

The funeral service was short, stark, unsentimental. According to Alicia's wishes, her lawyer read a short excerpt from Kahlil Gibran and played a recording of Handel's Sarabande. The casket remained closed, no floral tributes draped the coffin and cremation was to follow immediately, without witnesses.

Instead of raging at the injustice of life and death, Catherine allowed herself, just for the moment, to grieve untroubled by who and what had caused Alicia's early demise. She let scenes of her friendship with Alicia drift through her mind as the service unfolded. When she recollected the time Alicia had dyed her hair fluorescent orange —a protest against changing the official school colours—a smile glimmered on Catherine's lips. What a crazy, complex person Alicia had been! Even this funeral carried her unmistakable imprint. Who else would have written explicit funeral instructions and no will?

In addition to Catherine's sadly depleted group, Marsha and Alicia's other employees were in attendance, sniffing dolefully into designer handkerchiefs.

'What happens now?' Catherine quietly asked Marsha as they filed out after the brief ceremony. Marsha pushed back her heavy blonde hair. 'Alicia didn't have a will, so her estate goes to some third cousin in Halifax. We, the other girls and I, that is, have arranged to buy out the business assets. We'll carry on as long as possible at the boutiques. Alicia prepared enough clothes, patterns and sketches to last a year or two.'

'And then?'

A self-conscious blush crept up Marsha's face. 'I always wanted to be a designer. Maybe I'll give it a try. Alicia said I have a keen eye for fashion.'

'Sounds good. Alicia would be happy.'

'Yeah. I suppose so.' Marsha had aged in the days since her employer's death and she held herself carefully, like a fragile old woman afraid of falling. Catherine consciously fought the urge to droop similarly. I wonder if Marsha and Alicia were lovers, she speculated silently.

'Drop around to the boutique sometime, Catherine. I've taken over Alicia's apartment and I'd love you to come up for a drink. You can pretend I'm Alicia!' Marsha laughed nervously. 'You don't mind me moving in there, do you?'

'Of course not! Better you than anyone else.'

'Thanks.'

The swirling of the small crowd separated them at the lobby of the funeral home and Catherine drifted into a quiet alcove where she collapsed into a soft armchair, leaned back and closed her eyes. How much more could she take?

'Three down,' announced a deep voice from the depths of the companion chair.

Catherine snapped alert and peered around the wing back of her chair. Her eyes fell on Wilson Brandenburg's grinning countenance.

'You bastard!' she hissed. 'What are you doing here?'

'Alicia and I were good friends—very good friends.'

'Like hell!'

'Very good, very close friends, if you get my meaning.'

'You're insufferable!' Catherine jumped to her feet, intending to rush away from Wilson's unsettling presence but he thrust out a sinewy hand and gripped her arm.

'Let me go!' She tried to shake him off. He pulled her down towards him and she had to fight for balance.

'We were lovers, you know, me and Alicia. She couldn't resist me. I told her I was a married man but she couldn't help herself.'

'Liar! I know what Alicia thought of you. She thought you were scum.'

Wilson ignored the insult and drew Catherine closer. His wild eyes scared her and, mesmerized, she quit struggling.

'I had to break it off—told her my marriage was too important to risk. Alicia didn't take it well and she went to pieces. Remember her breakdown four years ago?' Wilson's smile gleamed. 'I felt so guilty, but what could I do? Peggy is my life.'

'You make me sick!' Repugnance twisted Catherine's face.

Wilson grabbed her other arm and jerked her towards him until his sour breath filled her nostrils with the stench of decay.

'That's what Alicia said.' His voice was cold and implacable. Catherine shivered. Abruptly Wilson released his pincer-like grasp and Catherine fled down the hall.

CHAPTER 20

'Daddy, why can't you stay home?' Melissa paused while eating her Raisin Bran and stared, pleading in her eyes, at her father. Calvin sipped coffee and read the *Globe and Mail* at the opposite side of the table.

'Daddy!'

'What do you want?' He rattled the newspaper impatiently.

'Do you have to go away again, Dad?'

'Yes.'

'Toronto?'

'Yes. Morgan's father will be around to pick me up in ten minutes and I want to finish the paper.' Calvin turned the page with a flourish.

'But Dad . . .'

'What is it, Melissa? Shouldn't you hurry? Aren't you going to be late for school?'

'Dad, my school play's in two days and you promised you'd come.'

Calvin rested the paper on the table. 'I know, honey, but I'm not sure I'll be able to make it. I've a lot to do in Toronto.'

'But I've been practising and practising. I want you to see me!'

'I'll try.'

'Please?'

'I said I'd try! Don't hound me!' Calvin folded the paper and got up. 'Give us a kiss.'

Melissa dutifully kissed his clean-shaven cheek when he bent over her chair. He smelled of a herbal aftershave which reminded Melissa of her mother. Mom would have come to see her play for sure.

'Say goodbye to your brother for me.'

'OK.' Melissa left the room, head hanging in dejection. She was the unluckiest person on earth! Not only had her mother abandoned her, but her father ignored her and even threatened to move her away from her friends. Toronto! She even hated the name.

Melissa kicked viciously at her brother's door. 'Time for school, creep!'

A few minutes later, Calvin threw his briefcase into the back seat and heaved a deep sigh as he climbed in beside Paul.

'Something wrong?' Paul asked as he pulled away from the kerb and headed the Volvo towards Toronto.

'Not really. Melissa's taken over Julie's role of complaining about my business trips. She expects me to come back by Thursday for some play she's in.'

'The all-candidates' meeting in Mississauga is on Thursday.'

'I know. I told her I might not be able to attend.'

'Poor kid,' Paul murmured, thinking of his own daughter.

'Yeah. It's too bad.' Calvin stared out of the side window, watching the dirty snow banks blur by. 'Julie would've gone.'

'You can't do everything, old man,' Paul comforted him.

Calvin turned his fine grey eyes on his friend. 'Does Catherine complain about your being away?'

'Not often—she's too busy herself to notice whether I'm home or not. But she worries about my letting my law practice atrophy.'

'Tell her you're working towards something better, more lucrative.'

Paul laughed ruefully. 'I do. Then she points out that your election's still not a sure thing. And that even if you do win and move to Toronto I'll have to go as well to reap my rewards.'

'So?'

'So she's a tenured professor at the university here. She doesn't want to move.'

135

'She'll come around when the time arrives,' Calvin remarked confidently. 'Catherine's the dependable type.'

'I'm glad you're so sure!' Paul recalled one of their more recent arguments on the topic. She had spoken of staying in Kingsport and spending only the Christmas holiday in Toronto.

'Don't be so sure I'll want to follow you, Paul,' she'd warned. 'I like it here. You used to, too, remember?'

'That was before I had a chance to get some real power. Calvin'll need me when he's elected and you can't expect me to quit once he gets to the top. Besides, if I don't go, I'll have spent the last two years for nothing.'

'Toronto's so big . . .'

'Think of the plays . . . the concerts.'

'Think of the pollution, the traffic jams,' Catherine countered, crossing her arms and staring at her husband. 'Maybe I could take it for a few weeks, but all year? No way!'

Calvin and Paul mused over their family problems for the next fifty miles.

Then Calvin's train of thought halted at a particularly unpleasant station and his interest in domestic affairs faded. 'Any more news on that damn book?'

'It'll be in the stores by July.'

'Have we seen the whole thing?'

Paul nodded. 'Except for the cover.'

'I hope I survive it.'

'You and me both!'

CHAPTER 21

'More coffee?' Marsha waved the ceramic pot in the air. Catherine, Peggy and Susan declined the offer. 'I couldn't manage another bite!' Catherine groaned. 'It was a fabulous meal.'

Murmurs of agreement came from all sides as the four women rose and moved to more comfortable chairs in the tiny living-room of the apartment above the boutique. Peggy surveyed the room critically.

Alicia's flamboyant, electric blue couches and chairs were gone. So were the sunny yellow cushions and the white free-form tables. In their place stood minimal Scandinavian pieces in muted shades of brown and green, the wood trim gleaming blond and clean-lined. The room, indeed the entire apartment, pulsed with a totally new feel. Alicia had imparted an atmosphere of stylish chaos; Marsha's taste spoke of aristocratic restraint.

'You're certainly neater than Alicia was, Marsha,' Peggy remarked, 'and your furniture makes the room seem bigger.'

Marsha was pouring Tia Maria into crystal liqueur glasses. 'Alicia's furniture is in storage right now until the "cousin in Halifax" gets a chance to look it over. He didn't even come to the funeral.'

'Just as well,' Catherine pronounced to general agreement.

'I've put her more personal belongings in the workroom for now. Somehow I don't really feel like setting up in there . . .' Marsha's husky voice faded into uncertainty.

Catherine shuddered. 'I wouldn't either! I can't shake the picture of her lying there, dead. Alicia was so alive, so vibrant—how could she just cease to exist?'

'Can you bear to be in that room long enough to pick out some mementoes? That's one of the reasons I invited you all over. The "cousin" won't miss anything and I doubt he really wants her clothes and knick-knacks anyway.'

'How thoughtful of you, Marsha!' Warmth suffused Susan's well-modulated voice. 'I would like a small souvenir of Brent's lifelong friend.' A shadow crossed her patrician brow. 'It will remind me of both of them.'

Since Julie's death, Peggy's animosity towards Susan had dwindled. Friends had become more precious as their numbers diminished. Peggy leaned forward to touch her sister-in-law's hand. 'I miss him too.'

Tears quivered on Susan's eyelashes as she fought for composure. 'Some days I still refuse to believe he's dead. I

137

want to call his name, find him in our bed. If it wasn't for my daughter I think I would've lost my grip.'

'Not you!' Catherine spoke firmly. 'You survived Brent's death and we'll all survive the loss of John, Julie and Alicia. We have to!' Catherine was reassuring herself as much as her friends. Maybe even more. The tragedies of the last few weeks had sapped much of her stamina, rendering her fragile and vulnerable to the eddies of fate. Small, inconsequential setbacks, which before she would have bulldozed through without hesitation, now depleted the few shreds of her self-confidence and became impassable obstacles. Her work, formerly a joy, enervated her, leaving her limp and disinterested. She knew her students were suffering from her lack of commitment just as Paul and Morgan were. At the moment, she was running on autopilot.

Marsha set down her empty glass and finally ended the oppressive silence. 'I'm going to the shop in the Mall for a couple of hours. I want you all to choose anything you like as a memento before you go. Don't hurry!' Tactfully Marsha left her guests alone with their communal memories.

It was with great trepidation that Catherine finally edged herself into the workroom. The stained corner of the carpet where Alicia's body had recently lain was mercifully hidden by a rack of clothes.

'Are you OK?' Susan asked with concern in her voice. 'You look awfully pale.'

'I'm fine,' Catherine lied. Her heart fluttered erratically and her palms were damp inside her rolled fists. She was blind to the room as it really was now. Instead she beheld Alicia's black enshrouded body lying in wait. In her mind, Alicia's tortured face pleaded for justice. 'Oh, Alicia,' her heart cried out, 'who did this to us?'

Peggy and Susan stared at the spot which drew Catherine's eyes like a magnet.

'Is that where you found her? Over there?' Peggy whispered.

Catherine nodded jerkily, like a marionette in unskilled hands.

138

'Is that where she hit her head?' Peggy gestured at the laden table, noting its sharp corners.

'If you believe the police report,' Catherine replied stiffly.

Susan and Peggy exchanged an uneasy glance. Paul had warned them against letting Catherine dwell on Alicia's death. 'She's just starting to get back to normal,' he explained, 'and I don't want seeing that apartment to set her off again. I wish Marsha hadn't invited her, but naturally she insists on going. It's up to you two to keep her off that topic!' Paul had pleaded.

'Right or wrong, the official verdict is accidental death and there's nothing we can do.' Peggy put her arm around Catherine as she spoke. 'Now we have to put this tragedy behind us. Come on, let's choose our souvenirs of Alicia.'

The three women wandered separately among the assembled memories. Catherine hugged the wall, unwilling to expose herself to the full impact of the room. As she slowly circled, she bumped into a tall, narrow cardboard box propped in a corner. She peered in. 'Skis,' she murmured. 'It's been years since I skied.'

Peggy crossed over to find Catherine examining a pair of old-style wooden skis. 'I'll bet these are the ones Alicia got for Christmas back when we were about fifteen! Imagine her keeping them all this time!'

Joining the other two, Susan ran her hand down the warm, smooth boards. 'Cripes! They're antiques!' She caressed their mellow surface. 'They don't make 'em like they used to.'

'They were second hand when Alicia got them,' Peggy explained.

'And then the rest of us scrambled around to borrow some so we could go skiing too!' Catherine started laughing and the black clouds parted for a moment. 'Remember that trip to Mont Tremblant? When Danny skied the longest run on his rump?'

A rich chuckle gurgled in Peggy's throat. 'Then you told him he didn't need any equipment and threw his skis in the garbage! Danny was furious.'

Catherine flushed guiltily. 'I didn't realize we'd have so

much trouble getting them back. How was I to know they were going to collect the garbage so soon?'

Peggy smiled at the memory. 'If it hadn't been for you, I would never have become intimately acquainted with the inner workings of a dump.'

'You're mother was very understanding about the whole incident, though, Peggy. I liked her a lot—she was my idea of a perfect mom. And she had a wild time without even going near the slopes,' Catherine recalled. 'Did your father ever find out about her escapades?'

Peggy shook her head vigorously. 'No way! Brent and I told him how bored she'd been and how strict she was with us—that way Dad let us go again.' Peggy sighed. 'Those ski trips were about the only times Mom managed to get away from him. He hated the idea of her having fun . . .'

'Your father was a real killjoy.'

'I think Mom died just to get away from him. And I never forgave him for not letting me go away to university with the rest of you.' Peggy laughed self-consciously. 'I might have been Mrs Parker instead of Mrs Brandenburg if I could've followed Calvin to Toronto.'

Catherine's soft grey eyes quizzed Peggy's blue ones. 'Do you really think so?'

Peggy dropped her gaze first. 'No. Even before he left town Calvin was running away from me as fast as he could go.'

Catherine nodded as her friend confirmed her suspicions. 'That's what I thought. One moment you and Calvin were as inseparable as Siamese twins; the next moment he bolted as if the grim reaper were after him.'

'Calvin thought he was . . .' The words trailed off as Peggy bent her head.

Forgetting the recent, grisly history of the workroom, Peggy perched on a carton of clothing. Her eyes unfocused and she stared backward down into the vortex of time. Sensing her mood, Susan and Catherine quietly made themselves more comfortable, Susan on another box and Catherine propped in the doorway.

'I got pregnant.'

The words glowed like a burning brand in the air. Susan and Catherine felt their stomachs lurch, sharing the terror they knew Peggy had felt. To be unmarried and pregnant in the early 1960s meant ostracism. Ruin.

'Oh Peggy . . .,' Catherine breathed. 'Calvin?'

Peggy nodded.

'Did your father know?'

'No! He would've thrown me out. Soiling the family name . . .'

'Did you tell Calvin?'

Peggy nervously licked her lips. 'He was furious. He said I should have been taking "precautions".' Peggy jerked her head up and her eyes blazed. 'Precautions? What did I know about "precautions"? I didn't know what the hell he was talking about!' Her voice dropped again and her companions had to strain to hear her.

'I said we could get married—that's what usually happened, isn't it?' She shot a challenging glance at her friends. 'Boy! Did that scare him! Calvin had big plans even then and a wife and a child right out of high school weren't part of them.

'Then he asked me if I was sure it was his baby. Can you believe it?' Peggy's restless fingers coiled and uncoiled a lock of her heavy hair as revulsion registered on the faces of her audience. 'He told me he didn't believe it was his but he'd help me "get rid" of it anyway.'

Tears welled in Peggy's eyes. 'I didn't know what to do! I couldn't tell my parents, Calvin literally ran away from me . . .'

'So you told Alicia.' Suddenly Catherine understood Alicia's oblique remarks.

Peggy nodded. 'Alicia wasn't quite as naïve as I was. She's the one who found the . . . the . . . abortionist. Don't ask me how.' Peggy stared into her past, living yet again the agony of those endless weeks of anguish. 'Alicia said I had to have three hundred dollars in cash before he'd see me.' Peggy's pain-filled eyes met Catherine's compassionate ones. 'Three hundred dollars! I had maybe forty or fifty at the most, so I had to go to Calvin even though I didn't want to. He asked if I could find somebody cheaper!'

'Bastard,' Catherine murmured in disgust.

'Did he give you the money?' Susan waited tensely for the response.

'Yes. I've always had the feeling he took it from his father's hardware store but I'm not sure. All I know is Mr Parker reported a break-in that week and just over three hundred dollars were taken.'

Catherine and Susan exchanged raised eyebrows. Cracks began to fracture Calvin's flawless façade.

'Where did you have to go for the . . . abortion?' The word left an odious taste in Catherine's mouth.

'Rochester. In the States. Alicia and I went down on a Thursday. We said we were planning a two-day shopping spree.'

'They'd believe that,' Catherine commented, 'since you have to stay out of the country forty-eight hours to avoid paying duty.'

'I still had a tough time getting my parents' permission, though.' Peggy scuffed her toe back and forth on the floor, leaving dull crescents in the wax shine. 'We took the bus. What an awful trip! I felt nauseous all the way—from fear or morning sickness, I'm not sure. Diesel fumes always remind me of that ride—I've avoided buses since that weekend.' Peggy leaned back and rested her cheek against the cool wall for a moment. Then she stood and began slowly pacing as she spoke.

'When we arrived at the bus terminal in Rochester, Alicia led the way to a grubby drugstore where she asked for "Dr Smith". The smirk on that ugly clerk's face! He knew why we wanted "Dr Smith". I would've bolted right then if Alicia hadn't been holding on to my arm.' Peggy rubbed her wrist as if she could still feel Alicia's iron grip.

'That toad-faced clerk gave Alicia directions to a run-down rooming-house run by a Mrs Croup.' Peggy shuddered. 'What a witch! Her clothes, if you could call them that, hung on her like rags on a scarecrow—and a scarecrow would've been better-looking. She waved a bottle of gin in our faces and spat on the floor. I had to pay her ten dollars before she led us to a room at the back of the house.' Peggy's lips trembled as she relived each horrifying minute of the ordeal. 'Just a bed—that's all there was in that god-awful room. The sheets were stained; the pillow wept feathers every time I shifted it. And as the naked light bulb swung back and forth on its frayed cord our shadows swooped down on us like God's avenging angels. I was terrified!' Tears, held back until now, coursed down Peggy's strained face. 'Oh my God!' She covered her face in her hands and her shoulders shook.

Catherine gathered her into her arms and smoothed the bright curls. Peggy's sobs diminished and then ceased. When she had released herself and vigorously blown her nose, she smiled wanly. 'After twenty years I can still cry . . . I wonder how many gallons of tears I've shed?'

'You don't have to tell us any more . . .' Susan said in a hoarse voice.

Peggy shrugged. 'I might as well finish—I'll be thinking about it anyway.' She strove for a matter-of-fact tone but the far-away expression, filled with gnawing pain, again established itself on her features.

'Alicia and I waited three hours in that hell-hole. We didn't dare leave to find a cold drink even though the sweat dripped off us. The water from the tap at the cracked sink came out brown but eventually we got desperate enough to drink it. By the time "Dr Smith" arrived it was almost dark outside.'

'Was he a real doctor?' Catherine asked.

'Who knows? Not a reputable one at any rate, but I was hardly in a position to demand his credentials! He, how-ever, was in a position to demand three hundred dollars, which he did. In fact, he tried for four hundred but we convinced him we had only the three.'

'Was he clean, at least?' To Susan, lack of personal hygiene counted as a capital crime.

'Reasonably, except for his fingernails. He had a little "Hitler" moustache which caught his spit when he talked. I couldn't take my eyes off it!' An hysterical giggle escaped but Peggy instantly crushed it and resumed her monotone.

143

'Before Smith would do anything he made Alicia leave.'

'Oh, no! You poor thing!' Susan cried.

'So there'd be no witnesses, I suppose,' Catherine grimly observed.

'Likely. I gather Alicia spent the ensuing hour with Mrs Croup—an edifying experience, she told me later.'

'And you?'

Peggy smiled bitterly. 'I undressed from the waist down while Smith hung a bag of cloudy liquid from a hook in the ceiling. A long tube dangled from it like a repulsive green snake and he forced a good three feet of that tubing into me! I kept my eyes on his face so I wouldn't see what he was doing. His obscene moustache was twitching with excitement. I think he enjoyed hurting me.' Peggy clamped her teeth shut as her gorge rose. Sweat glistened on her forehead. She cleared her throat to continue.

'As soon as Smith released the clamp on the tube the liquid began to flow—it was icy cold just like the tube had been.'

'What was in it?' Catherine demanded.

'I asked. He said someone in my situation should learn to shut up and not ask questions.'

Susan and Catherine cringed at the loathing in her voice. They knew Peggy was hating herself as much as she hated the despicable 'Dr Smith'.

Peggy continued. 'I guess the poison wasn't running fast enough because Smith jumped on the bed to squeeze the bag—almost stepped on me in the process. God, it hurt! Now I know what a balloon feels like.' She laughed pathetically at her joke. Her composure began to crack again but the gesture which dashed away her tears was an angry one.

'Smith ordered me to lie absolutely still for an hour and then leave. He promised I'd abort before morning but when I screwed up my courage and asked him what to expect he just walked out on me!'

'Were you in pain?' Peggy's agony mirrored itself in Susan's face as she asked the question.

'Not then, except for a heavy, distended feeling, but by the time we got to our motel the cramps had started. I

144

didn't think it possible to survive that much pain! All night I writhed and sweated—Alicia gagged me with a nylon stocking so my screams wouldn't be heard. At about five in the morning the bleeding started and I watched my life leaking away.' Peggy shivered. 'Even now I can see that room—blood in the toilet, blood in the bathtub, on the sheets, on the rug. The entire room screamed murder at me!' Peggy shrieked the last sentence and then pressed her fist to her mouth.

Catherine and Susan watched helplessly as Peggy vented her raw emotions.

After a moment Peggy continued in a low voice. 'I was sure I was dying, and so was Alicia, but we didn't know what to do. Stranded in a foreign country . . . we'd broken the law . . . we'd no one to turn to and we were almost out of money . . .

'I fell unconscious but my bleeding had slowed by then so Alicia just kept me warm and waited. I suppose she had as horrible an experience as I did in a way. Poor Alicia; I put her through a lot that weekend.'

'Thank God she was with you!' Susan exclaimed. 'You could never have made it alone.'

Peggy nodded solemnly. 'It's a debt I'll never be able to pay. Alicia was holding my hand when I finally woke up. I still felt as if my insides were being twisted and wrung by a sadistic washerwoman but I knew the baby was gone.' Peggy regarded her friends steadily. 'Know what? I was sorry! I knew part of me was missing and I've never got it back. Even my three wonderful children haven't replaced my lost one.'

'You didn't have a choice,' Susan whispered.

'There's always a choice. However, I've paid for my sins —I've lived with that memory for twenty-five years.'

Susan needed to hear the end of Peggy's sordid tale. 'You got back to Kingsport all right?' she asked.

'Yeah. We had to stay an extra day until I could travel and even then it was dicey. Alicia had the sense to buy a few sweaters and stuff to make our trip look authentic. To explain why I looked so sick I told my mother I'd picked up a 'flu bug.'

'So for all those years only Alicia and Calvin have known about the abortion?' Catherine asked.

'Now you and Susan know too.' Peggy wearily brushed back her hair. 'Since Alicia died I've felt I had to tell someone—I can't carry this burden all alone.'

The three women hugged each other and cried. It was a long time before they were able to rein in their seething emotions, but when they did they gravitated back to the living-room and the liquor cupboard. Their errand in the workroom was forgotten.

'Alicia wondered if you were going to tell that reporter, Millikin, your secret,' Catherine remarked.

Peggy jerked her head up. 'Alicia told you about the abortion?'

'No. No,' Catherine hastened to reassure her friend. 'She just said you knew something unflattering about Calvin and you could exert some influence on his behaviour if you wanted to.'

'I've never blackmailed him, if that's what she meant!' Peggy was incensed.

'She said that you could, not that you would, or did.'

'I'd never use my pregnancy and abortion against Calvin. He didn't act well, but then neither did I. He did what ninety per cent of boys in his position did. He ran!' Peggy laughed ruefully. 'Believe me, I would've run too if I could!'

'It isn't fair,' Susan murmured over the rim of her brandy snifter. 'All the danger and disgrace are on the girl's side.'

'Unless you're in politics. An illegal abortion in his past could stop Calvin's campaign dead in its tracks,' Catherine pointed out. 'He must be worried.'

'I doubt it,' Peggy disagreed. 'If I'd planned to make trouble I would've done it long ago.'

'But you can't deny Calvin's worried about something. He's very tense about Millikin's book,' Susan, still smarting from the fall-out of the photograph fiasco, said with feeling. She leaned forward on the couch and stared intently at

Peggy. 'Is it possible Wilson knows about you and Calvin? Would he have talked?'

Peggy chewed her bottom lip with her even, pearly teeth. 'Wilson knows I had an abortion in my teens—that's why my children were delivered by Caesarian section. Frankly, I'm surprised I managed to have any kids at all after that butchery.'

'Then Wilson must have guessed Calvin fathered the child,' Catherine declared. 'He's not that stupid.'

'Wilson isn't stupid at all. Don't let him fool you. However, I told him it wasn't Calvin.'

'So who did you pin it on?' Catherine asked with curiosity.

A guilty smile tugged at the corner of Peggy's pink mouth. 'I didn't actually name anyone but I led him to believe it was Danny.'

'Danny Retson?' Incredulity resonated in Catherine's voice as she raised her eyebrows in disbelief.

Peggy nodded. 'Danny was dead so Wilson couldn't ask him. Or hurt him for that matter.'

'And Wilson believes you had an abortion before you were sixteen?'

'Yeah.' Peggy blushed.

'And Danny was the father?'

'I assume so.' Peggy tossed her head defiantly. 'Sorry, Catherine, but it was the best solution I could think of. I know Danny was your boyfriend but I implied he was cheating on you.'

'That's OK.' Catherine flicked her hand, dismissing Peggy's concern. She remembered that day in the bushes with Danny. The day before he was killed. Neither of them had thought of "taking precautions" so it could just as easily have been Catherine making that horrifying visit to Dr Smith. And all for what? That first sexual encounter had evolved clumsily and painfully. Catherine felt reluctant but Danny forced her—not physically, but with the age-old arguments used by teenage boys the world over.

'Everyone does it, Cathy, they just don't always admit it. You love me, don't you?' Danny's voice, with its exact timbre and inflections sounded again in Catherine's ears.

'You know I do.' The stock answer.

'Well then, prove it. We love each other. That's all that matters.' Danny caressed her back.

'I don't know . . . I don't think we should. It's a sin, Danny.'

'To love each other?'

'No . . . The other.'

Back and forth they argued for weeks. The discussion was never cool. Instead it took place in snatches, between kisses and groping, each session going farther than the one before. They ended with Catherine pulling away, flushed and breathing hard.

'You're a tease, just a tease, Cathy!'

'I'm frightened, that's all.'

'Of me? You know I wouldn't hurt you. I love you!'

And so it would start again. But one day it ended differently since Danny had another powerful argument on his side. 'You know what I want most of all for my birthday?'

Catherine shook her head coyly.

'You.' Danny's open mouth fastened on to hers and his tongue thrust deeply.

'Oh, Danny,' she had managed to gasp as they briefly surfaced for air.

They were in their secret nest in the ravine. Soft grasses grew tall and waving in thick green tufts under the branches of three huge oak trees. A circular wall of dense underbrush screened their hideaway from all angles while in the dusk hung the heavy, sweet smell of summer. The grass, still warm from the sun's heat, tickled Catherine's thighs when Danny pulled up her gingham skirt with one hand and pushed her back against the ground with the other. Her pink blouse already hung open and two rosy nipples thrust themselves skyward, demanding attention. Danny began mouthing them but his attention was focused on his hands. So was Catherine's. This time she didn't grasp his fingers as they tunnelled under her white panties. This time she didn't stop him from dragging them down. In fact Catherine had helped by arching her back and momentarily

148

lifting her weight from the ground. She felt the lightest flutter against her skin as her body tensed in uncontrollable anticipation.

But in his haste Danny got the white cotton tangled around her knees. Then, while fumbling with his buckle he scratched her naked stomach with its prong and dug his elbow in her breast. Catherine kept her eyes closed but she clenched her teeth involuntarily. Danny's full weight lunged on top of her and she felt something probing, searching between her legs. Danny's nails ripped her flesh as he fought to find the entrance he sought. His heavy body crushed her lungs as he stabbed home. Catherine sobbed and clutched his back as Danny shuddered in release.

They had dressed in silence, turned away from each other, and Danny pretended not to notice the smear of blood on the dark green of the grass. Before they left their bower, however, Danny held her gently in his arms and kissed her hair.

'You're beautiful.'

'Happy Birthday,' Catherine whispered.

'Maybe you'll give me another present tomorrow night, after the dance?'

She had tightened her hold around Danny's neck while saying nothing.

But Catherine knew if Danny hadn't been murdered the very next night she would have done it again. A visit to Dr Smith or his equivalent would have been simply a matter of time.

'Wilson's trying to make things difficult for me,' Peggy was saying when Catherine surfaced from the past. 'He's supposed to have the children every second weekend, you know . . .'

Susan nodded.

'But he keeps changing the date and messing up my plans. Then, when he does take them, he never returns their clothes or brings them back on time.'

Susan steepled her fingers pensively. She spoke with hesitation in her musical voice. 'Do you worry that one day Wilson won't bring them back at all?'

149

'No. Well, only when I'm expecting them and they're late,' Peggy admitted sheepishly. She took a sip of her Tia Maria and crossed her ankles. 'Children require time and effort—things Wilson's unwilling to give.' A shadow settled on Peggy's features. 'Lately Wilson's begun acting strangely.'

'So what else is new?' Catherine quipped and instantly regretted her flippancy.

'No, really, Catherine. He stalks the house at night trying to scare me.'

'What do you mean?'

Peggy described the eerie night visit which had scared her so badly. Although she recounted only the bare bones of the story, her friends shivered at the fiendishness of the trick.

'You're sure it was Wilson?' Catherine demanded sharply. She stood up and began to pace, eroding an elliptical trail in the beige carpet. If Wilson got a charge out of terrifying his wife, what kind of a kick would killing her friends give him?

Peggy shrugged. 'Who else could it be? No thief would be bothered with my junk!'

'Did you call the police?' Susan asked. It was typical of her that she thought first of the authorities.

'By the time I got to the telephone he was gone.'

'You should put a phone in your room.'

Catherine studied her friend. 'Are you really finished with Wilson this time?'

Peggy hesitated.

'We worry about you, you know.'

'Yes. Yes, I am.' Peggy at last knew it was true. She sighed deeply and then smiled. 'Wilson doesn't hold any attraction for me any more.'

'So you're not seeing Calvin to make Wilson jealous? It would be a dangerous game,' Catherine warned, anxiety sharpening her voice.

Peggy misinterpreted Catherine's tone and frowned. 'I'm not "seeing" Calvin as you put it, though I admit I offered to be a hostess for him. And I'm certainly not trying to make

150

Wilson jealous. He's developed enough emotional problems without any extra help from me.'

Catherine still couldn't let the topic rest. 'Do you still have feelings for Calvin despite what he did to you?'

'What is this? The third degree?' Peggy inquired hotly, her patience stretched to the limit. She stood up and faced Catherine, hands on hips. 'Haven't I bared enough of my soul tonight?'

Susan glanced from one to the other as if preparing to jump in as umpire. 'Who's for coffee?' she asked, to ease the tension. 'I think we could all use some,' she said, heading for the tiny kitchen.

Catherine backed off, her sense of propriety and fairness coming late to the situation. 'Sorry. I've no right to ask.' She perched on a straight chair across the room.

'No, you haven't, frankly.' Peggy eased herself into her chair again and they sat in silence until Susan returned with three steaming cups.

'You think I should hate Calvin.' Peggy twirled her spoon and stirred the coffee after the cream was thoroughly mixed. 'I did for a while,' she admitted. 'After all, he deserted me. But eventually you all drifted back to Kingsport and, except for Danny, we were all together again. I'd married Wilson whom I still adored, Calvin married dear Julie . . . It was hard to keep hating him.'

Emotions flickered across Susan's face as she experienced vicariously everything Peggy spoke of. 'Did you and Calvin ever mention your . . . your abortion?' she asked.

Peggy curled her legs up underneath her and smoothed her burgundy wool skirt down around her knees. 'Once. Obliquely. We were at a barbecue, at your place, Susan. We were all talking about growing up—about taking responsibility.' Peggy paused reflectively. 'I happened to be standing by the pool next to Calvin so I looked at him. I couldn't help it!' She smiled quickly. 'He spoke so quietly I could barely hear him. "When I was young," Calvin said, "I didn't accept responsibility for something . . . someone . . . when I should have. I'll carry the guilt my entire life."

151

Then he walked away. That's when I knew I couldn't hate him any more.'

'I wonder if he meant it?' Catherine mused aloud.

'Why else would he say it?' Peggy demanded. 'You're too cynical. Lately you're very suspicious of everyone's motives.'

Catherine's eyes flashed angrily. To hide them she turned her gaze to the floor and traced figure eights with the toe of her shoe in the thick pile of the rug. 'Sorry,' she mumbled.

'Have you considered seeing a therapist?' Susan asked gently. 'You haven't been your usual wonderful self lately.'

'Since the fire, you mean.' The bitter note in Catherine's voice made Susan wince.

'I suppose so,' Susan admitted lamely.

'I am expected to see three of my friends die in as many months and almost die myself and not be affected in any way?' Catherine fought to keep the shrill tone out of her voice.

'That's not what she meant!' Peggy rose to Susan's defence. 'Of course you should be affected. But the rest of us don't see a murderer lurking behind every friendly face. We don't impute hidden motives to every word or action.'

'If Alicia had she might still be alive today!' Catherine exploded. 'She was afraid—that's why she was going away —but she wasn't careful enough. Alicia invited a murderer into her home!' Catherine's laboured breathing punctuated the tense silence. She stood abruptly and faced her friends. 'I realize you think I'm crazy. Know what? I wish I was! It'd be much easier to cure my delusions than unmask this maniac!' She took three deep breaths before she continued more calmly. 'Please be careful!' She held out her hands to Susan and Peggy. 'Humour me. Tell me you'll take care.' Her hands dropped. 'I need you,' she whispered.

Peggy and Susan exchanged worried glances.

'Of course,' Susan finally assured her. 'We'll be very careful.'

'Right,' Peggy echoed nervously. 'We'll be fine and so will you.'

These hollow words of comfort returned to torment Catherine in the horrifying days to come.

CHAPTER 22

John Warshinsky wiped the sweat from his eyes. He'd put in seven days straight at the police station and now, on his day off, he was stuck in the basement putting up dry wall. A hell of a life, he thought savagely as he banged in yet another nail. An hour later he had had enough.

'How's it going?' Vicki, his wife, inquired when he rumbled into the bright kitchen. She was elbow-deep in bread dough and wore a white smudge of flour coquettishly on her dimpled cheek.

'One more wall to go!' John grunted, making a beeline for the refrigerator. 'Want a drink?'

'Not yet. I don't have a free hand.'

John rummaged in the fridge for the Coke and then fetched the rum bottle from its home on the top shelf. All the everyday glasses were dirty so he grabbed one of the sparkling crystal ones from the depths of the cupboard.

'Not that glass, John!'

He stopped with the rum bottle poised in the air. 'Why not?'

'It's part of our good set. We don't use those unless we have visitors.'

'Then what the hell am I supposed to use? Do you want me to drink out of the bottle?'

'Rinse one of the others.' Vicki gestured with her shoulder to the stack of dirty dishes in the sink.

With a sigh John put the crystal glass back in the cupboard. 'The things I do to keep you happy . . .'

Viki's dimple deepened, 'I know. You're so wonderful . . .' She stood on her tiptoes and kissed her husband lightly on the lips.

Smiling, John retreated to the living-room, flopped on to the couch and rested his large feet on the battered coffee table. He reached for the television remote control but

153

didn't immediately turn on the set. Instead he studied the plain glass in his hand and thought about Catherine Edison and the late Alicia Castelvetri.

Peggy sat in her cluttered kitchen, her tired feet propped on one of the mismatched chairs. She was thirsty but didn't even have the energy to walk the few feet to the refrigerator. Is this living, she asked herself, surveying the havoc created by seven active children. Is this all life has for me?

She crossed her arms on the table and, laying her head on them, sank into a miasma of self-pity. No money, no fun, no man, and no relief in sight. Even Wilson had disappeared, and Peggy didn't know whether that made her happy or sad. At least Wilson had been interested in her in some capacity; the combat had kept her mind and spirit alive. All these children, both her own and the ones she babysat, sucked her energy, leaving only an automaton. Cook, clean, tidy. Her head throbbed in rhythm with her thoughts. No Wilson, no Calvin, no money. No future.

She sniffed and struggled from her chair. Shuffling to the buffet, she pulled out a half-empty bottle of cooking sherry and splashed a generous portion into a cracked plastic tumbler. 'Cheers!' She toasted herself with bitter mockery.

Who was she trying to fool anyway, with her new haircut and fancy clothes? A middle-aged, lower-class woman. A nobody. Gilding the outside wouldn't change anything. And as for chasing Calvin . . . Now she'd really blown it!

Peggy's cheeks burned at the memory of how she'd thrown herself at him. She'd seen the pity in Catherine's eyes that day at Calvin's house but still she'd forced the issue with him. Not satisfied with the polite brush-off, she'd made him say those hateful words. Her shrill pleading and his harsh response replayed themselves ceaselessly in her mind.

She pressed her hands to her hot cheeks as she remembered yesterday's incident. To start with, she made the mistake of seeking him out at his campaign headquarters. Of course Calvin had been less than thrilled to see her there, disrupting his tight schedule. Peggy could see that now. Confronting him there had been a tactical error.

Backing him into his tiny office, she again offered her services as hostess. 'You'll have to get back into the social whirl, Calvin, a politician must be accessible.'

'I can attend functions without holding any myself,' Calvin replied, sitting on the corner of his desk and swinging his leg impatiently. 'No one expects me to hold a grand ball, and as for business gatherings, I'm better off alone. It's easier to get down to business without wives in the way.'

Peggy changed tactics, sidling up closer to him and letting her voice drop to what she hoped was a seductive whisper. 'It's not just for your job that you need someone, Calvin. You're so busy . . . You need someone to look after you and the children. We were close once, Calvin, I know your needs, I can smooth your way.'

Instead of melting before her, he edged away. 'No. No, thanks, Peggy, I can manage on my own.'

'But Calvin, you loved me once. You said you did!'

'That was years ago. We've both changed, moved on.'

'You could love me again if you tried . . .'

Calvin got up and moved away from her. He stood behind his desk, his hands on the back of the chair, positioning it between them like a shield. 'I've decided to concentrate on my work, Peggy, so I'm not planning to remarry, or even date, for that matter.'

'Then why are you seeing that McAuliff woman?' As soon as the words left her lips Peggy knew she'd made a fatal mistake, but even then she couldn't let it rest. There, in his office, her voice shrilled on with a life of its own. 'I know you're seeing Brianne McAuliff! I've seen you sneaking into her apartment late at night!'

Calvin's knuckles gleamed white against the black chair. He pushed it to one side and stalked up to Peggy. He thrust his face so close to hers she could smell the stale coffee on his breath. 'You've been spying on me!'

Peggy quailed. 'No! No! I happened to be passing, that's all!'

'You bitch!' The words exploded like spit from his lips. 'You think you can blackmail me about that abortion and force me to marry you,' he hissed.

'No, no! I'd never do that!' Peggy cringed, her back to the wall.

'Just try! Tell anyone—it won't hurt me. It's ancient history now. People will feel sorry for the "confused" teen-ager but they won't pillory me!' Calvin shook his fist in Peggy's white face.

'No, I won't tell, Calvin! I swear!' Peggy was blubbering like the schoolgirl she'd been at the time of her unwanted pregnancy.

Calvin gripped her shoulders, shaking her in cold fury. 'All these years I've let you and that unspeakable husband of yours call me "your friend" so that you'd keep your mouth shut. And now, Peggy, I discover I don't even care! Once I get to Toronto I won't be surrounded by hicks like you. Get out of here and do your damnedest!'

Peggy had fled, weeping, from Calvin's office and car-omed off a horrified Paul.

She giggled drunkenly into her sherry. Poor Paul! His carefully planned election strategy hadn't allowed for scan-dals from Calvin's past. He'd probably been as upset with Calvin as he was with her. Now both men would be biting their nails, waiting for the storm to break.

But Peggy did not hold a press conference. She didn't write letters, anonymous or otherwise, to newspapers and television stations. Instead she crept home and shut herself away to lick her wounds. She knew she was no match for Calvin.

CHAPTER 23

Catherine spent many tortured hours of indecision before she knocked at the door of Mildred McKeown's apartment. Even now, she had to suppress the urge to slink away into the darkness. All her training, even her very nature, pro-

156

tested against belief in the supernatural. If any of her colleagues from the biology department saw her now . . . !

She checked her watch. Nine-thirty—she was right on time. At least Mrs McKeown hadn't insisted on a midnight appointment. She licked her lips nervously as she heard a bolt being drawn back. The door opened with a squeak and a small, drab woman stood before her squinting into the dim hallway.

'Dr Edison?'

Catherine stepped forward hesitantly, as if entering an unknown landscape enshrouded in dense fog. She wanted to go forward but the way was unclear. Safety lay behind her. Danger lay ahead.

'May I take your coat?' Mrs McKeown's voice was thin, without resonance, and she gave her vowels the flat enunciation of a Newfoundlander.

'Thanks.' Catherine shrugged her jacket from her shoulders and put it into the woman's outstretched hand. 'I'll just take off my boots.' She waited for her hostess to turn away before pulling them off and slipping brown, knitted slippers over her scarred feet. Since the fire they were very sensitive to cold.

'Make yourself at home, Dr Edison, while I put the kettle on.' Mrs McKeown gestured at a well-worn armchair in front of a low table. A similar chair faced it from the other side.

Sitting stiffly in the chair, her handbag clutched on her lap, Catherine surreptitiously studied the room. It was unremarkable. The chair where she sat was in a shallow alcove which might have been originally intended as a dining area. Both the alcove and the rest of the living-room were painted institutional beige—probably the colour used throughout the high-rise apartment building. She glanced at the picture above the blue brocade sofa—a large, garish oil painting depicting a rural scene. She grimaced. Why on earth had she come here?

Catherine half rose from her seat. Should she leave? Furtively, she looked around. Mrs McKeown wouldn't see her slip out . . .

157

Her attention was caught by a bookshelf almost hidden in the gloom at the far end of the room. Maintaining that a person's choice in books revealed a lot about their character she put her purse on the arm of the chair and tiptoed over to examine them.

The first shelf was crammed with *Readers' Digest* condensed versions of the best-sellers of years gone by: *To Kill a Mocking Bird, All The President's Men, Silent Spring*. Beneath these were paperbacks, mysteries mostly, and a few westerns by Louis L'Amour. Lining the bottom shelf, the unmistakable yellow bindings of *National Geographic* magazines glowed in the dim light. Can Mrs McKeown really be this ordinary, Catherine wondered?

'They were my late husband's books,' Mildred McKeown said quietly, coming up behind Catherine and making her jump. 'I'm not much of a reader myself.'

Flushing guiltily, Catherine slunk back to her chair. She was a schoolgirl who had left her seat without permission.

In her absence a silver teapot and a delicate china cup and saucer had appeared on the table. Mrs McKeown held out an ornate silver dish and a spoon which she was cradling in her hand. 'Would you put some tea-leaves in the pot, please?'

'Of course.' Catherine tried to keep her hand from trembling—not entirely successfully.

'Take your time.' The gentle smile on Mildred's face transformed her from a soulless cut-out to a charming hostess.

'I don't know why I'm so nervous,' Catherine lied as she finally negotiated the transfer of the dry black leaves to the pot.

'Are you comfortable, my dear?'

'Yes, thank you,' Catherine murmured politely. Physically, she was comfortable enough, but emotionally? A frisson of dread ran down her spine. Calm down, she chided herself. You can always leave if it gets too strange. Or too ridiculous.

While the tea brewed the two women conversed in a desultory fashion about the weather (grim), recent movies

158

(violent) and local politicians (incompetent). By the time the tea was steeped Catherine had relaxed enough to pour the fragrant drink without spilling it.

'You're not having any?' she asked after filling the single cup.

'No, my dear. Caffeine keeps me awake.'

Catherine sipped the hot tea, but didn't enjoy it's smoky flavour. She identified the variety as Lapsang Souchong, one of her university room-mate's favourites. Wouldn't ordinary tea-leaves work for fortune-telling?

'I know who you are, of course,' Mildred stated quietly. 'Your name has appeared in the newspaper on two recent occasions.'

Catherine nodded. Both the fire and her discovery of Alicia's body had rated mention in the local rag, and her theory of foul play had briefly piqued the attention of the crime reporter.

'So you know why I'm here.'

Not precisely, Dr Edison. You yourself aren't sure why you've come.' The psychic settled more comfortably into her chair and nested her hands in her lap. She blinked at Catherine with her faded blue eyes.

Catherine had to admit the truth of this. What on earth did she hope to accomplish in this prosaic apartment? To rend the curtain between present and future? To make the past clear and banish her present uncertainties? Or did she want her worst fears confirmed? Catherine gripped the delicate teacup with both hands, nursing it, absorbing its comforting warmth into her trembling body. Fear clawed at her heart.

From beneath her lashes and behind her tinted lenses, Catherine studied the woman seated opposite. How ordinary she appeared—grey hair ranged in lacquered waves and her steel-rimmed glasses pinching her snub nose. A faint moustache fringed her short upper lip. Mildred McKeown wore sensible shoes. Could such a woman be in touch with the unknowable? Nonsense. Catherine swallowed the last of the pungent brew.

'May I?' The psychic reached for Catherine's empty cup.

She leaned forward and tilted the leaves against its white china sides. Then she gazed pensively into its depths while she cradled it as her reluctant guest had done. 'Shall we start with your fear?' Mildred asked after a considerable silence.

Bobbing her head, Catherine assented. How could tea-leaves reveal anything? Her natural scepticism momentarily took precedence in her mind.

As if sensing Catherine's doubt, Mildred smiled slightly. 'First of all you fear you've made a fool of yourself in coming here.'

Catherine flushed.

'Don't worry, most people feel that way at first. It's only natural. But in addition to that small anxiety,' she continued, 'you fear I might actually be able to sense something which you can't sense yourself—something your science can't explain.' Mildred studied what she could see of Catherine's face. 'But most of all you fear what I might see. Are you and your friends in danger? Or are you imagining the entire plot?' Mildred gestured helplessly. 'Neither possibility brings you any comfort.'

At this Catherine raised her head and exposed her misery to her inquisitor. 'As you say, I'm confused. Is there any hope for me?' she joked desperately. A tear trembled on her lash but it concealed itself behind her dark glasses.

'Dear Alicia was confused too. And frightened,' Mildred stated abruptly. 'She told me you thought the fire wasn't an accident.'

'And she told me *you* knew that John would die.' After a small pause Catherine whispered, 'I suppose, in the final analysis, that's why I've come to you.'

The older woman tilted her head to regard her visitor. 'You were close to the dead man . . . this John.'

'Childhood friends,' Catherine replied firmly.

'I see . . .'

Catherine ran the tip of her tongue over her bottom lip.

Mildred steepled her fingers over her mouth, her thumbs braced under her chin. 'The fire which injured you and killed your friend wasn't centred on Alicia, so from her the

160

emanations were faint. But I did sense a malevolence.'

'And now? Now that I'm here?' Catherine leaned forward in her chair, unconsciously holding her breath.

'Your own belief in a human agent is so strong I can barely probe it.'

'Please . . .' Catherine exhaled the word on a thread of breath.

As Mildred's eyes rolled up, her sight seemed to turn inward and Catherine felt the woman no longer saw her, at least not her physical presence. The psychic sat so completely still she became an integral part of the room. Catherine waited in an agony of suspense, her own mind willing the woman to see the unknowable. Her hands balled into clenched fists and she breathed in short, irregular gasps.

'Evil . . .' The word sprang into the air between the women but Catherine couldn't be certain Mrs McKeown had actually spoken it. It hung there as a sinister presence. She shrank deeper into her chair but couldn't drag her gaze from Mildred's pale, immobile face and vacant eyes. In her ears, Catherine's pulse throbbed and beat like a caged bird's wings against bars.

'Death. Many deaths . . .' The words formed in the psychic's mouth but her lips never moved. The voice that spoke was not her own wispy soprano but rolled deep and rich, echoing through unimagined distances with multiple eerie harmonics. Catherine held her breath and clenched her fists so tightly she embedded her nails into her palms.

'Danny.' The voice rose and fell, stretching out the name like an elastic band under maximum tension.

'Danny?' Catherine whispered, terrified. 'Danny Retson?'

Without altering her blank expression, Mrs McKeown's blue-veined hands scrabbled weakly at her neck. Catherine recollected Danny had been shot in the throat. She was too petrified to scream. Too scared to ask questions.

'One,' the hollow voice intoned. 'Two . . . three. Dead.'

A sob broke through Catherine's clenched jaws. John, Julie, Alicia.

'Not finished yet!' The voice sounded querulous now.

'. . . can't stop me. . . . more work to do . . .' A thread of Mildred's own high tone wove through the other voice, weakening its fabric. 'Catherine . . .'

As the last syllable of her own name sounded, Catherine heard only Mildred's flat enunciation. Behind Mrs McKeown's eyes her spirit took up residence once more and her body slumped in its chair.

Mildred's eyes fluttered closed, then blinked open again a moment later. 'What happened? Did I speak?'

Catherine nodded and shuddered.

'What did I say?' Mildred's hand fluttered feebly on the arm of her chair. 'I don't often go into a trance.'

'You spoke of evil. Death. And you said the name Danny.' She wiped her sweaty palms on her skirt and leaned forward. Urgency gripped her. 'Why did you say Danny?'

With sad and weary eyes Mildred scanned Catherine's tense face. 'I don't know,' she finally answered. 'Do you know someone by that name?'

'Yes. No.' Catherine paused. 'He's dead.'

'Perhaps his death is connected with the recent . . . misfortunes of your other friends.'

Tears of frustration and exhaustion welled up in Catherine's grey eyes. 'He died more than twenty years ago!' Her emotions had suffered such a roller-coaster ride since she passed through Mrs McKeown's door that she hardly knew what she was saying. Coming here had been a terrible mistake. She wanted desperately to leave but Mildred reached across the table and clutched her sleeve.

'Something *is* wrong, Dr Edison. Very wrong.'

'I *know* that!' Catherine cried. 'But *what* is wrong? Who is doing this? And why, for God's sake. Why? You're supposed to know!'

Mildred didn't need to be psychic to sense Catherine's desperation. 'Sometimes I see things so clearly—events, people, from the past and future—that I confuse them with present reality. But I cannot command this muse, this power, if you like. I can't control what I see and sometimes the more urgently I want to know, the less I sense.'

162

'You warned Alicia of John's death. And her own.'

'Yes,' Mildred admitted, 'and without going into a trance.' She remembered Alicia's visit vividly. 'Alicia's aura flickered so dimly the last time she came here—it was as if she were already dying.' Mildred smiled a little. 'Usually her aura was so vibrant, crackling with life and mischievousness.'

'And that's why you told Alicia she was in danger?' Catherine asked with a puzzled frown. 'Because her aura, whatever that is, was pale?'

'More or less.'

'And how is my aura?' Catherine challenged.

Withdrawing protectively into the shadow cast by the wing of her chair, Mildred hesitated in confusion.

'Well?'

'I've never met you before, Dr Edison. I'm unfamiliar with your usual emanations. It's more of a comparison process, you see, and I don't have a baseline for you.'

Catherine almost snorted. She had yo-yoed from disbelief to fear to awe and now to scorn. Mrs McKeown was trying to apply scientific methods to something totally outside the realm of experimental procedure! But touching base with her more accustomed world helped anchor Catherine now. Relief cascaded through her. She felt safer with scepticism and decided to stick with it. 'So you can't help me, can you? Auras, trances, evil powers—it's all bunk!' Catherine snapped to her feet, marched towards the door, and struggled into her boots and coat.

'Dr Edison! Catherine!' Mildred called out, alarm lending her voice the edge it usually lacked.

Despite herself Catherine hesitated.

'Be careful!' Mildred quavered. 'Someone you know is not what they seem. You're in very real danger!' Mrs McKeown stood stiffly, one hand on the back of her chair and the other stretched out towards Catherine in supplication, willing her to believe. 'The carnage isn't over yet!'

For ten minutes Catherine huddled miserably inside the comfortable shelter of her car. She couldn't go home. Paul and Morgan would question her brittle mood and she shrank from admitting what she'd been doing. But when her body shivered uncontrollably in the cold, she reluctantly started the engine and pulled away from the kerb. Where should she go? Somewhere anonymous where no one knew her.

Catherine drove along the dark streets of Mrs McKeown's neighbourhood, unaware of her surroundings as her mind leapt and spun around the events of the last hour and a half. Whenever her mind skittered close to focusing on the hollow, dead voice which had emanated from the psychic during her trance, her grip on her scepticism slackened. Mildred McKeown's narrow throat could never have formed those sepulchral reverberations. Mildred couldn't have known about Danny. Could she? Had Alicia mentioned him, perhaps? Spoken of the impact his death had had on her and all Danny's friends? Maybe that was the explanation. Her heart slowed again as that comforting thought settled briefly in her mind but then the doubts battled back. The voice had counted the dead and had spoken of a job not yet completed. How many more deaths did it seek? The psychic thought Catherine's was one of them. Was she fated to die too, like John and Alicia and Julie?

'Oh John, I need you!' Catherine whispered through her white lips. A sob caught in her throat. She ached to feel his strong arms around her, his lips kissing away her fears. 'Why are you gone?'

Tears traced glistening paths down her cheeks as she randomly turned left or right. She was in unfamiliar territory geographically and emotionally. Catherine had always despised self-pity and now she wallowed in it.

'John wouldn't have believed you any more than Paul does, Catherine,' she admonished herself aloud. 'He had even less appreciation for the abstract.'

'Yes, but he wouldn't have mocked you,' another part of her replied indignantly.

'Paul isn't mocking you. He's worried about you and is doing what he thinks best.' Catherine's critical self spoke up again. 'And maybe he's right!' Catherine smacked the steering-wheel as she said this. 'Visiting psychics! Believing in spirits! You're losing your grip, old girl.'

Eventually her erratic course spilled her on to a busier avenue where small stores and businesses were interspersed with dilapidated houses. The familiar white and yellow sign of a doughnut shop penetrated Catherine's fog and instinctively she turned into the small parking lot. Hot coffee and a sugar fix would do her good.

Bending her head against the wind, Catherine scurried into the warm, bright restaurant. Then, armed with a large coffee and an apple fritter, she retreated to the back table and sat facing the wall.

The combination of warmth, caffeine and the very ordinariness of her surroundings soon brought a modicum of sanity and order to Catherine's chaotic thoughts. Smiling at her own gullibility, she set about banishing her fears. Talk about overreacting! She'd fallen for one of the oldest tricks in the 'spiritualist' book. Trance indeed! Mildred McKeown said nothing any informed person of average intelligence couldn't have said. Granted she was a good actress. But psychic? No way! Catherine's tense muscles relaxed and her headache faded to a distant drumming. What a fool she'd been to have visited the woman! To indulge her love of the dramatic, Alicia had sought out odd people dabbling in the occult, but she, Catherine, had her feet firmly on the ground.

She stirred her coffee absently as another unpleasant thought worried her. Whether or not Mildred McKeown turned out to be a charlatan, she was still the only person who shared Catherine's belief the three deaths weren't accidental. So what did that say about Catherine herself? Was she nuts? Just what evidence did she have? She reviewed her case.

John. Fighting the wave of sorrow and loss which threatened her every time she thought of him, Catherine considered the circumstances of his death. She claimed a country lane in the dead of winter, in the middle of the night, was an unlikely spot for a hit-and-run accident. No one denied this. Only she concluded that it had to be murder.

Julie. The intruder and the half-remembered smell of gasoline. Without the midnight caller, the gasoline was no evidence at all. John himself might have left it there beside the electric heater. And only she had heard the uninvited visitor. With her doctor explaining to everyone she could be unconsciously manufacturing excuses, her own claims were received with polite scepticism.

Alicia. A shifted table and a fancy wine glass. After her interview with Sergeant Warshinsky, Catherine knew how seriously those ideas had been considered!

Catherine dismally swirled the dregs of her cold coffee as doubt engulfed her. If even she herself wasn't convinced . . .

A familiar voice, coming from the front of the shop, penetrated her consciousness.

'It's about time you got here,' a man declared with annoyance.

Catherine swivelled in her chair, her face draining of blood. Wilson!

Her questing eyes easily located him slouched at the front table. Her heart resumed beating. He wasn't talking to her. At first she didn't recognize the muffled figure facing Peggy's estranged husband.

'Let's talk in the car. Bring your coffee with you.' The clipped, well-modulated voice of the stranger shocked Catherine even more. Calvin!

Catherine ducked her head and turned back to face the wall. Let them not see me, she prayed.

'What's the hurry? 'Fraid to be seen with me?' Wilson sneered.

'Just come on.' Calvin turned on his heel, not bothering to check if Wilson followed.

Catherine heard the door bang open and, in the side of the chrome napkin container, saw two wavy reflections disappear through it. She ventured a careful peek. Calvin and Wilson had vanished.

Feverishly she sought an explanation for this bizarre

166

encounter. Obviously it had been planned. Who had instigated it? Calvin? Wilson? And why? Did it involve Peggy? An ice worm coiled in Catherine's stomach and sent its bloodless children oozing through her veins.

She staggered to her feet and headed for the pay telephone near the door. With trembling fingers she fed coins into the slot. Let her be all right, she entreated as she listened to the ringing at the other end.

'Peggy? Thank God you're OK!' Catherine sagged against the wall.

'I'm fine,' Peggy replied, mystified. 'Why wouldn't I be?'

Now Catherine felt foolish. 'No reason . . . I was just thinking of you, that's all,' she explained lamely.

'Oh.' Peggy wasn't convinced. 'You sound strange. Is anything wrong?'

'I saw Wilson today—that's what started me thinking about you. Have you talked to him recently?'

'Briefly. Just about the kids.'

'He's not bothering you? Not coming around at night any more?' Catherine forced herself to speak normally and prevent the panic she felt from transmitting itself to Peggy.

'No. I told him the police were watching the house.'

Catherine drooped, weak-kneed with relief. Peggy would be safe. 'Great! You finally filed a complaint against the snake.'

Peggy hesitated. 'Not exactly. I just told Wilson I did.'

'So the police aren't watching your house?' Dismay jerked Catherine rigid again.

'Of course not. They haven't the time or manpower to guard all threatened wives.' Peggy's light tone belied her worried frown. Her friend was acting very oddly. 'How about coming over for a drink or something?'

'It's late . . .'

'I don't mind. I'm not doing anything.'

'No, but thanks for the offer,' Catherine replied, anxious to hang up. 'I've got to run. See you soon.'

Catherine replaced the receiver and stood irresolute. Prickles of alarm danced along her spine but cold reason fought back. Wilson couldn't hurt Peggy while Calvin was with him. Unless he killed Calvin first. Or Calvin could kill him. Or Peggy might kill them both. Or . . .

She clapped her hands to her head. Paul was right about her. She'd make an appointment with a psychiatrist in the morning.

CHAPTER 24

A worried frown still creased Peggy's brow when she hung up the receiver. She was becoming increasingly concerned about Catherine's mental health. If only her friend could let go of the recent tragedies—continually rehashing the events led her farther and farther from reality.

Since respect had always played a large role in Peggy's complex feelings towards Catherine, she had seriously considered her friend's case for murder. But in Peggy's opinion it didn't stack up. Sure, the deaths were tragic; sure, the odds against three friends dying so close together were astronomical; but it could happen. And it had. Catherine would have to accept it—the sooner the better.

Peggy climbed the stairs to check on her children. Peter lay sprawled across his bed, his covers bunched underneath him as usual. He looked so beautiful when he slept, the shutters down on his manic energy. Kissing Peter gently on his soft cheek, she manœuvred him back under the blankets and tucked him in. The resemblance to his father was striking . . . she smoothed his tousled hair, her fingers absorbing the warmth of his scalp.

Tiptoeing out, she silently closed his door and moved along to the next room where her two daughters lay asleep in their twin beds. Picking her way carefully around the scattered clothes and toys, Peggy brushed each forehead with her lips and tucked them in too. Tonight the mess didn't bother her; instead she focused on just how much she loved her children. Peggy had been born for motherhood and whatever else Wilson had or hadn't done, he'd given her her children. As her friends died one by one, or turned away from her, these three small beings became even more important in her life.

Parental duties done, Peggy retired to her own room at the back of the house. She went over her mental checklist: lunches made, children's clothes ready for the morning, doors locked, stove off, dog tied outside. Peggy yawned luxuriously—bed at last.

Gradually she returned to consciousness. No, the noise didn't originate in her dream—she could still hear Rex, the hound, howling urgently, the note high-pitched and piercing. This odd behaviour was unprecedented. Even when strangers approached, he characteristically wagged his tail and danced around. So what was his problem?

Peggy plopped the pillow over her head and tried to ignore Rex's baying. She squeezed her eyes shut and pressed the pillow to her ears but still the barking penetrated.

'Damn!' She threw aside the pillow and lay tense, listening to the dog and the clattering of the freezing rain on the roof—like a million tiny claws trying to dig their way in to her. Why did Rex have to make a fuss on a night like this? The old snow would be slick and treacherous underfoot and the night was black as death.

'Let him howl,' she grumbled, huddling into the covers and ramming a second pillow over her head. But Rex's bark altered to sharp, pain-filled yelps, impossible to ignore.

Peggy's heart sank and she groaned. She'd have to do something. Even though the neighbours lived too far away to hear and the children wouldn't awaken, she'd never get back to sleep knowing he was in pain. But a cold shard of fear knifed her gut as she climbed out of bed. She peered out at the driveway from the window in the stairwell before she continued down to the main floor. No car, no person, no animal crossed her line of sight.

She bundled her parka over her nightdress, donned heavy work boots, grabbed her old, unreliable flashlight and inched open the door. The light from the porch pierced the

169

blackness for twenty or thirty feet, far enough to see Rex wasn't in his usual spot, tied to his dog house.

'Rex!' Renewed howling rose from far back behind the pond. 'Rex!' Peggy bawled, exasperation overtaking the quaver of fear in her voice. 'Rex! Get over here, you stupid animal.'

The baying didn't come any closer, so, swearing under her breath, Peggy grimly started picking her way through the freezing rain, watching carefully for the edge of the pond and the stakes which marked the thin ice. As her flashlight flickered and dimmed to amber, she doubled her pace. She altered course to make straight for the dog, but as she started across the pond she searched alertly for the markers. There they were, unexpectedly far away to her right. Peggy breathed more easily; she must have become disoriented in the dark.

Crack! The ice beneath Peggy's feet rocked and parted. Unbalanced, she fought against sliding into the black water but her tiny ice floe tipped up. Peggy plunged into the frigid pond. Her shriek of terror choked off suddenly as freezing water rushed into her mouth and nose. Fighting against the dead weight of her heavy boots, she clawed for the surface, gasping as her head broke through to the night air.

'Help!' But she didn't waste much energy in pointless screaming. Who would hear? She had to save herself. Every sensor in her body shouted with the pain of extreme cold. She had only minutes to live before her body temperature plummeted below the critical level.

She propelled herself to the edge of the ice and scrabbled on its slick surface with her gloved fingers for any sort of purchase. None. Peggy kicked harder, launching her upper body on to the ice. She writhed, snakelike, to push herself forward. Just as she got a knee up on to the ice another chunk broke off, flipping her helplessly back into the killing cold water and under she went again.

The chill began to affect Peggy's muscle control as she kicked, more sluggishly this time. Her lungs were in spasm before she resurfaced to flail weakly back towards the ice shelf where she clung, unable to pull herself up.

170

'Help! Help me!' Peggy cried feebly into the black night. From the direction of Rex's howling a beam of light suddenly flickered into being.

'Over here!' Hope gave renewed power to Peggy's lungs.

The light approached, but stopped several yards short of her perilous position.

'Help!' The light blinded Peggy as it swept over her and then came back to rest where she clung, her head barely above the oily waters.

'I can't,' a voice whispered out of the dead night.

'Get a pole!' Peggy pleaded weakly. 'You can reach me with a stick.'

The light did not waver.

'Help me . . .' Peggy's cry was a mere thread of entreaty, lost instantly on the night breeze.

A minute later, framed in the beam from a powerful flashlight, Peggy slowly slid into her frigid tomb.

A sigh of satisfaction escaped from the watcher who turned in the direction of the still howling Rex.

'OK, boy, I'll let you go now.' The rope, which had cruelly forced the terrified animal's head against the frozen ground, suddenly released and, skirting the broken ice, Rex bolted for the house.

After this humanitarian act, the watcher walked carefully along the edge of the pond and pulled out the markers misleadingly placed earlier in the evening. The black figure tossed them, like lilies on a grave, among the ice floes. 'Sweet dreams.'

CHAPTER 25

Catherine heard the side door click behind Paul and Morgan and realized she was running late again. She tossed her papers into her briefcase and grabbed her coat and handbag. When the telephone rang shrilly in the hall her hand was already on the door.

'Drat!' She paused in indecision. Should she answer it?

Glancing at her watch, she reached for the telephone. 'Yes?'

'Aunt Catherine?'

'Is that you, Ashley? It sounded like Peggy's twelve-year-old daughter.

'Yes.' The child paused. 'Is Mom over at your house?'

Catherine felt bewildered. 'No, honey. Isn't she at home?'

'No . . . and Mrs Pouget's here with Brandon, and me and Leslie and Peter got to get to school.'

The receiver felt slippery in Catherine's hand as she broke out in a cold sweat. She struggled to keep her voice even and light. 'When did your mother leave?'

'I dunno. She wasn't here when I woke up. I got breakfast for Peter and Leslie but it's time for the school bus and she still isn't here.' With every passing second Ashley sounded younger and more lost.

Catherine dropped heavily on to the hall bench, letting her briefcase slide unnoticed to the floor. What in heaven's name had happened? 'Can you get yourselves off to school?' she asked.

'I guess so. Mom made our lunches last night . . .'

'Then put Mrs Pouget on the telephone and you three get on your bus as usual. I'm sure there's nothing to worry about.'

'OK.' Ashley seemed happier now that she had shifted the responsibility to someone else. 'Will you ask Mom to call the school when she gets home?'

'Of course. Don't worry, honey.'

Her briefcase still lying abandoned in the hallway, Catherine drove towards Peggy's house, running stop signs as the speedometer crept well past the speed limit. Dread wove its icy tentacles through her flesh and squeezed at her heart. Peggy would never have left her children alone, especially without telling them. Something had happened to Peggy.

Catherine fleetingly considered calling the police, but worried that if she gave her name, her concerns would be ignored. So she raced to the scene, fast, alone and very, very worried.

172

Sitting at the end of the Brandenburg driveway, Rex wagged his tail in welcome.

'Why aren't you tied up?' Catherine chucked him under the chin as she hurried by and was surprised at his yelp of pain. She didn't stop to investigate.

Catherine knocked at the door and rang the bell in the faint hope that Peggy had returned. But she didn't wait long before pulling out her own copy of Peggy's house key.

'Peggy?' Catherine's tremolo died in the still air and she tried to ignore the fear that sped with her up the stairs to Peggy's room.

She braked at the bedroom door and peeked inside. The curtains still covered the long windows and the bed stood rumpled and empty. She tiptoed into the gloom and hesitated before snapping the light switch. When she did, the light chased the ghosts away to reveal a perfectly ordinary bedroom.

Catherine gingerly lifted the dented pillow. No nightdress. It seemed Peggy had slept in the bed, got up, and without dressing, had disappeared. In the ensuite bathroom the tub felt dry. So did the sink and Peggy's toothbrush. Catherine slowly descended the stairs, uncertain of her next move. Should she call the police? Didn't the person have to be gone for twenty-four hours before they were officially missing?

Down in the kitchen, chaos reigned. Ashley had got herself and her brother and sister to school but she hadn't spent any time cleaning up. On the table, indistinguishable brown lumps lay congealed in the bottom of three cereal bowls. Milk rings decorated the table-top and neither the milk carton nor the pitcher of orange juice had been returned to the refrigerator. Automatically Catherine put them away, scraped the bowls and loaded them into the dishwasher.

Rex watched her from the yard, staring hopefully through the french doors.

'What do you know about all this?' Catherine asked him through the glass. Rex wagged his tail like a semaphore signal.

The car! Suddenly she remembered Peggy's car. Was it still here? Dragging on her boots without pausing to fasten them, she heaved open the door and raced around the house to the garage. This unfinished building squatted in a dense clump of cedars behind and to the side of the house itself. She peered through the tiny window, cupping her hands to block out the daylight. Peggy's battered station wagon stood there, squeezed in among the junk filling the rest of the double garage. So Peggy hadn't driven away—at least not in her own car. Again, dread gripped Catherine. Neither Peggy nor anyone else would go walking out here in the middle of the night.

Hands thrust into her pockets and head down, Catherine headed slowly back towards the house. Rex danced around and between her legs.

'Come on, old boy, let's tie you up again.' Catherine grabbed his collar. He yelped when she touched his neck and this time her curiosity was aroused.

'What's wrong?' Gently she explored his neck with her bare fingers. As they moved around to the left side, probing under his coarse hair, Rex flinched. 'You've been cut!' Catherine exclaimed. 'You poor thing.' She patted him reassuringly. 'I guess I won't tie you up after all—your collar would rub.'

Leaving Rex to take up his station by the kitchen door again, she returned to the empty house. The state of the kitchen reminded her of the three Brandenburg children. What about them? What if Peggy hadn't been located by the time school finished? Calling Wilson seemed like a betrayal of Peggy—she'd be terribly annoyed to find Wilson ensconced in her house if . . . when, she returned.

'When Peggy returns,' Catherine stated aloud. Her voice quavered eerily in the expectant house. 'Not if.' But despite her attempts at optimism, Catherine's heart lurched with the sick certainty that Peggy was dead.

For the next half-hour Catherine paced the silent rooms, her mind seething with pointless conjecture. She desperately hoped to hear Peggy's distinctive step in the driveway. Finally, unable to bear the oppressive atmosphere any

174

longer, she pulled on her coat and boots and stepped out into the watery sunlight. The trees dripped softly on to the dead leaves. The musty smell of spring filled her head and lifted her spirits. Rex rubbed against her legs and the scent of wet fur eddied in her nostrils. Catherine strolled under the trees whose naked limbs gleamed black and wet against the faded sky. Not trusting the ice, she halted at the edge of the pond and inhaled lungfuls of the pungent air. The outline of the rink was faint under the crusty, porous old snow and the scattering of puddles.

At the periphery of her vision a black outline demanded Catherine's attention. Something lay in the snow at the edge of the old rink. Gingerly she edged closer, testing the ice with each step before resting her full weight on it. The ice seemed firm so she picked up her pace until she could identify the item. A black flashlight lay abandoned in the wetness. Beyond it, the colour of the ice changed from bluish white to beige and a pattern of white fractures criss-crossed it. In one of them a red marker stick had wedged itself. Catherine's scalp tingled as the hair on her neck bristled. Ignoring the sting of cold, she formed a snowball in her bare hands and threw it with all her strength at the cracked ice. As the snowball smashed into dust the ice beneath the point of impact rocked and an inch of open water appeared.

'Oh no . . .' Catherine wailed piteously. Rex howled one long mournful note into the sky.

Noon had come and gone before Staff Sergeant Warshinsky pulled up in the unmarked police car. He walked slowly up to the house where Catherine waited in the open doorway.

'So we meet again, Dr Edison.'

'Come in.' Catherine stood back for Warshinsky to enter. His eyes darted around, taking in the worn furnishings and the general disorder. Catherine's cheeks reddened as she imagined his contempt.

'Seven children play here, you know!' she defended her friend.

'So you said on the phone.' Warshinsky strolled through

the living-room without bothering to remove his boots. Wishing she had done some cleaning while she waited, Catherine trailed along behind him.

In the kitchen Warshinsky stopped in front of the french door and stared into the back yard. He blew his nose on a large, crumpled tissue.

'I see your friend has a dog.'

'Yes. His name is Rex. He's a beagle. He's usually tied up over by the trees but his neck's sore so he's free.' Catherine knew she was babbling. She clamped her lips shut.

Warshinsky turned away from the window, pulled over a chair and straddled it backwards. 'OK, tell me again in a hundred words or less. Just hit the high points.'

Catherine kneaded her damaged left hand in her right as she marshalled her thoughts. 'I spoke to Peggy Brandenburg on the telephone last night, about ten-thirty. Nothing seemed unusual. This morning, at about eight o'clock, Peggy's elder daughter, Ashley, phoned to say her mother wasn't home and hadn't been since Ashley got up. So I came over. Peggy's bed has been slept in but I can't find her nightdress. Her car is in the garage. There is a flashlight in the snow beside the broken ice in the pond.'

Warshinsky chewed on his lip, his adam's apple bobbing up and down. 'Maybe your friend just got fed up and left.'

'In the middle of the night? Without a car?' Catherine demanded hotly.

Warshinsky shrugged. 'Someone could've picked her up.'

'She wouldn't just leave the children.'

'So you say. Sometimes people suddenly flip out.'

'Do you really believe that?' Catherine stamped her foot in fury.

'Not really.' Warshinsky swung off the chair. 'Let's go outside.'

Catherine led the way. They didn't talk and the only sounds were made by the dripping trees and the splashes when they stepped into some of the many pools collected in the hollows of old snow. Under the puddles lurked a mixture of mud and ice, making the footing treacherous.

What could have brought Peggy out into this in the middle of the night, Catherine wondered yet again.

She stopped at the edge of the pond and pointed. 'Over there.'

Squinting, Warshinsky peered ahead. He couldn't make it out. I'll have to get those damn glasses soon, he thought; I'm as blind as a bat. 'That black thing?' he asked, locating a dark blur against the white of the snow.

'That's the flashlight. The ice beyond is unsafe.'

Picking his way carefully, Warshinsky edged closer until he could clearly see both the torch and the broken ice. 'What's that red stick?'

'A marker,' Catherine explained, sidling closer to the detective. 'Peggy used a row of them to mark the thin ice.'

Warshinsky grunted and stared around. 'No hope for footprints.'

What about fingerprints on the flashlight? Catherine suggested.

'Bound to be your friend's. What would that prove? Anyways, this isn't even a missing person investigation yet.'

Tears of frustration and fear stung Catherine's eyes. Every second was precious if they were to find Peggy. 'So what do we do?'

'Wait. If Ms Brandenburg isn't back by tomorrow we'll initiate a search. Drag the pond maybe.'

Catherine shut out the implications of Warshinsky's last sentence. 'Wait?' she shrieked. 'What if she's hurt? What if Peggy's been kidnapped or something? We can't just wait!' Catherine gesticulated wildly. 'And the kids? What about the three children?'

Warshinsky retraced his steps to the edge of the pond. God, he hated outdoor jobs in the winter! He lowered his head into his upturned collar and strode as rapidly as the terrain allowed towards the house. Catherine scurried after him, straining to keep up.

'These kids got a father?' Warshinsky's voice died in his scarf.

'What?' Catherine slid on the ice and almost lost her balance. Warshinsky sighed but slowed down and erased

177

the exasperation from his voice. 'I asked if the Brandenburg kids have a father.'

Reluctantly, Catherine nodded.

'Call him. Best to let him know the situation anyways.'

Catherine invited him in for coffee but Warshinsky wouldn't stay any longer. 'I shouldn't be here at all, you know. Ms Brandenburg isn't missing, at least not officially, and there's no indication of foul play that I can see.' He clapped his numb hands together, trying to stimulate his sluggish circulation. 'My visit here today is unofficial, Dr Edison. I came as a favour to you.'

Confusion covered Catherine's features. 'As a favour to me? Why?'

Warshinsky shrugged, sorry he'd mentioned it. 'I don't know . . . You've had a rough time lately . . .' Abruptly he turned towards the drive way. 'I've gotta go. Call me tomorrow if your friend doesn't show up.'

Catherine fixed herself a cup of hot chocolate and sat at the kitchen table. Warshinsky's softened attitude had been totally unexpected. Had he begun to believe her? Or at least have doubts about the 'accidents' to John and Alicia? Far from reassuring her, Warshinsky's manner frightened Catherine. She shivered with fear. Was Peggy the next victim? Was she Wilson's victim?

She toyed with the idea of staying with the children herself but in the end realized it wasn't practical. Their father had to be informed. 'If he doesn't already know,' she murmured aloud. Still, she had to give him the benefit of the doubt. If he wasn't responsible for Peggy's disappearance the children would need him. And if he was? Catherine prayed the children would be safe. She'd keep an eye on them.

Over the telephone, Catherine questioned several surly men and heard a mind-expanding selection of lewd comments before finally locating Wilson. She unearthed him at Chuck's Truck Repairs—one of his more regular and less salubrious haunts.

'Why the hell did Ashley call you instead of me?' were Wilson's words of greeting when he burst into the house.

178

'Were you home?' Catherine demanded, the sharp edge of her voice cutting like a knife.

Wilson ignored her remark but didn't pursue the topic. Instead, he began attacking his missing wife. 'Peggy left our kids to run off with some man,' he raved. 'She's run off with Mister high-and-mighty Calvin Parker, I'll bet. She's no better than a whore! I could take her to court and any judge in the land would give me custody. She's an unfit mother!'

'Aren't you the least bit concerned?' Catherine asked in astonishment. Even for Wilson this behaviour was unexpectedly vitriolic. 'Aren't you worried something happened to Peggy?'

Wilson slouched down on the sofa. 'Why should I be? She never worried 'bout me.' He sucked on his white teeth and leered at Catherine. 'Frankly I hope she never returns. Then I'd have the house, the car . . .'

'And the children, Wilson. Seven days a week. Fifty-two weeks a year. Think about it!' She tried to ignore the wave of panic rising in her as Wilson exposed his malice and his avarice. Had his greed erased even the most basic of human ethics?

Wilson eyed Catherine with malevolence. 'I'm here now. You're not needed. Beat it, Professor, and don't come back till I say you can. This is *my* place now!' Wilson leaned forward, waving a fist in her face.

'Just wait till Peggy returns!' Catherine retorted. 'I'll be watching you!'

Wilson's harsh laughter echoed as Catherine fled the house.

CHAPTER 26

At seven o'clock the next morning Catherine telephoned the Brandenburg house. Ashley just had time to say her mother hadn't returned before Wilson snatched the receiver

179

and barked into it. 'It's none of your damned business, Professor.'

Catherine ignored his animosity. 'I'm reporting Peggy missing. The police'll be around whether you like it or not.'

'You can't do that! You can't stick the police on me in my own home. I won't let them in.'

Catherine smiled sourly. 'They'll be very interested to know where you were the night before last.'

'I was home, you bitch.'

'Prove it!' Catherine slammed the telephone down. She felt soiled by mere telephone contact with Wilson. He became ever more unstable, increasingly unpredictable, and, Catherine felt, dangerous. Wilson had always had a cruel, wild streak, a feral edge to his character, but it had become the dominant trait.

All too clearly she remembered Ashley's kitten—a fuzzy ball of frenetic energy. Emerald eyes blazing with curiosity, it raced through the house investigating everything it could get its black nose into. The children, and Peggy too, loved Midnight.

A year ago, just before Wilson had walked out on his family, Ashley had given Catherine a demonstration of Midnight's skill.

'Watch, Aunt Catherine,' Ashley cried, dragging a string across the kitchen floor.

Midnight stalked the end of the string on her padded feet and then launched herself into the air, landing squarely on her prey. Shrieking with delight, Ashley jerked the string forward and again Midnight crept up on it. Peggy and Catherine watched grinning from the sidelines. Wilson, beer at hand, lounged at the table, the sports page spread open.

'She plays baseball too, Aunt Catherine,' the young girl cried. 'Watch!' Ashley threw a yellow foam ball gently at the kitten. Midnight balanced on her hind legs and swiped at it, sending it rolling under the table. She scrambled after it, attacking with her needle-like claws. Ashley wrestled the ball away from the kitten and threw it again. Midnight

180

batted it into the air and it landed on Wilson's lap. Quick as a hunting lion, the kitten followed it.

Wilson roared in fury as the kitten's claws dug into his leg. 'Shit!' He grabbed Midnight but she slipped from his grasp and leapt up on the table, knocking over the bottle of beer.

Teeth clenched in fury, Wilson lunged across the table and caught the fur ball as she scurried for cover.

'Gottcha!' Wilson gloated and bared his teeth. For a moment he let it dangle, mewing in fright, and then juggled the cat so that it faced him, its tiny neck between his fingers. Holding the kitten's head still and staring straight into its terrified eyes, Wilson began twisting its body.

'Daddy, you're hurting her!' Ashley tugged frantically at her father's arm.

Wilson shook her off.

Peggy, white-faced, stared in horror. Catherine's voice shook as she pleaded for the kitten's life. 'Don't kill it, Wilson. Let it go.'

'Shut up,' he growled, darting a savage glance at his horrified audience.

The mewing grew hoarse and strained. Midnight's tail lashed from side to side as she struggled to escape.

'You're killing it!' Catherine tried to pry apart Wilson's fingers.

He kicked Catherine's shin with the sharp toe of his cowboy boot.

With a yelp of pain Catherine jumped out of range.

'Daddy . . . Please!'

Ashley's terrified squeal seemed to inflame him even more. He snapped the kitten's neck with a last vicious twist and hurled the limp body out of the open door. 'Take your goddamned cat and stop yer whining.' Then he turned on Peggy. 'Get me another damn beer.'

Wordlessly Peggy fetched a bottle from the refrigerator and handed it to him. Then she put her arms around her sobbing daughter. 'I'm sorry, honey. I'm sorry,' she murmured into the girl's soft hair.

'How could you?' Catherine whispered. 'How could you

do such a thing?' Her wide grey eyes glittered behind her glasses as she stared at Wilson.

The intense rage transfixing Wilson dissipated, leaving only his usual sour expression.

'Piss off,' was all he said as he pushed by Catherine and left the house.

Catherine shivered as she relived the scene. Now Peggy was missing and her children at Wilson's mercy. She was afraid for Peggy's children. She was afraid for herself.

All afternoon Catherine hovered in Peggy's backyard, watching the activities of the three uniformed policemen. Their progess seemed agonizingly slow, and several times she caught herself on the verge of screaming in frustration. Why did it take hours to arrange a search of one small farm pond? Staff Segeant Warshinsky directed operations with succinctly worded orders and the same curt tone he'd used to banish Catherine to the sidelines.

The cold, damp April day seeped through into her very marrow and she shivered uncontrollably as she sat on an overturned garbage can. On a telephone wire above, eight crows perched. A flock of crows was called a murder, she recollected. Appropriate. Murder had been done here—she was sure of it. The birds cawed in their guttural voices as first one flew off, then another and another until only two remained to oversee the event. Calvin and I, Catherine thought. Only two of us left. An evil omen indeed. She shivered again, not with the cold.

As she watched the search proceed, Catherine felt Wilson's hostile eyes drilling into her back. He hadn't left the house but peered constantly through the net curtains of the bedroom window.

The last rays of the sun gleamed golden on the horizon when the police diver let out a shout. He had surfaced, towing behind him a pale shape rippling amorphously in his wake.

Catherine jerked up her head and stared intently at the sodden object. Her stomach somersaulted with a sickening heave. Even though she couldn't identify the diver's find, she knew it meant Peggy was dead.

Like a rabbit to a snake, Catherine was drawn to the pond. In their excitement neither Warshinsky nor the other officers noticed her silent approach, so she watched unmolested as the white bundle was hoisted ashore. Grounded, the billowing cloud collapsed into a beige jacket and a white nightdress. And the body wearing them.

'Peggy . . . !' Catherine stumbled forward only to be caught ten feet from her goal by a massive policeman.

'No, ma'am,' he said sternly. 'Not yet.'

'But . . .' Catherine struggled weakly.

'Not yet!'

While Warshinsky knelt down and carefully shifted the wet folds of the jacket away from the head of the corpse, Catherine's eyes were riveted on the legs. These waxen forms extended whitely out from the huddle of clothing. One bare foot pointed skyward and the nightdress was hiked high up on the pasty thighs in a parody of seduction.

'Pull down her skirt,' Catherine whimpered. 'Pull down her skirt.'

The policeman holding Catherine nodded slightly at another officer. With a quick jerk the man tugged the nightdress as far as it would go.

Catherine's tension diminished. She let her eyes wander over the bundle of clothes to the face. Peggy's empty face.

Warshinsky scrutinized Catherine as she homed in on the dead countenance. He caught the involuntary flinch when the moment of recognition came.

'Is this Mrs Peggy Brandenburg?' he asked formally. His words failed to penetrate Catherine's consciousness. 'Dr Edison?'

In slow motion she turned to Warshinsky and pinned him with her misery. 'Yes.'

CHAPTER 27

Warm spring sunshine bathed Catherine as she sat at the cluttered desk in her office. She didn't notice it. Neither did she hear the low hum of activity from the hall and adjacent labs and offices. Everyone in the biology department went out of their way to avoid disturbing her, but Catherine was the subject of the whispered conversations being held in every corner of the building. She was the last to know of Staff Sergeant Warshinsky's arrival.

The knock at the door roused Catherine from her reverie. 'Come in.'

Warshinsky's ruddy face peered around the edge of the door.

'Oh, it's you.'

Undeterred, the policman entered, took in the untidy room at a glance and then dragged forward the rickety chair which stood against the bookcase. 'May I sit down, Dr Edison?'

Catherine pulled herself together. 'Certainly. Would you like some coffee? Or tea?'

'No, thanks.' He arranged his large form as comfortably as possible on the wooden chair. 'I thought university professors had fancy offices in ivory towers and ate caviar.'

'Don't I wish! Reality is being squashed like sardines in broken-down buildings and drinking instant coffee.'

'Not so different from the lot of a policeman, then.'

'In some ways.' Catherine folded her hands on her desk and eyed her visitor warily. At least this time she had home turf advantage. 'What can I do for you, Sergeant?'

'I'd like you to tell me about the night Mrs Brandenburg disappeared.'

'I wasn't there. I don't know what happened.'

'Tell me about your evening, then,' he invited.

'Again?'

'Yes. In more detail. For instance: where did you telephone her from? Your house?'

'No. I called from a doughnut shop.'

'Which one?' Warshinsky crossed his ankles, revealing his lime green socks.

Catherine refused to squirm under his stare. 'I'm not sure . . . They all look the same.'

'I don't care whether it was Tim Horton's or Dunkin' Donuts, Dr Edison. Where was it? What street?'

'I don't remember!' The pitch of Catherine's voice rose as her nerves tightened. 'I phoned from a doughnut shop. What difference does it make which one?'

'Was someone with you?'

'No. Why?'

'You were alone, late at night, in an unknown restaurant and you suddenly got the urge to telephone Mrs Brandenburg?' Scepticism dripped from every word as Catherine's actions took on a sinister aspect. The temperature of the room dropped several degrees as the two eyed each other frostily.

Catherine shifted in her chair. 'That's more or less the way it happened. I was worried about Peggy.'

'Why? Why at ten-thirty at night?' Warshinsky persisted.

By this time Catherine felt almost as unsettled as she had the night she'd called Peggy—the night she'd seen Calvin and Wilson together after her interview with the psychic. But how could she admit to visiting a fortune-teller? Warshinsky already thought she was nuts. He didn't need proof.

'Dr Edison, why did you telephone Mrs Brandenburg? You did call her, didn't you?' The police detective leaned forward on his chair while his fingers drummed rhythmically on his knee. His dark eyes never left Catherine's face. She wasn't a good liar, he decided. She was hiding something, but not *the* something. Or, maybe she was very good and that demure exterior hid a murderer.

'Of course I called her—that's what I told you from the start. Peggy'd been having trouble with her husband and I wanted to be sure he wasn't hanging around.' Catherine stabbed her finger in the policeman's direction. 'You've met

Wilson Brandenburg. You saw what he's like. Peggy was afraid of him. You should find out where Wilson was that night and forget about me.'

'We're working on that angle as well.' Warshinsky whistled tunelessly through his uneven teeth and Catherine fidgeted with the sheaf of papers in front of her. Somehow she'd lost any advantage she might have started with. 'Anything else?' Catherine's voice quavered slightly.

'Where were you the night Ms Alicia Castelvetri died? Or the night Mr John Retson died?'

Catherine froze as the implication of his questions hit her. She was sinking even deeper into the quagmire which had sucked at her heels ever since John's death. 'How dare you!' she croaked.

Warshinsky sat relaxed and at ease on his wooden chair. He felt sharpest when his prey squirmed. It meant he'd hit a soft spot. 'You're the one who first mentioned a serial killer. You discovered every body but the first. You've been the one constant throughout this entire series of deaths.'

Struck dumb with horror, Catherine could only gape uncomprehendingly at the policeman. She couldn't marshal any coherent thoughts as her mind spun off on a thousand simultaneous tangents.

Warshinsky watched emotions chase each other across her face. Finally, the racing scenes in Catherine's mind slowed enough for her to zero in on the only encouraging aspect of the horrible interview. The rest she locked away under severe restraint. 'So you believe me, then. You believe there's a killer . . . that the deaths haven't been accidents.'

'Not really,' Warshinsky replied, 'but if I do decide to treat Mrs Brandenburg's death as a homicide, then I'll have to reconsider the verdict on the others.'

Catherine kept her thoughts focused tightly on the policeman's words. Other ideas fought for attention but she held them back. 'Are you treating Peggy's death as murder?'

'Not officially. There's no evidence of a struggle, no evidence, in fact, that anyone else was in the vicinity when she died.'

186

'But why would she go out walking in her nightdress in the middle of the night?' Catherine demanded.

'That is the question.'

Meeting Warshinsky's steady stare was one of the hardest things Catherine had ever done but she did it. 'I had nothing to do with Peggy's death—or any of the others.' She gripped her hands together tightly but not so tightly that her knuckles whitened. She'd already provided more than enough body language for the policeman to read. 'You're welcome to investigate me and my movements, provided you investigate others as well.'

'Like who?' Warshinsky tensed. He wanted the answer to this question.

'Wilson Brandenburg, for one.' Catherine found it easy to point a finger at him now that he'd shown his true colours. But what if it wasn't him? Who then?

'Yeah,' Warshinsky nodded. 'He warrants some attention. A nasty piece of work, he is. I feel sorry for the kids.' He slipped a notebook from his pocket and flipped it open. 'Give me the names of the others in your group—the ones still alive, I mean.'

Catherine hesitated. Since John's death she'd pushed for a full inquiry. As her friends died one after the other, she worked harder and harder to convince the authorities to undertake an investigation. But now that the Staff Sergeant hovered on the brink, Catherine wavered. What would he discover?

'Dr Edison?'

'All right,' Catherine said. 'There are only myself and Mr Calvin Parker left of the original group. Brent Wellwood's widow, Susan Wellwood, still lives in Kingsport, however, and is a friend of ours.'

Warshinsky raised an eyebrow. 'Wellwood? I don't think you've mentioned a Brent Wellwood before.'

'He died of a heart attack two years ago. He was Peggy Brandenburg's brother.' Catherine outlined the relationship of the original eight. 'The likelihood of six of us dying before ther age of forty-five is very low,' she concluded.

'Check the actuarial tables if you don't believe me. Something's wrong.'

'Maybe,' Warshinsky replied noncommittally. 'And your husband? Where does he fit into this picture?'

'Paul didn't meet any of the others until thirteen years ago when we moved here from Toronto. He is close to Calvin Parker but has little to do with the rest.'

Warshinsky grunted as he finished scribbling in his book and snapped it shut. 'Right now I'm going to concentrate on the Brandenburg death. Perhaps if I dig a little deeper something'll turn up to convince me it wasn't an accident. Or suicide. Meanwhile, madam, you'd better come up with some convincing alibis for yourself. You're in this up to your elbows!'

With these words of warning the policeman scraped back his chair and rose to his feet. He picked his nose delicately with his little finger. 'I'll be back,' he said and ushered himself out of Catherine's office.

When John Warshinsky climbed back into his car, he didn't immediately drive off. Catherine Edison puzzled him. When he talked to her, the logic of her theory appeared solid. He could feel himself wanting to believe her. But away from her influence, doubts flooded back and the complete lack of evidence overwhelmed her argument. As for motive, even she couldn't come up with one of those. And if murder had been committed, Dr Edison herself was the obvious choice. Talk about coincidence! What were the odds of the same uninvolved person being on the spot every time a body turned up?

Nor could he ignore the possibility she was seriously disturbed. Warshinsky had met multiple murderers who appeared to be perfectly normal, intelligent, compassionate beings most of the time. The policeman slapped the steering-wheel in frustration. Better just to stick to facts, meagre as they were, and forget Edison's flights of fancy.

In bed that night, Catherine recounted the story of Warshinsky's visit to Paul. 'He told me to prepare my alibi!' she concluded, her stomach churning again in fear.

'That's what you get for babbling on and on. I told you you'd only cause trouble.' Paul punched his pillow angrily. 'Now I suppose that Warshinsky guy will be nosing around Calvin and me. Nice work!'

'I only want to discover the truth.'

'The truth? The truth?' Paul's voice cracked. 'I'll tell you the truth. You're crazy!' Paul shook his finger in his wife's face. 'You've got it in for Calvin and me. Julie's death was bad enough—we couldn't avoid being involved in that. But to send the cops after Calvin, like he's a common criminal . . . Wait till the press gets hold of this one.'

'But Paul . . .'

He twisted around and sat up. 'But Paul,' he mimicked sarcastically. 'But Catherine! Do you hate me that much?'

'I don't hate you. I love you!'

'Well, this is a fine way of showing it. Sabotaging Calvin's future is like stabbing us both in the back. And it's a great way to treat your friends—dragging their names through the mud.'

'I just need to know,' Catherine wailed, clutching at his sleeve.

'Oh, get a grip on yourself and leave me alone. I have to plan some damage control.' Paul lay down, his back to his wife who stared miserably at the rigid line of his spine.

Tears rolled silently down Catherine's cheeks as she lay stiffly at the very edge of their huge bed. John, her mind cried out. John, I need you! She spent a comfortless night as somewhere, someone plotted yet another untimely death.

CHAPTER 28

Susan lunged for the ball but her weak volley dribbled off the net. On the opposite court Catherine grinned and wiped the sweat from her face. 'Had enough?' she called out. 'Our hour's almost up.'

'I sure have,' Susan panted. 'Let's call it a night.' She fetched the ball and slid her tennis racquet into its case.

189

'God, am I ever out of shape,' she moaned as she and Catherine headed for the showers. 'Your burned feet seem to be OK, though.'

'Not bad,' Catherine agreed, collecting her soap and towel from her locker. 'My ankles are stiff but they'll loosen up in a week or two. They don't look so great but they're functional.'

After showering and changing, the two women retired to the club restaurant for a drink. Catherine felt pleasantly tired—the healthy tired which results from physical activity, not the draining fatigue caused by mental stress and worry.

'Exercise doesn't seem so torturous once it's over and I'm clean and dry,' she remarked sipping gratefully on her vodka and orange juice. 'You could convince me I'm human again without calling in a hypnotist.'

Susan groaned. 'Speak for yourself! Exercise, in my opinion, is a vastly over-rated activity. Give me a good book and a rocking-chair any time.'

They sat in companionable silence, watching other tennis players sweating it out on the courts.

'You know,' said Catherine, 'this is the first time since it happened I've forgotten about Peggy's death? Even for a moment?'

'Me too,' Susan answered soberly. 'Have you heard how her kids are doing?'

'Morgan spoke to Ashley a couple of times but she hasn't said much. I hope Wilson's behaving himself.'

'I wish there was some way we could keep an eye on them,' Susan worried. 'If our kids went to the same school as the Brandenburg children we'd have something to go on other than rumours. Yesterday I heard young Peter was in a fight.'

'Wilson must be pleased. That's the kind of behaviour he approves of.'

'How did Peggy ever get hooked up with that jerk?' Susan demanded. 'I know Calvin didn't treat her well but that's no reason to go running off with the likes of Wilson!'

Catherine sipped her second drink—a Perrier and lime

190

this time—and remembered the young Wilson. 'He was very attractive at the time, Susan. Handsome, sexy . . . verrry sexy. And charming in an earthy way. Lots of women chased after him, many older and more sophisticated than Peggy. But Peggy outshone the lot. She was really something when she was younger.'

'I know.' Susan set her glass down on the small table and reached for her handbag. 'I brought over the photographs Millikin's using in his infamous book. Peggy's in one of them.' She sorted through the small pile. 'Here. The one of Calvin and Peggy's on top.'

Catherine hesitated before accepting the proffered pictures. She felt strangely loath to reawaken the past. As she studied the photograph of Peggy and Calvin tears filled her eyes. Poor Peggy! She had everything going for her but success and happiness always eluded her. And now there could be no second chance.

Catherine flipped rapidly through the other pictures without paying them much attention. One showed Calvin with Danny wearing his beloved leather jacket. Then Calvin was pictured with the rest of the school football team —Calvin had been quarter back, of course. Then there was Calvin with his parents, in front of his father's hardware store, and at his high school graduation.

Catherine handed the stack back to Susan. 'Brent took some good photos.'

Susan nodded. 'These aren't his best but I guess Millikin was concentrating on Calvin, our up and coming politician. Brent took some gorgeous pictures up north at summer camp. He made quite a collection of wild flower photographs too.'

Catherine stared into her glass, searching for enlightenment in the effervescence of the tiny bubbles. 'Do you think Peggy committed suicide?' she asked abruptly.

'Of course not!'

'So you think her death was an accident?' Catherine persisted.

'It must have been . . .' Susan had no wish to wade into these waters, especially with Catherine.

191

'Why did Peggy ignore the markers and walk on the unsafe ice? Why was she outside at all?' Catherine leaned forward and regarded Susan intently. Tension furrowed her pale brow into an imitation of corrugated paper.

'I don't know. No one knows,' Susan replied reluctantly.

'Maybe someone called her. Maybe someone was calling for help and Peggy ran out.'

'It's possible, I suppose,' Susan admitted. 'But who? And why haven't they come forward with information?'

'Because the person was faking it. All they wanted was for Peggy to drown. Perhaps they even moved the markers to trick her.'

'Catherine . . .' Susan took a deep, calming breath. 'No evidence suggests anything like that happened.'

Catherine wasn't fazed by Susan's discouraging response —after all, she was used to it. 'But what evidence would there be if my theory is correct? That crusty snow wouldn't hold a footprint. No one else could've heard a shout. There wouldn't be any sign of a struggle because there wasn't one.'

Susan mulled over these arguments, unwilling to believe such a diabolical plot. Suddenly she looked up eagerly. 'Rex! You told me Rex was loose. Peggy likely went out to tie him up!'

Catherine shook her head, her short dark hair flying in her eyes. 'Peggy leashed him near his dog house, not on the other side of the pond.'

'But if he wouldn't come she would have had to chase him.'

Catherine still shook her head. 'Rex always came for Peggy; he worshipped her.'

'I hope Wilson feeds the old fellow,' Susan said, glad for a chance to change the topic. 'He isn't very fond of dogs.'

'Unlike you.' Catherine smiled and relaxed marginally. 'Ashley will look after Rex,' she reassured her friend. 'That girl loves animals so much she wants to be a vet. Frankly I'm much more worried about the kids, but Wilson won't let me see them.'

'He has become very peculiar lately,' Susan agreed,

replacing the photographs in her bag. 'He was unbearable at Peggy's funeral. Thank God the kids weren't there!'

'Calling his dead wife a "thieving whore" was definitely beyond the pale,' Catherine agreed. 'Poor Peggy! She tried so hard to be dignified despite him. To have her funeral almost degenerate into a brawl . . .' She shuddered.

'I have to give Paul credit for hustling Wilson out of there as quickly as he did. Paul seems such a calm, reserved man —a real pacifist. But he used a very professional-looking head lock to toss Wilson out of the funeral chapel.'

'Paul was on the wrestling team at university,' Catherine explained. 'But he did do a good job on Wilson, didn't he? And you know, he even managed to calm Wilson down! He can be very persuasive at times.'

Susan smiled. 'Maybe that's why Calvin chose him for his campaign. By the way, how's that campaign going? According to the last report I heard, Calvin is running neck and neck with that real estate tycoon, Dressler. You may find yourself heading for Toronto before long!'

Catherine sighed. While she did wish Calvin well, a win for him would mean a loss for her. Once Paul took up his promised post at Queen's Park, either her marriage or her career would have to be sacrificed. Catherine wasn't sure which one it would be.

Academic jobs, particularly for plant pathologists, were rare. To leave her present post would be to leave science and her career behind. What would she do with herself then?

But to stay behind . . . To shrug off seventeen years of marriage. Could she really do that? Granted, she and Paul fought a lot lately, but they were both trying to function under extreme stress. Time would ease the tension and then they could return to their normal, comfortable relationship. If, that is, Catherine moved to Toronto.

'A penny for your thoughts?' Susan's voice broke into Catherine's musings. 'Why are you frowning?'

Catherine laughed and waved away Susan's concern. 'No reason. I'm not going to worry about moving until after the leadership convention. Dressler's still the favourite, you know. Calvin has lots of hurdles to jump before he becomes party leader.'

'And that book about him hits the shelves before the convention,' Susan added, biting her lip. 'I'll never forgive myself if anything in it scuppers Calvin's chances . . .' She swirled her empty glass on the marble table, leaving a wet trail in its wake. 'What do you think, Catherine? Will any of those photographs cause him trouble?'

'I don't see how,' Catherine replied, but a niggling doubt began tickling her brain. Something about the pictures wasn't right.

Not noticing the faint overtone of reservation in her friend's voice, Susan relaxed again and picked up her tennis gear from the chair beside her. 'Then I'll quit worrying about that damn book. God knows I have enough problems of my own without worrying about Calvin's.'

Nothing more was said about the photographs, but Catherine's memory itched all the way home. Maybe if I sleep on it . . .

CHAPTER 29

Despite his threats, Staff Sergeant Warshinsky didn't come back to hear Catherine's alibi and whenever she telephoned he was out. It seemed official interest in the death of Peggy Brandenburg had not awakened after all. This inaction pleased Paul who regained his usual calm demeanour. But again Catherine felt alone in her struggle to find the truth.

At odd moments during her lectures, while making meals or talking to Morgan, a vague unease would grow inside her. She feared she was missing the clues pointing to the answer. If she studied the problem face on, however, even the hint of a solution faded. The flicker of enlightenment glimmered on the fringes of her consciousness only when her attention was elsewhere.

In Catherine's dreams the group of eight were reunited. Danny was always sixteen and wearing his black leather jacket but the ages of the others varied. Sometimes Catherine was ten and playing in the ravine with an adult Alicia. Sometimes John, the man, lay with her on a soft blue blanket, cradling her in his protective arms. But he whispered words she couldn't quite make out. Once John and Alicia entwined themselves while Danny and Brent boxed at a fund-raising dinner for Calvin. For reasons which seemed sensible in the dream, the dinner took place in the hardware store owned by Calvin's father. Officer Warshinsky looked on. Between these surreal sequences the stark black and white images of Susan's photographs inserted themselves, disrupting the fantasy and leaving behind a nimbus of apprehension both in the dream and later when Catherine would awaken depressed and uneasy.

'Take some of those sleeping pills the doctor gave you,' Paul suggested one night after Catherine's tossing and turning awakened him as well. 'We both need some sleep.'

'I don't want to,' Catherine obstinately replied. 'I'll go sleep in the guest-room so I won't keep you awake.'

'Don't be silly! Taking one or two pills won't make you an addict, for God's sake!'

'Julie might still be alive if she hadn't been taking sleeping pills. I never want to be drugged into oblivion!' Catherine was determined to work her way through her troubles without drugs.

'Suit yourself,' Paul sighed in defeat, 'but you don't have to leave. How about some hot milk? Or a back rub? Would that help?'

'A back rub would be nice.' Catherine rolled on to her stomach and Paul knelt over her, one leg on each side of her body. With firm, clean strokes he worked the tight muscles in her back. Up and down his strong fingers travelled digging out the knots of anxiety. 'Better?'

'Mmmm.'

He bent to kiss her neck and his hands left her back, moving down to cup her buttocks. 'I know what would take you mind off your troubles . . .'

She wriggled around under his hands, twined her arms around his neck and sought his lips with her own. They

195

hadn't made love since the night Peggy died. He felt good inside her.

When the doorbell rang, Catherine tensed. She wasn't expecting anyone and the slightest deviation from routine started her stomach churning. She ran into Morgan'a bedroom which overlooked the front door and peered cautiously through the white net curtains. At first she didn't recognize the foreshortened figure waiting on the porch but when she shook out her long, honey hair in a characteristic gesture of impatience, Catherine realized who it was—Paul's secretary, Gretchan Busch.

By the time Catherine finally opened the front door, Gretchen had turned away and was half way down the walk.

'Gretchen!' Catherine called.

Her visitor turned and retraced her steps. 'Hello, Catherine. I didn't think you were home. I didn't mean to disturb you.'

'You're not disturbing me. Come in out of the wet.' She stood back to let the other woman enter. 'Let me take your coat.'

'Thanks. I hope this rain stops soon. I'll soon be growing mould!'

Catherine laughed. 'Mould's my speciality.'

'Then you must love this weather! I won't stay long, though,' Gretchen added as she slipped her damp coat off her shoulders and handed it to Catherine. Her perfume wafted on the air current. 'I came to collect some of Paul's business papers—stuff from the law office, if that's all right.'

'He didn't mention you were coming.'

'I'm not surprised. He's so busy with the campaign these days . . .' Gretchen swept back her hair as she spoke. 'How've you been?'

'Not too bad.' Neither Gretchen not Catherine herself found the answer convincing. Catherine rushed to fill the sceptical silence. 'Could I get you some tea? Coffee maybe?'

'No, thanks. I really must collect Paul's papers and get back to the office.'

'Well then, let's go into the study—that's where Paul keeps his business papers.' As Catherine stooped to pick a piece of fluff from the carpet, Gretchen went on ahead. Catherine had to rush to catch up. 'I'll turn on the light for you . . .' she was saying as Gretchen snapped on the switch.

Catherine walked over to the desk. 'All the papers in the desk are mine. I sort of took over the study after being injured in the fire.' She closed her eyes for a moment, fighting the rush of emotional pain that flooded her as she spoke. So many tragedies in so short a time. What disaster lay in wait even now?

Gretchen turned to the large filing cabinet in the corner but didn't open either of the top two drawers. Instead, she put her hand on the third. 'I'll be as quick as possible, Catherine, but you don't have to stay with me. It may take a few minutes to find what I'm looking for.'

'I don't mind.' Catherine felt strangely unwilling to leave the other woman alone in the room.

Gretchen turned back to the cabinet. 'What a day I've had,' she said. 'Car trouble, computer trouble, headache . . .' She pressed her hands to her temples. 'Do you have any aspirin? This damp weather always makes my sinuses act up.'

'I'll get you some.' Catherine frowned unconsciously as she headed to the bathroom. When she returned with the pills, she stood quietly inside the door, watching Gretchen's sure movements. She'd emptied the fourth drawer of the filing cabinet on to the armchair.

Turning around, Gretchen noticed Catherine. 'Thanks so much.' She hurried over for the painkillers. As she did so, another wave of her perfume pulsed through the air.

Catherine's brow cleared. 'It was you.'

Gretchen stopped. 'I beg your pardon?'

'You're the one who searched the study a few weeks ago.'

'What are you talking about? I've never been here before.' Gretchen backed away from Catherine's determined stare.

197

'Yes you have. I recognize your perfume. I could smell it when I came in here that day.'

'I don't know what you're talking about,' Gretchen protested again. 'It's a popular scent.'

Catherine moved forward, cornering the other woman in the alcove between the windows. A note of satisfaction crept into her voice. 'You led the way to this room today. You knew where the light switch is located. You even knew my things are in the top two drawers of the filing cabinet—that's why you skipped them and went straight to the third.' Catherine sat on the corner of the desk and eyed Gretchen with more curiosity than animosity. 'What were you looking for? And how did you get in?'

Gretchen wilted under her accuser's gaze. She licked her dry lips before answering the second question first. 'Paul keeps a spare set of keys in his desk. I used them.' She wiped her sweating palms on her elegant black skirt and swallowed nervously. 'I was looking for proof. Proof that Paul's embezzling from the trust funds.'

'Paul? Embezzle?' Catherine couldn't believe what she'd just heard. 'Paul would never steal from his clients. Or anyone, for that matter.'

'But I think that's exactly what he's doing, Catherine. I'm almost certain, but it's been cleverly done. I still need proof.' Tension showed in every line of Gretchen's body.

'Well, I won't help you find it.' Somehow Catherine forced the words past the constriction in her throat. 'You're badly mistaken about my husband. He's the most honest man I know!' She put her hand on the back of a chair to steady herself but didn't back away. Her clouded eyes flickered over Gretchen, around the room and back to the secretary.

'I couldn't believe it at first either,' Gretchen said defensively, 'but money is disappearing from several accounts. Accounts Paul administers.'

'Then obviously someone is trying to shift suspicion. Hell, Paul's never even at the office any more!' Catherine's hands flew out as she punctuated her words with jerky movements.

'He comes in occasionally to use the computer.' Gretchen pointed to the machine on the desk. 'Besides, he could do most of the manipulations from here. Your computer can be linked up to the one at the office.'

'Paul uses it for campaign work, not for theft.' Catherine stared accusingly. 'How could you betray him like this? Paul trusts you!'

'And I trusted him. But I can't deny the evidence. Someone is stealing funds and he's the only one with the power and knowledge to do it.' Gretchen's voice shrilled as she pleaded her case and red blotches blossomed on her cheeks.

How could I ever have thought her beautiful, Catherine wondered irrelevantly. 'My husband's not a thief and I'm going to tell him about your treachery as soon a I possibly can. For the moment, though, I suggest you leave. Right now!'

Daunted by Catherine's now blazing eyes, Gretchen inched past her and scuttled for the door with Catherine right behind. 'I'm not any happier about this than you are, Catherine . . .'

'You'll be even less happy after I've talked to Paul. If I were you, I'd pick up a newspaper and check the "Help Wanted" column!'

Catherine grabbed the doorknob but Gretchen put out a hand to stop her from opening it. 'I'll tell Paul's partners what I suspect,' Gretchen threatened. 'It's out of loyalty to Paul I've kept quiet this long.'

'I'm not a fool!' Catherine let out a shout of derision. 'If you had enough evidence to blow the whistle, you'd have done so. Instead, you ransacked my home. You didn't find anything when you broke in before—you're really obsessed to try it again now.' She opened her arms and swept the room with them. 'There's nothing here! There's nothing here because there's nothing to find.' Catherine's head throbbed and her vision blurred. A full-blown migraine had set in. Damn Gretchen.

'What about the computer? How do you know there aren't any secret files in it?' Gretchen leaned forward as she issued her challenge.

Catherine put her palms to her temples and spoke through gritted teeth. 'I use the computer. I know what's in it.'

'But files can be hidden. Let me take a look, Catherine. If I can't find anything, I promise I'll say nothing more.'

'No.'

'If you're so sure Paul's innocent you have nothing to lose . . .'

'No!' Catherine shrieked. 'Shut up and go! Tell Wilf your suspicions if you want—he won't believe you. Paul's always been scrupulously honest and his partners know it. What's *your* track record?'

Gretchen flinched, remembering an unpleasant episode soon after she'd started working for Paul. She'd told a crown prosecutor details of the defence Paul intended to use for a client. The small bribe hadn't been worth jeopardizing her job for.

'I'm a good worker,' Gretchen answered in a faint voice.

'Not that good. You'd better think carefully before you say anything. Now get out of my house!'

Catherine slammed the door behind Gretchen's retreating figure and then slumped against it. Paul. She had to talk to Paul.

CHAPTER 30

As soon as Gretchen left, Catherine raced for the telephone. She had to talk to Paul. But as she started dialling the number for the campaign headquarters, she hesitated. He likely wouldn't be there and she'd have to leave a message. What could she say? 'Come home, Paul, your secretary thinks you're a thief'? Hardly. 'Please call your wife. Urgent'? Paul wouldn't necessarily comply. Lately he mistrusted her sense of what was important and, besides, anything unrelated to Calvin's political future held no urgency for him.

Catherine dropped the receiver back into its cradle. She

200

would wait until he came home. Talking to him face to face would be better. Gretchen's accusation was too terrible to deliver over the telephone.

Checking her watch, Catherine pursed her lips in exasperation. Only four o'clock. She didn't expect Paul before six— if then. He worked a good eight to ten hours even on Sunday as the leadership race entered the final stretch.

Pulling on an old coat, Catherine went into the backyard to get some air. A hint of green peeked through the brown, dead grass and the buds on the trees were swelling. A brave robin picked in the moist earth and flew away with her wiggly prize. Catherine patted the rough bark of the gnarled oak in the corner before leaning her cheek on it. The tree felt strong and good and non-judgemental.

She turned her face to the pale sunlight, seeking its healing warmth. The cool breeze fluttered her dark hair and tugged at the hem of her skirt. I must start my field work, she thought. God's nature is my tonic.

Catherine propped herself against the old tree and closed her eyes. Bird songs trembled on the breeze and the scent of the pungent earth filled her head. Gretchen's treachery shrank to more realistic proportions.

Gretchen had to be wrong. Paul's high principles were one of his main attractions for Catherine. At university, too many students had cared only about their marks and not how they got them. Calvin proved to be one of them in his first year as an undergraduate. After too much to drink one night, he let slip that he'd purchased an essay for the compulsory philosophy course.

'That's dishonest, Calvin,' Catherine protested, aghast.

'No way! I don't want to take philosophy—I want business courses. If the administration can make me waste my time on something utterly useless, I've the right to make it as easy as possible.'

The majority agreed with Calvin's point of view, but she didn't change her principles or give up hope of finding someone whose ideas meshed with hers. Paul turned out to be the one. Hell! He'd never even run a stop sign! Catherine smiled, remembering an incident from their university days. He'd tried to trace the owner of a tattered one-dollar bill he found at the door to the cafeteria.

'Buy yourself a sandwich,' Catherine had advised.

But Paul cupped his hands around his mouth and yelled into the crowded room, 'Who lost a dollar?'

After their surprise wore off eight students approached.

'Now what?' Catherine chuckled.

'New or old bill?' Paul questioned. Four said old.

'Serial number?'

'Hey, man, who notices serial numbers?' one acne-scarred claimant complained and turned away in disgust.

'Wait,' Paul called. 'Tell you what. Any of you got four quarters for change? You can split the dollar.'

'Get real,' another student mumbled as they all headed back to their seats shaking their heads.

'Looks like you're stuck with it, Paul,' Catherine remarked, putting a comforting arm around his shoulders. 'You'll have to buy *me* a sandwich. That way you won't profit from another's misfortune.'

Catherine turned up her collar against the freshening wind. As time passed, she and Paul seemed to value security over excitement. Paul now wanted order in his life and, until recently, Catherine had supplied a firm anchor. Since John's death, however, her own emotions dripped like blood from a raw wound and Paul couldn't cope either with her or his own response to her pain. Their relationship skittered from argument to misunderstanding to hurt silence and rarely had a chance to renew itself. But Catherine's resentments receded before Gretchen's attack on Paul. She would close ranks with her husband.

'Mom? Mom!' Morgan's voice roused Catherine. 'What are you doing out there?' Her daughter leaned from the upstairs window.

'Just getting some air. I'll be right in.' Catherine's unease wrapped itself around her again, trying to smother her new spark of life, but this time she refused to submit to it.

As Catherine made dinner, Morgan chattered away about her friends and their crises. Catherine let her rattle on, enjoying the wonderful normality of it all. Except for a sensitivity which Morgan occasionally exhibited, the terrible winter had left little impression on her.

At seven o'clock Paul still hadn't returned so Catherine served up Morgan's dinner and sat with her while she ate. The edge to her hunger assuaged, Morgan settled back and surveyed her mother. 'Are you OK, Mom?'

'Of course.'

'You look tired . . .'

'Maybe I am, just a little,' Catherine admitted, 'but I'll be fine after a good night's sleep.'

Morgan slipped off her chair, circled the table, and put her arm around her mother. 'I'll listen, Mom. That's what friends are for.'

Catherine hugged her daughter convulsively. Easing her grip at last, she stroked Morgan's fragrant hair. 'I love you, honey.'

'I love you too, Mom,' Morgan whispered.

Catherine gave a final squeeze and let Morgan go. 'Just hearing that makes me feel a hundred per cent better!' she declared with a smile. 'Now you go do your homework and I'll clean up here.'

With Morgan in bed and the hour advancing, Catherine paced restlessly. She had tried reading and working at the computer but Gretchen's accusations reverberated in her head, blocking out everything else. She had just begun rearranging the books in the bookcase for the second tine when she heard the scrape of a key in the lock. Catherine sprang to her feet and raced for the door. Paul stepped in to find his wife in front of him.

'At last!' Catherine ejaculated.

'I couldn't help it,' Paul began, misunderstanding her words.

'It's OK,' Catherine broke in. 'Here, let me hang up your coat.'

Mystified, Paul let her remove his coat and whisk it into the closet. 'What's going on? I thought you'd be in bed by now.'

'I have to talk to you. Come and sit down.' Catherine dragged him into the living-room. 'Are you hungry? Do you

203

need something to eat?' Never tell bad news to an empty stomach, was one of her family's favourite sayings.

'I had a hamburger' Paul replied.

Paul chose an armchair and Catherine sat on the ottoman facing him. With Paul regarding her warily, she had difficulty starting her story. Catherine chewed her lip and frowned at the rug.

'Well? What is it? Bad news, obviously. Someone else been murdered?' Deep in concentration, Catherine didn't hear the sarcasm in her husband's voice.

At last she looked up and cleared her throat. 'I had a visitor today. Gretchen, your secretary.'

'Oh?' Paul stopped drumming his fingers. 'What did she want?'

'At first she said she needed some papers from the study —and you knew she was coming over.'

Paul shook his head.

Catherine continued. 'Then I noticed she knew where the study was and where you keep your papers—even though we shifted everything around after the fire so it'd be more convenient for me.'

'Odd,' Paul remarked, a worried note creeping into his voice.

'Then I recognized her perfume as the strange scent I'd noticed in the study the day it was searched.'

'You mean *Gretchen* did that? Gretchen broke in and ransacked our house?'

Catherine nodded vigorously. 'She used the keys you keep at the office.'

Paul's brows creased and he rubbed his chin. 'Did she admit it?'

'Yes.' Catherine swallowed hard. 'She said she was looking for proof you're embezzling from the trust funds.'

Silence stretched the atmosphere taut like a rubber band.

'Paul,' Catherine ventured in a small voice. 'Did you hear what I said?'

He nodded, still silent and then hid his face in his hands, his elbows on his knees.

An awful dread oozed into Catherine's mind and an icy

tingle tiptoed up her spine. 'Paul, it isn't true, is it?' she whispered.

Paul's head jerked up. 'Of course it isn't true . . .' but his voice faded out and his head fell back on his hands.

Catherine stared at him, unblinking. Slowly, ever so slowly, Paul lifted his eyes to hers.

'Yes. It's true.'

'Paul . . .' Catherine breathed. 'Oh no . . . Why?'

Paul groaned and slumped back in his chair. 'For Calvin's campaign. We needed more money.'

'But Calvin couldn't expect you to provide it,' Catherine objected.

Paul snapped to his feet and began to pace, slamming one fist into his other palm. 'Calvin thinks I have connections on Bay Street. He thinks I just have to snap my fingers and corporate donations will flow into the coffers.' Paul snapped his own fingers as he emphasized his point.

'Why would he think that?'

'Because I told him so,' was Paul's strangled response.

Catherine felt ill.

Suddenly, Paul crouched before her and stared into her face. 'Don't you see, Catherine? Calvin's going places—I knew that the moment you introduced us—and I knew I had to be part of it. Calvin expected me to know important people since I was a lawyer from a prestigious Toronto firm. How could I admit all I did was legal aid cases and I never so much as entered a corporate boardroom?'

'That's nothing to be ashamed of, Paul. I was proud of you!'

'But helping the weak and the poor isn't an activity Calvin values. He's interested in the big players, the powerful men. So I told him I knew some of them.'

'And then when Calvin decided to run for political office he called your bluff.' Catherine bowed under the weight of understanding. Poor Paul.

Paul recommenced his pacing. 'As soon as Calvin wins the leadership, I'll be able to pay back all the money. I'm not stealing, Catherine. I'm just borrowing.'

'Oh, Paul,' Catherine moaned. How he'd changed! He had become exactly what he used to despise.

Paul stopped in front of the fireplace and turned abruptly. 'You said Gretchen was looking for proof. Did she find any?'

'Of course not! As soon as I knew what she was doing, I threw her out.'

'Good.' Paul tapped on his teeth with his thumbnail. 'I doubt she can find any.'

'She can prove there's money missing,' Catherine pointed out.

'Yeah, but she can't prove I took it,' Paul replied. 'It could just as easily have been her. More easily, in fact.' He continued talking, almost to himself. 'If I went to Wilf and said I suspected her . . .'

'Paul! You can't do that! You can't accuse an innocent person of something you've done.'

He recollected Catherine's presence. 'Of course not. Only a criminal would do something like that. I was merely considering the possibilities.'

'It was a stupid, stupid thing to do, Paul,' Catherine said in despair.

He crossed the room and took Catherine's unresisting body into his arms. 'You're right. But you do understand why I did it, don't you? Calvin pushed me into it?'

Catherine nodded against his shoulder. 'I understand, but you must have known it was wrong . . . that you'd be found out . . .'

'I didn't think about that. I only thought about getting Calvin the leadership. Once he's the top man I'll have the power to fix my mistakes.'

'Mistakes!' Catherine pulled away. 'Gretchen's going to tell Wilf and Jan. I don't know what your partners will do but I don't see how you'll be able to keep this quiet. Calvin will be forced to drop you.'

Paul moved away, thinking as he walked. 'I must talk to Gretchen. Maybe we can work something out.'

'Like what?' Gretchen hadn't seemed very conciliatory to Catherine.

'A repayment scheme or something. At the very least I can get her to hold off blowing the whistle for a few days.'

'Probably . . .'

'And you won't tell anyone about this, will you, Catherine?' Again Paul took her in his arms. 'I need you on my side now more than ever.'

'I'll stick with you.' Catherine hugged her husband tightly. 'For better or for worse. Remember?'

CHAPTER 31

Despite lack of sleep and constant worry, Catherine insisted her research not suffer. Consequently, she spent longer hours in the laboratory, poring over petri dishes and at her desk writing papers and analysing data. The school year had finally ended, so, with the undergraduate students away, Catherine made rapid progress and almost caught up with the schedule she had set herself. In another week she would be ready to head out to collect fungal samples. She hoped field work and its calming influence would bring relief.

At eight-thirty on a drizzly Thursday evening the telephone in Catherine's office at the university rang shrilly. Compressing her lips in annoyance at the disruption she answered it.

'Dr Edison?' The identity of the voice floated tantalizingly just out of reach.

'Yes? Who is this, please?' Catherine's stomach muscles tightened involuntarily.

'Mildred McKeown.'

Now Catherine's chest constricted painfully and she almost hung up. Like a mouse mesmerized by a snake, Catherine eyed the telephone receiver for a minute before putting it back to her mouth. 'Hello, Mrs McKeown. How nice to hear from you,' she lied.

'You're in danger, Dr Edison—great danger,' the psychic blurted out in a rush.

'Nonsense.' Catherine's voice cracked and her knuckles whitened on the receiver.

'It's not nonsense! You've haunted me since the night you visited. I see you always in my mind, in my dreams. Do you think I like it? Do you think I want to be obsessed with you?' Mrs McKeown quavered to a crescendo.

'Why are you telling me this?' Catherine sat on her right hand to control its trembling.

'Because I know you're in danger. Right now! I see hands at your throat. A film over your face. A man is murdering you and he's smiling!' Mrs McKeown's voice took on a faraway, sing-song resonance. 'He has killed before . . . he pushed Alicia against the table. You are the last one on his list . . . When he kills you he will be safe. He wants you, Catherine . . .'

'Stop it!' Catherine shrieked. 'Stop it! You don't know what you're saying.'

'I predicted Mr Retson's death and that image was much fainter in my mind,' Mildred pleaded in her own voice. 'Your death is clear. Clear!' She ended on a note of rising urgency.

Catherine's thoughts tossed in a sea of confusion and fear. If her own sense of unease hadn't been so strong she would have slammed the receiver down instantly but she couldn't do it. Mrs McKeown believed in murder.

'Can you see the man's face?' Catherine demanded sharply.

'Not clearly. He's around forty . . . not fat . . . tallish . . . He wears a suit.' There was an agonizing pause before Mildred McKeown spoke again. 'Politics. Politics,' she repeated with greater conviction. 'The man is involved in politics.'

Staring blindly ahead, Catherine let the receiver drop back on to its cradle, cutting off Mrs McKeown's frantic repetition of her name.

Forty. Tall. Suits. Politics. Calvin! But why? Catherine lurched to her feet and staggered down the hall to the washroom where she ducked her head right under the cold water tap. The graduate student washing her hands backed away

208

from the next sink and left quickly, without even drying off. Gasping from the cold, Catherine groped for a paper towel and wiped ineffectually at her face with its hydrophobic folds. Calvin. Why? Her stomach churned and her lips trembled as she leaned against the stained sink and wrung her hands. Calvin. Why?

In the mirror her reflection showed a pale, hollow-eyed spectre. Catherine shrank from the image, afraid of seeing strong hands clasped around her thin neck. She would be so easy to kill! One good squeeze and the fragile spinal column would separate. Crack! She would die.

Returning to the illusory safety of her office, Catherine laid her head on her arms. Calvin. Why? I must think. I have the answer if I only could find it!

Calvin's face floated before her eyes and she instinctively recoiled from the image manufactured by her mind. Calvin at sixteen raising his arms in victory at a football game —he had strong, dexterous hands. Calvin at university, debating hotly, rising in anger to shake a fist in the astonished face of his opponent. Calvin at his wedding to dear Julie—how proud and happy they looked. Calvin's grim face as he and Paul assessed the strength of Calvin's principle opponent for the political leadership. Catherine shuddered. Calvin Parker had the iron will and the single-minded determination to kill if it served a purpose. But what purpose could be served by the deaths of his friends? Was Calvin insane?

Fragmented scenes kaleidoscoped in Catherine's head. Death. Danny's first. Who killed Danny? Did Calvin have bloodstained hands even then? But how could he have killed Danny—he was with Brent Wellwood, Brent who took pictures. It was Brent who took the last photograph of Danny and Calvin together—a photograph where Calvin held a rifle and Danny wore his new black leather jacket.

Understanding dawned like the sun gleaming through a chink in black, roiling storm clouds. Calvin *had* killed Danny! Danny had worn that jacket for only an hour or two before he died—for the time when Calvin told the police Danny had gone off by himself. But in that hour he and Calvin and Brent had been in the ravine with Calvin's rifle—the rifle Calvin claimed to have lost months before.

Catherine shook violently as the full implication hit her. Calvin was killing anyone who would understand the significance of that photograph! For twenty-five years that picture had remained in obscurity, hidden in a dust-covered photograph album. But then Millikin had chosen it for his biography of Calvin and soon the picture would be exposed for all to see. John, Julie, Alicia, Peggy and she herself would sooner or later have realized what the photo meant. It meant Calvin had killed Danny. But what about Brent? He'd been there too . . . But Calvin could easily have dominated him, convinced him it would be better to keep silent. Maybe Calvin even threatened him.

Catherine trembled as the chill sank deep into her soul. Calvin would do anything to become Premier, she knew that. But to murder even his own wife to keep his secret safe . . . Millikin's book had sealed the fate of everyone in the group. Mrs McKeown was right. Catherine's death would complete Calvin's list if she couldn't stop him. She reached for the telephone.

CHAPTER 32

As the approach of measured footsteps echoed eerily in the deserted corridor, Catherine tensed. Her enormous eyes riveted on her office door as the footfalls halted outside and the doorknob turned. She didn't breathe.

'Catherine?'

She let her breath out in a rush. 'Paul!' Catherine flung herself on his chest, sobbing with relief.

'There, there, honey.' Paul's strong arms held her close and he stroked her hair. 'What's wrong? You act like you're expecting Jack the Ripper.'

Catherine pulled away far enough to see Paul's face but she didn't let go of him. 'Calvin the Ripper would be more accurate.'

An unreadable expression passed over her husband's face. 'What are you talking about?'

In her haste to explain, Catherine's words tripped over themselves. 'When I saw the photograph . . . you know . . . the one Susan had . . . of Danny in his brand-new black jacket . . . standing with Calvin and holding the gun? Then I knew Brent and Calvin *did not* leave Danny at the end of the street the night he died. They all went down into the ravine together—that's where the picture was taken.' Catherine gripped Paul's shoulders, willing him to understand. 'They had the rifle with them . . . the one Calvin said they'd lost long before.'

'So?' Paul pulled her hands from his shoulders and gripped them between his own.

'So don't you see? *Calvin* must've killed Danny and then forced Brent to keep his secret. Brent never showed us that picture, Paul. Never! He knew what it proved. Danny wasn't killed by a marauding psychopath; he was killed by his best friend!'

Paul shook his head. 'It doesn't prove Calvin killed Danny. Maybe Brent did it.'

Catherine laughed harshly. 'No way. Calvin's not the type to risk his own neck covering for someone else. Besides, Brent was too weak to control Calvin. Calvin's always called the shots.'

Paul detached himself and tried to pace in the cluttered office. He kicked the battered garbage can out of his way and it cluttered metallically against the filing cabinet. 'Even if you're right, Catherine, that was twenty-five years ago. It's ancient history.'

Catherine felt like screaming with impatience. Why didn't he understand? 'But that photograph is about to be published in Millikin's book, Paul. *Julie* would see it. *Alicia* would see it, *John* would see it. *Peggy* would see it. *I* would see it! And we'd understand what it meant! Ancient history is about to reawaken and swallow Calvin and his golden future.' Exhausted, Catherine dropped into her chair and watched her husband with fever-bright eyes.

Paul paced rapidly, hand over his eyes, his expression

hidden. 'You're trying to tell me Calvin killed John and Alicia and Peggy? And even Julie—his own wife?'

Catherine nodded in relief. At last he had the picture. 'So when Millikin's book came out there'd be no one left who could figure out Calvin killed Danny twenty-five years ago. He's desperate to win that leadership race, Paul. Desperate enough to kill. Once I'm dead, there will be no one left to testify.' Catherine sank her face in her hands and groaned. 'I just called him and told him I knew what he was doing. He's on his way over.'

'You think Calvin's going to kill you and yet you invited him over here?' Disbelief resonated in Paul's voice. 'You're nuts.'

Catherine reached out her arms to her husband. 'But I called you first, honey, and we live closer. I knew you'd get here before Calvin did. I need you as a witness when I confront him.'

'You're crazy. Smart and brave, but definitely crazy.' Paul moved around behind Catherine and rested his hands lightly on her shoulders.

Catherine smiled at these words. 'That's where you're wrong, Paul. I'm finally sure I'm *not* crazy, and believe me, it's a relief!' Catherine leaned her cheek on Paul's wrist. 'All these months everyone has thought I suffered from delusions, or paranoia—I began to think maybe they were right.' She twisted under Paul's hands so that she could see his eyes. 'You believe me now, don't you? You see that Calvin's been murdering anyone who could stand in his way?'

Paul gently turned Catherine around and began massaging her neck with firm, even rhythm. 'It's hard to believe. He's our friend, after all.'

'But you have to admit it makes sense,' she persisted.

'It will mean the end to Calvin's political career,' Paul remarked softly.

'If we still had capital punishment it would mean the end to his life!' Catherine retorted. 'I'm more concerned about his victims than his damn career!'

'But I've invested a lot in Calvin's success. I've spent

two years working on his campaign without any pay-off.'

Catherine grasped his wrists. 'I know, Paul, and it's a shame, but you didn't know what kind of a man he really was. Neither did I for that matter, and I've known Calvin longer than you. At least you still have your law practice.' As Paul's fingers spasmed, she remembered the embezzlement. 'You did tell me you'd managed to convince Gretchen not to say anything, didn't you? And you're going to pay the money back quietly?'

'Don't worry. She won't talk. But I don't have much of a law practice.' Paul snorted. 'Wilf took over my clients months ago. I've nothing to go back to. If Calvin fails, so do I.'

'If?' Catherine tried to turn around but he increased the pressure of the massage and forced her to stay still. 'You're hurting me, Paul.'

Paul eased his kneading and resumed speaking in a conversational tone. 'I always knew you were smart, my dear, but figuring out the reason for the deaths from one photograph—that's impressive.'

'Calvin almost got away with it! He's been very clever.'

Paul ignored the interruption. 'You have one detail wrong though, Catherine.'

'What's that?'

'Calvin didn't kill anyone except Danny, and that was an accident.'

It was Catherine's turn to snort. 'And how do you figure that?'

'Calvin told me about Danny's death over a year ago. He told me how the gun accidentally went off and he and Brent made a pact to say nothing. If that bitch Susan hadn't given the photos to Millikin no one else would have had to die.'

'So why are you saying Calvin didn't kill the others? It's obvious you already suspected him,' Catherine whispered. 'Or did you know for sure?' She wrenched herself free of her husband's grip and whirled to look him in the eye. 'Tell me you didn't know!'

Paul's hands reached out and clutched Catherine's shoul-

213

ders again, yanking her towards him. She tried to pull away but he slid his grip up from her shoulders to her neck. 'Calvin didn't eliminate them . . .' His thumbs dug sharply into her windpipe while his fingers pressed on the spinal cord at the back of her neck.

'No!' she mouthed. 'Please, Paul . . .' Why was he massaging her neck so roughly? Why did his fingers press . . . ?

He loosened his fingers fractionally, and she tore at his hands. 'Paul . . .'

He released her. 'Something wrong?'

She drew in great gulps of air, and her panic subsided. 'No . . . noth . . . nothing . . . just you're pressing a little too . . . much.' God, woman, get a hold of yourself, she thought. That fortune-teller's been playing with your mind so much soon you'll suspect your husband's the killer . . . that he's going to kill you.

'It's OK, Paul,' she said shakily when his fingers slid back to her neck. 'That's enough massaging for one day.' She reached up to pull his hands away. 'As I was saying, 'Calvin had . . .' Paul's thumbs sank into the sensitive flesh of her throat, cutting off her words.

She kicked out as her breath stopped. He leaned forward over her and she stared up into his eyes. Recognition dawned as darkness began to descend. Paul! Her husband . . . oh God . . . and her murderer.

Again he released her. Again she choked as she coaxed air into her lungs. And then again his fingers pressed on her neck. 'This won't look like an accident,' she managed to croak. 'Gretchen . . . will . . . talk . . .' Paul's thumbs punched cruelly into Catherine's throat and silenced her.

'No, she won't. My nosy secretary had a little accident earlier this evening.' His hold eased marginally and the fanatical light in his eyes dimmed. 'I saved you for last . . .' he murmured. 'I don't want to kill you . . . you must understand I have no choice.' Paul's voice grew tender and caressing. 'I do love you, Catherine . . .' He bent to kiss her lips.

Catherine clawed at Paul's hands and face, scratching

214

and drawing blood. Paul jerked his head out of range, gasping in pain, but his grip tightened.

As her tongue pushed against her teeth and her eyes bulged, Catherine saw Paul's face looming above her. His bared teeth grimaced below his glittering eyes. An engorged vein pulsed beneath the film of sweat on his forehead. The cords of his neck stood out with the effort of strangling her.

While her lungs fought for air, Catherine thrashed violently, knocking papers and books off her desk. Her groping fingers found the telephone. She grabbed it and swung wildly at Paul's head. Her arm vibrated with the impact but Paul didn't let go. Again she bashed at his temple. He ducked but couldn't get completely out of range without releasing her. Blood trickled over his ear and into the corner of his mouth. He licked it away, his red tongue smearing it over his white teeth.

Fog swirled in front of Catherine and the rushing sound of her life's blood filled her head. She struggled to maintain consciousness.

As blackness slid like a shutter across her eyes, another face swam into view. Calvin. She hadn't heard him arrive. Would he tear Paul's hands from her throat or help him murder her?

CHAPTER 33

Eternity passed before Calvin acted. Paul's head snapped back from the blow and he lost his choking hold on her neck. Catherine coughed and slid to the floor, gulping air into her lungs, unmindful of the new battle being fought over and around her.

When she was finally able to think beyond her next life-giving breath she looked up. Calvin, fists raised, stood over Paul who lay crumpled in the corner. Her husband was conscious but no longer in fighting shape. Blood dripped from his split lip and his swelling nose blossomed purple

215

and off-centre. On Calvin's cheek a bruise swelled and reddened.

Catherine got unsteadily to her feet. 'Calvin?' she croaked, wobbling in his direction.

Calvin took his eyes from Paul long enough to appraise Catherine's condition. 'Thank God! I thought he'd killed you!'

'Almost.' She wanted to say more but each word tore at her bruised vocal cords. Gingerly Catherine fingered her mutilated neck.

Calvin directed his attention back to Paul. The madness had faded from his eyes and he looked shrunken and defeated. 'Phone the police,' Calvin ordered Catherine.

'That won't be necessary.' Staff Sergeant Warshinsky filled the doorway. 'What's been happening here?' His darting eyes took in the situation. 'Dr Edison, you left me a message about a matter of life and death. Explain.' As he stepped closer, he saw Catherine's bruises and winced. 'I guess you weren't exaggerating this time.'

As Catherine struggled to find the words to explain her nightmare, Warshinsky had to lean close to understand the hoarse sounds which passed for a voice. Though on the point of collapse, Catherine couldn't rest until both Calvin and Warshinsky understood the catastrophe which had befallen her friends. 'He killed them all,' she cried. 'Don't you understand? My husband killed them all!' She spoke compulsively, describing the insane ambition which had driven her husband. 'He wanted power and he planned to get it through you, Calvin. He told me he'd be the real "power behind the throne".'

As soon as he understood the bare bones of Catherine's story, Warshinsky called an ambulance. Murderer and victim lay side by side as the vehicle screamed towards the hospital. The policeman kept a heavy hand on Paul Edison's chest and a worried eye on his white and shivering wife.

Alone in the hospital that night, Catherine lay in bed, dry-eyed, with despair filling her soul. She stared out of the window at the rain weeping on the black world. Death, she thought, would be preferable to living in this reality.

Paul's docility after his arrest astounded Catherine. The madman who had tried to strangle her become a cooperative witness in his own prosecution.

Staff Segeant Warshinsky stopped by the Edison house two weeks after Paul's arrest. 'Your husband told us how he committed those four murders,' he said, sipping a cup of coffee. 'You were right on all counts. You both have very devious minds.'

He noticed the horrified look on Catherine's face. 'Sorry! I didn't mean to imply you think like he does.'

She smiled bleakly. 'I knew someone had to be insane. I just didn't think it was Paul.'

'During our perhaps less than thorough investigations he implied you were the one with problems.'

'Most everyone agreed with him—including you, as I recall.'

'*Touché.*'

'Will Paul be sent to trial?'

'I doubt it. But he won't be out on the streets. He'll be locked up for a long, long time.'

'Good.' But Catherine wasn't really sure how she felt about Paul. She still loved the man she'd married. Was he still in there somewhere? Driven to find out, she made one attempt to visit him at the mental institution but he refused to see her. Relieved, she started divorce proceedings.

Until the fickle wind of notoriety blew in another direction, Catherine and her daughter led reclusive lives, avoiding the hordes of reporters camped on their doorstep. They permitted only a few close friends to visit.

A month after Paul's arrest, Susan and Catherine were settled in a sunny corner of the living-room.

'How are Peggy's children adjusting?' Catherine asked.

'OK, I think. We're a little bit cramped but we'll work

it out. Maybe I'll move to a bigger house now that I've four kids instead of one.'

'It's quite a responsibility you've taken on, Susan.'

'It's the least I could do for Brent's nieces and nephew —I couldn't leave them with Wilson.'

'I wish I could help, but in the circumstances . . .' Catherine rubbed her forehead wearily. 'This isn't the future I would have predicted for that carefree group of children from Kingsport,' she murmured. 'We had plans . . . dreams. And to think I'm the one who brought Paul into our circle!'

'No one blames you, Catherine.'

Catherine laughed. 'Who's left to blame me? Except myself, that is. And Calvin.'

'Have you talked to Calvin since . . . since Paul was arrested?' Susan asked.

Catherine shook her head. 'Calvin may still be alive but I ruined his life as well as everyone else's the day I brought my "darling husband" back to Kingsport.' She laced and unlaced her fingers.

'But at least Calvin isn't going to be charged with Danny's death. All the witnesses from the original investigation are dead.' Susan regretted her choice of words as she saw Catherine flinch.

Catherine moaned and covered her face with her pale hands. 'Even so, he has no political future. Paul and I saw to that.'

'You can't change anything, so don't torture yourself. It wasn't your fault anyway. You didn't make Calvin kill Danny or force Paul into insanity.' Susan got up and prepared to leave. 'Look to the future, my friend, and put the past behind you.'

'That should be simple!' Catherine grimaced.

Summer had come before Catherine visited Calvin. When she arrived at his home she found him weeding Julie's perennial garden.

As her shadow fell on him, he straightened to greet her. 'How are you?' Concern darkened his handsome eyes.

'OK, I suppose.' Catherine plucked a scarlet poppy and twirled it between her fingers. 'You look well.'

Calvin gestured at the garden. 'Lots of fresh air. I never realized how much work Julie did out here.' He cocked his head at his visitor. 'What brings you here?'

'I'm sorry I believed you were a murderer,' Catherine said in a rush.

Calvin laughed. With the leadership irrevocably lost, he was no longer a driven man. 'I presented a more likely suspect than Paul did.' He ran his fingers through his wind-blown hair. 'And I planted the seed for this disaster over twenty years ago when I shot Danny and covered it up.' Calvin glanced at Catherine but her head was lowered and he couldn't see her expression.

'It was an accident, Catherine—I never meant to kill Danny. Believe me.'

'I do,' Catherine murmured to the grass.

'If only I had had the courage to own up to my mistake!' Calvin's voice resonated with his bitter regret. 'But it seemed so much easier to convince Brent to back up my story of leaving Danny at the end of the road.'

They ambled in the garden, soaking up the healing sunlight which glinted off the new threads of grey lacing Catherine's hair.

She paused to study her companion. 'How could I not know, Calvin? How could I live with Paul day after day and not see?'

Calvin shrugged. 'I worked with him twelve hours a day and didn't see.' He kicked a pebble which skipped over the grass and landed with a tiny plop in the goldfish pond. 'I have to live with the fact that Paul killed for me.'

'No, he didn't,' Catherine retorted. 'He killed for himself. Paul wanted power and wealth and you just wrote his ticket.'

'I pushed too hard. I'm the one who forced him to contribute more money than he had to give. I'm the one who first saw a pre-print of Millikin's book and explained the dilemma it created. Paul interpreted it as an order to solve the problem.' Calvin spun around on the grass,

219

flinging out his arms. 'Oh Catherine! How have the mighty fallen!'

The two old friends walked on in silence and by unspoken consent sat down on the garden swing where they rocked gently back and forth.

'Why did you have a secret meeting with Wilson?' Catherine asked into the silence.

'Me? A secret meeting with Wilson?' Calvin's mouth opened in astonishment.

'At a doughnut shop on the far side of town. The night Peggy was killed. The night Paul murdered Peggy, I should say.'

'Oh, that. I remember now.' Calvin nodded. 'How on earth did you find out about that?'

'I was there. At the back of the restaurant. The meeting looked planned.'

'It was.'

'Why?' she persisted. 'What could you and Wilson possibly say to each other?'

Calvin remained silent for a long time while Catherine listened to the creak, creak of the swing moving gently back and forth. At last, with a sigh, Calvin spoke. 'It was guilt, I suppose. The day before, Peggy and I had a terrible row —I literally screamed at her—and I felt awful about it. She needed more from me than I wanted to give. Than I could give, perhaps, but I felt I had to do something for her. So I decided to pay off Wilson.'

'Pay off Wilson?' Catherine's brow creased in confusion.

'I told him I'd pay him three hundred dollars a month,' Calvin explained, 'if he'd agree to stay completely out of Peggy's life. And stay away from the kids too.'

'And what did Wilson say?'

'He swore at me and called me a number of names I won't repeat, but in the end he agreed. He said he had no use for that "two-timing bitch" as he called Peggy.' Calvin's fists clenched as he remembered. 'I almost ploughed him one right then and there.'

'Did you give him the money?' Catherine asked.

'Oh yes. Three hundred in cold hard cash. I know Wilson doesn't like dealing in traceable funds.'

Catherine shook her head. 'All that money the night Peggy died. You must've been awfully suspicious!'

'I was, believe me, but I had no proof Wilson killed her. Nor, to be honest, did I want to advertise my stupidity. Wilson would never have kept his end of the bargain.'

Catherine relaxed in the swing, lulled by its gently rocking motion. She let the sunshine do its healing work and the gentle breeze blew some of the cobwebs from her mind. It was good to be out in God's green world. Perhaps life could be worth living after all.